THE
DARKEST STREET

A BLADES OVERSTREET NOVEL

THE
DARKEST STREET

GLENVILLE LOVELL

CHATTEL HOUSE BOOKS

PRAISE FOR GLENVILLE LOVELL

"Lovell has crafted a novel of style as well as substance, building with exquisite process to a shattering conclusion that in retrospect seems the only one possible. Along the way he skillfully weaves several subplots into the main story, and the novel's rich but seemingly unconnected strands meet to form brilliant patterns, completing a portrait of a village straining under the weight of secret lives."

—*The Washington Post*

"Mr. Lovell, who was born in Barbados, has a sharp eye for the extraordinary tropical landscape and the eccentricities of his characters."

—*The New York Times Book Review*

"A new generation of West Indian Writers have arrived full tilt on the literary scene, and one of the most arresting voices belong to Glenville Lovell of Barbados."

—*Paule Marshall*

"Snuggle up in your most comfortable spot... You will soon be swept away by Glenville Lovell's prose as he takes you on a journey..."

—*Emerge*

"Novelist Glenville Lovell joins the ranks of of such writers of magic realism as Alejo Carpentier..."

—*Library Journal*

Read these stories and share in their bold experiences. Lovell quickly draws you in and grips you in his tropical alchemy to the final pages of this book.

—*African American Literary Book Club*

ALSO BY GLENVILLE LOVELL

Fiction:
Fire in the Canes
Song of Night
Too Beautiful To Die
Love and Death in Brooklyn
Going Home in Chains

Plays:
Panama Silver
Simone's Place
On the Block

ABOUT THE AUTHOR

Glenville Lovell grew up in Barbados surrounded by sugar-cane, shadows and word-magicians. He is the author of five novels, several short stories and a number of prize-winning plays. This is his third Blades Overstreet book. Visit his website or follow him on Facebook or Twitter.

www.glenvillelovell.com
www.facebook.com/lovell.glenville
twitter:@glenvillelovell

1

That winter morning in 2005, I looked out into the early light and saw a purity I'd never expected to see in New York. The way the sunlight drizzling through the branches illuminated our bedroom was the stuff of lush poems and made me think of Barbados. The bone-colored sky was that flat and still.

The vista before me offered a stark contrast to the images conjured up by the song playing on WBAI, which was doing a special on the consequences of wars raging in different parts of Africa. The singer bemoaned life in exile, life on the run from the dictator who ruled his country.

I could relate to his feeling of exile. Born in the '60s to a black father and white mother, I've felt all my life as if I'd been born at the wrong place or time in history, that I should've made my arrival another century or two into the future, after the cracks across the American racial divide had been filled in.

As I listened to the song, I remembered something my friend, Noah Plantier, said to me one day. The notion of man living harmoniously regardless of race was a figment of my imagination. And that, in fact, disunity among men had little or nothing to do with race or class or creed; it was simply a condition of man's inability to be happy.

Recently, I've been suffering a disunity of a different sort. You could call it psychological disunity. Or maybe spiritual disunity. No difference to me, really. I'm not much on labels. The core of it all was that I've been having terrible dreams—nightmares, to tell the truth—which often felt so real they seemed like snippets of buried experiences. Each day for me was becoming a steadfast march toward confusion.

I glanced over at Anais, curled in a fetal pose, her cotton nightgown wrapped around her like a wayward shawl. Delight and love swelled in me along with the urge to kiss her, waking her to the smell of distant rain and marble daylight broadening across Brooklyn. It was hard to imagine a more beautiful sight than that of my wife asleep in our bed.

As I leaned close she arched and stretched, opening her eyes a crack. Her cheeks dimpled in smile.

"Morning." I kissed her lips.

"You're up early." Her feline eyes widened slowly.

"I got up to watch you sleep."

A soft, girlish giggle. "You must be horny."

"Come on," I said, feigning offence. "Why it always gotta be about sex?"

"Because you're a man, and I'm going away in two days. I know how you get when I have to go away."

"How do I get?"

"You're all over me like the chicken pox."

I got up from the bed. "I'm going for a run. You're making me out to be some love-starved puppy."

"Come back here."

I stopped.

"I love you," she said. "Go sweat your manly sweat, but leave some energy for me. I'll make breakfast and then we can get back to bed after Chesney leaves for school. We have all day to exhaust each other."

A stiff wind greeted me as I left my Prospect Lefferts home in a black vinyl tracksuit. The brisk five-minute walk to Prospect Park was enough of a warm-up for my run around the three and half mile circuit.

As I climbed the hill toward the park's northern entrance the wind became bitter, leaving a rancid taste in my mouth, and like a fluent conjurer it poured the remnants of last night's dream back into the chamber of my thoughts.

It was late evening. My father had just returned from an event important enough for him to wear a suit, a sight most unfamiliar to me. I must've been about six or seven; busy, as most boys that age are, playing in the living room with my action-figure toys: Captain America and GI Joe. My father knelt down beside me, putting his arm around my shoulder. Hunched over my toys making crazy battle noises, I paid little attention to him. He stayed there for a few minutes, saying nothing. I looked at him and he smiled, then he tousled my hair and went out.

A short time later, I heard a ruckus in the kitchen. I did not think to look up because my father was home. It always felt safe with him in the house. He was a big man, a giant in my eyes.

Then I heard loud sobbing. Behind that came my father's cannon voice. I'd never heard his voice this loud before, so full of anger. I got up to see what was going on.

I saw my mother hunched at the kitchen table, her body rippling with sobs. My father stood behind her, a menacing dark look in his eyes. He stared at me and said something. Whatever he said never registered in my head; I was paralyzed by the sight of my mother crying like a baby.

I felt clean inside after my run, the sweating having swept last night's toxins from body and mind. Exhausted but feeling blessed that I would be going home to an incorrigibly sexy wife, who was also a great role model for my young daughter, I crossed a Flatbush Avenue already teeming with people moving ghostlike through the cold like wanderers in an epic story.

I reached my house and was fumbling for my keys when Anais came from the backyard with a fat garbage bag.

"Weren't you supposed to take this out last night?" she said.

I grinned. "Sorry. Forgot."

Sunlight settled on the bulging black bag as she set it down on the lawn.

"Do you want me to take it?" I said.

Anais shrugged. "Noah is waiting for you in the den."

"Noah? What's he doing here so early?"

She turned away. "He's not alone."

"Who's he with?"

"Some guy named Chancellor something."

I blew my nose, wiping my hands in the wool cap covering my head and opened the door.

2

As laughter filled their Douglaston home, retired judge Rupert Foder beamed at his beautiful family gathered around him, and the exquisite feast he'd prepared for the event. Expensive French wine. Trays of braised lamb and veal cutlets. Just-baked Italian bread from DelMonte's. He looked across the table at his daughter, Zoe, and was almost overcome with pride. What a beauty she'd become. And so brilliant.

The Foders had come a long way since Rupert's grandfather emigrated from Italy to work on the dockyards of Brooklyn, before changing his name and opening a grocery store in Red Hook. Rupert had worked in that store before enrolling in law school at NYU. His success enabled him to send his children to private school and now they had gathered to celebrate Zoe's tremendous achievement.

His only daughter had recently become a partner with Loeb and Grosse, a team of pioneering plastic surgeons whose work in mesotherapy was making wrinkles disappear in Hollywood and on Park Avenue. Zoe would be in charge of their New York office, an opportunity that could make her very wealthy. And she was only twenty-eight.

Chancellor, a fledgling playwright, sitting to his father's left, appeared to be happy for his sister. He looked at his immigrant mother, Maria, and fed off her smile. She was a beautiful woman, her radiance in a purple velvet dress filling the entire room.

Chancellor got up to make a toast.

"I would like to congratulate my lovely sister on her meteoric rise in the world of body-magicians. As a writer, I hope to make the world a more beautiful place by leaving a mark on people's minds, but Zoe is already making women much more beautiful without leaving any marks. And that makes the world a much more enjoyable place for men like me. To have achieved so much so early can be a burden to some, but Zoe has handled her success like a true Foder. With humility and class. With that said, can I borrow fifty thousand dollars for my next production?"

The others laughed. Maria took her son's trembling hand and kissed it, the way she always did when she wanted to convey her love. She did the same to Zoe.

That's when the doorbell rang. Lourdes, the Nicaraguan housekeeper, a compact woman in her late-forties, answered the door. A minute later she returned to the dining room, a look of terror filling her brown eyes. Behind her were two masked men clad from head to toe in black. A contrast in size if not style, these leftovers from the last Ninja movie waved shiny guns in the air like toy swords.

Just like that, their night of celebration turned ugly. Laughter and merriment stopped. Fear paralyzed the family. Only the echo of the intruders' boots as they marched over to Rupert Foder penetrated the hot silence settling on the room.

The bigger of the two men, a dark hunched bear, whipped the gun in a wide arch and smashed the butt against the side of Rupert's head.

Rupert burped involuntarily and his head thudded to the table, a rope of blood streaking down the side of his face.

The housekeeper screamed. The smaller man served her a cold stare, immediately killing her voice. Her mouth froze open. She felt something hot running down her legs and tried to squeeze her thighs together to halt the flow. But every muscle in her body had turned to salt. She could not scream. She could not move. Her bladder, the only other outlet valve for her fear, had burst.

Lourdes' pee trickled along the floor, surrounding the larger man's scuffed boot. He glanced down, saw the river, looked into her eyes and held her gaze long enough to make her bite her lip.

She was a good Catholic, but here she was locking eyes with the devil, unable to turn away.

He smiled, mockingly puckering his lips, inviting her kiss. She shuddered and tried to look away. She couldn't. His gray eyes held hers in a frightening grip and she felt ashamed that she was so weak.

The smaller invader shuffled over to the table. With a peculiar forward lean to his body, he placed a piece of paper on the table in front of Maria.

ONE MILLION DOLLARS. NO TRICKS.

CONTACT THE POLICE AND HE DIES.
FURTHER INSTRUCTION LATER.

The stone-white tablecloth now boasted a bright triangle of blood, pooled next to the tray of chops. Numbed by fear, Maria looked at the note, her eyes flitting from the almost indecipherable scrawl on the paper to the blood scribbled across her husband's wrinkled forehead.

Zoe opened her mouth to speak to the bully with the bear's gait but her words seemed to flow backwards. Tongue-tied is what she was. The woman who woke in the morning giving notes to herself, the woman who out-talked everyone in college had been struck dumb.

Maria began to sing in Spanish. But it wasn't really singing. It was a raucous noise, a cawl ungoverned by any rhythm, a moment of complete and naked abandonment of sanity. Her head shook from side to side, her hair becoming loosened as she reached across the table to stroke her husband's head.

Thank God! He was still breathing.

The bear grabbed Mrs. Foder by the hair. Her head jerked up and he swung her around to face him. There was a mystified savage look of pain in her eyes. He must've seen arrogance. How dare she look him in the eyes? He put the gun to her head.

Chancellor finally found his voice.

"No!"

The diminutive gunman marched over to Chancellor. He carried the gun as if it were too heavy. But he had no trouble lifting it to Chancellor's temple, his free gloved hand moving quickly to clamp Chancellor's Adam's apple.

Chancellor became heavily aware of his own lips clutched together, dry and swollen. The cold metal scorched the side of his face. He closed his eyes to keep the fear inside.

He heard a faint click. Then an explosion. Loud and hollow at the same time, echoing for seconds in his brain. Then he realized he couldn't hear anything anymore. Was he dead or just dying? Was that bright light his life flashing before his eyes?

An urge to laugh. How long did he have to recap his life? How long before the light disappeared?

He regretted not being able to make his father as proud of him as he was of Zoe. He regretted not finishing that play he'd started two years ago. That could've been the one. Why didn't he finish it? That one could've taken him to Broadway.

The bright light disappeared.

Laughter now. Full and unrestrained. Hearing restored. Was it real?

The laughter receded. He opened his eyes.

The burly one swept Rupert up from the chair, flung him over his broad shoulder as he would a sack of rice, and plowed toward the exit, swinging his captive's body through the air barely missing the chandeliers.

Chancellor looked up and saw the hole in the ceiling and cried with relief.

Seconds later, the house was plunged into darkness.

Chancellor Foder finished the story of his father's kidnapping and glanced over at Noah then looked at me with eyes that stared wide, yet gave him an odd frozen presence. He seemed utterly lost.

Anais brought a pot of coffee and three cups on a tray, setting the tray down on the circular mahogany table she'd bought at a flea-market last summer.

"I'm going to get my nails done," she announced, then left with an arrogant sway of her hips, no doubt admonishment for my not getting rid of the intruders in timely fashion. Sun steamed through the glazed window, but did little to warm the room.

I poured coffee for the three of us. Chancellor pulled on his ponytail, then leaned forward, picked up the black mug and lifted it to his mouth. He might've been forty-five, give or take a few years with receding reddish-brown hair whisked with grains of gray.

I lifted my mug and instinctively blew into the cup. Anais always served her coffee steaming hot. I could feel Noah's eyes vetting my face, trying his best to read my mind.

"Why did you come to me?" I asked.

Noah spoke, "I brought him here. I told him you could help find his father."

"One million is a lot of cheese, I said. "Who put up the money?"

Chancellor wet his lips and sat back. "We got it from my father's bank account."

"He had that kind of cash?" I said.

"He did well in the gold rush of the eighties and nineties."

"What time did your sister make the drop?" I said.

"Around seven."

"What happened after that?" I said.

"Nothing. My father was supposed to be released after she delivered the money. Twelve hours later and we still haven't heard anything."

"When did you call the police?" I said.

"Late last night."

"And they haven't turned up anything yet?" I said.

Noah said, "Let's face it, Blades. We know how slow they work. Chancellor called me late last night to cancel a reading we were supposed to do at a church in Harlem. He told me what happened. I told him right away he needed to get somebody else on this."

We drank our coffee without further conversation. It was a silence that comes when you build the right fences, and I had erected not just fences around me but a sign saying keep out.

A swift appeared at the window, wavering momentarily before alighting on the ledge. When the silence had built to a crescendo Noah and his playwright friend got up and left.

3

Let me tell you about my city, this bazaar of world cultures. Half the population is descendant of immigrants, unless they've just stepped off a plane or boat themselves. It can be a wild, ugly city, but there's no place to match its creative personality and its passion, especially for the hustle.

They come from all corners of the globe, and whether they park themselves on wide cracked sidewalks, or get ensconced in large glass cages high above ground, they are united by one thing. The hustle. Speaking in silver tongues, some foreign, some familiar; selling knock-offs from Gucci to Groucho, from junk bonds to bail bonds, from cocaine to Coca-Cola, they make it all seem so authentic. On any given day, from Canal Street to Delancey Street, from Madison Avenue to Fashion Avenue, you can hear the clear refrain of the hustle. One man. Every man. Each true to a dream, his own hustle.

And for those who crave instant gratification, for whom the hustle is too slow a dance, there's always the big score. Lotto. A bank robbery. A kidnapping.

Sometimes it makes you wonder if there was anything real in this city. The New York skyline brimmed with stunning beauty, a striated, mauve and blue sunset, which I glimpsed standing at the intersection of Ocean Avenue and Avenue K with Anais who'd dragged me out of the house to check out a yard sale.

The raw images that Chancellor had painted on my mind were prodding me into uneasiness and Anais easily picked up my distraction.

"What's on your mind, honey?"

"Oh, nothing." I said, mechanically.

"Then how come you haven't responded to anything I've said for the past five minutes?"

"I was thinking."

"Not about anything I was saying, clearly."

"I'm sorry."

"What do you think about this lamp? It's a Tiffany."

"I don't like it."

"Why not?"

"Why can't I just not like it?"

She set the lamp back on its roost on the cluttered table. "Okay, Blades. Let's go. You shouldn't have come if you weren't up to it."

"I'm sorry, babe. I was thinking about that guy who came to see me this morning."

"Why'm I not surprised," she groused.

I knew I already had one foot in the dog house so I said nothing.

"Have they found his father?" Anais probed.

"I don't know. I suspect not. Families always make that mistake. Thinking that if they give into the demands the thugs would respect their own promises. His father's probably dead."

We left the yard sale and walked along Avenue K to our car, passing a group of fresh-faced youngsters rapping with feverish intensity.

Anais opened the door on the driver's side. She looked at me, her eyes sad. "That could've been you, Blades. I think about it sometimes, you know. About you being a target. You're a successful businessman."

"I'm always armed."

She bared her teeth in disdain. "One day your big gun isn't going to be enough."

"We'll see when that day comes."

I didn't have any bad dreams that night for which I was thankful. Indeed, when I woke next morning and realized that I'd slept the night through it was both a relief and a joy. But the joy was short lived.

It began to rain just after ten o'clock. With the rain came a zealous wind darting quicksilver through the swaying branches, its white tail lashing the windows with a graceful violence. I could only watch in admiration.

Negus Andrews, my partner in Club Voodoo, called to ask if we could skip our regular Saturday meeting; he had a brunch date. Knowing Negus, that meant he'd gotten himself involved with a new woman and things were looking good. The way the wind was whipping up leaves in the yard I didn't mind at all.

Chesney came downstairs and found me in the living room reading the newspaper. As energetic as any ten-year-old, my daughter looked unusually despondent that morning.

She kissed my cheek. "Morning, Daddy."

"What's wrong?"

"The world is so sad," she mused.

"It's not so bad if you're a bird," I joked. "You can fly away when you don't like your surroundings. When it's cold you can fly to warm places."

"I'm serious, Daddy. I was just watching a program on TV. All those poor people in Africa starving to death and dying of AIDS. Why don't we help them? We have so much food here. All the stores are full of things."

I didn't have a quick or easy answer for Chesney. If I tried I couldn't even explain it to myself. The phone rang, saving me further embarrassment. It was Noah.

"They found Judge Foder," he said.

"That's good."

"They found him dead."

I left home after lunch. A driving rain still blanketed the city. Water splashed off the highway hiding cars in a balloon of gray froth.

Driving carefully, I hit all the right exits off the Parkway to Northern Boulevard, then through the winding tree-lined streets of Douglaston, reaching my destination on Shore Road fifty minutes later.

The roar of water rushing down storm drains filled the afternoon as I parked on the inclined driveway and got out in the rain. The wind had died down and the rain no longer slanted in ropes but fell in noisy heaps to the ground.

The large cream and brown two-story house was partially hidden by two huge oak trees out front. Beneath the portico two white stone lions guarded the entrance.

Several cars were parked in the driveway. One I recognized as Noah's. However, none I could mark as police.

I rang the front door and watched mist float off Little Neck Bay as I waited. Chancellor opened. Face tight. Lips bleached. He ushered me inside with a solemn handshake. The house seemed even bigger from indoors. Chancellor took my coat and led me to a wide living room that boasted of genteel living: plush stone-colored couches, expensive-looking rugs, art work on pastel yellow walls.

The air was heavy with the anguish of a damaged family. They did little to hide the wreckage. Not that they needed to. Was their house. Their grief. Two weeping women sat together on a couch holding hands, the bags under their eyes deep enough to hold a roll of pennies.

Noah was there, sitting by a fireplace. Standing near a window was a tall busty brunette who had the haughty bearing of a frigate bird: long limbs and a fitful glare in her dark eyes. She crossed the room to greet me, her step light and soundless on the rug.

"I'm Honor Foder, Chancellor's wife," she said, and then smiled as if she'd just salvaged the last smile from the cliff of disillusionment.

"Blades. Nice to meet you," I said.

She introduced me to the wailing women on the sofa. The older woman with the ancient face and scooped eyes was Maria. Next to her, Zoe strained to camouflage her pain by forcing a smile, but her tiny mouth seemed unable to span her teeth.

The other woman in the room whose patient eyes lapped up her surroundings needed no introduction. She stood taller than almost everyone else, her unshackled dreadlocks falling past her shoulder.

"Blades, so nice to see you," she said.

"River, what are you doing here?" I said.

She took a step toward me. Her eyes smiled. "I was about to ask you the same question."

"After you turned us down, we went to her," Noah said.

River Paris was an old acquaintance who once managed my club. But she was no stranger to detective work. She'd been a cop in Miami some years ago where she'd built a reputation for ruthlessly hunting lowlifes. I hadn't seen her since I fired her about a year ago. I'd heard that she'd opened her own P.I. business in Brooklyn. Though she once saved my life, I hesitate to call her my friend. Around that same time we found ourselves on different sides of an issue involving our fathers which almost ended tragically.

I turned to the widow. "I'm deeply sorry for your loss."

She held what looked like a scarf in her hand, a thick yellow cloth which she intermittently lifted to her face, either sniffing or rubbing her cheekbone. She looked at me and tried a smile. Her eyes were red from crying, but I sensed a determination beneath them. "Help us find who killed him."

I said, "I'm sure the police will find them."

Zoe spoke for the first time. "We're not putting our faith in them. My father used to call them a bunch of uneducated morons. He had little faith in them. Why should we?"

Honor Foder cursed under her breath and marched from the room.

"Police work has as much to do with instincts as with clues," I said. "Little things could be important markers in developing a case. Kinda like being a good doctor."

Zoe's eyes focused on mine. "I know a little about the police and how they develop cases. And you're out of your league trying to compare it with medicine."

"I was just saying…"

She cut me off. "I know what you were trying to say. But I know more about the police than you know about medicine. They were here all night last night. And most of the morning. They just left half an hour ago. All they could tell us was that they think it's the work of professionals."

"Except for the slug in the ceiling, practically no evidence was left here or at the murder scene," River said. "I spoke to the lead detective."

"Where was the body found?" I said.

Zoe answered. "In an abandoned warehouse in Long Island City."

"When did you get the first call?" I said.

Zoe said, "Around seven next morning. To find out if I had the money. I told him it would take a few hours."

"What were your instructions?"

"I was told to put the money in a black knapsack and be waiting in my car for further instructions at seven o'clock that evening."

"What happened then?"

"It's still a jumble in my head. I was so scared." She paused. "The call came to my cell phone at exactly seven o'clock. I was told to drive south on the Belt. I wasn't told where I was going. About two minutes before I got to Kings County Mall they told me to go into the parking lot. I was told to take the money and buy a ticket to whatever was showing in theater three. I was to sit in the first aisle seat in the front row. Don't ask me how he knew that seat would be empty."

"My guess he was already in the theater," I said.

Zoe continued. "I was to put the bag in the seat and leave. The movie had already started when I got there. It was so dark. I did as I was told. But before I could get outside there was an announcement over the PA, that everyone in the theater should leave in an orderly fashion. Someone in the back screamed. 'It's a bomb.' That's when pandemonium broke out. I was almost trampled by the mad rush for the exit. I made it to my car. I sat there unable to turn the ignition. I wasn't crying. I can't even say I was upset. I was just numb."

"Did you notice anyone in the seat next to where you put the bag?" I said.

Zoe said, "No."

"The police already ran a trace on the phone," River said. "Burner."

"Your father, he was retired, right?" I said.

"Two years," Chancellor said.

"Criminal court?" I said.

"Civil," Zoe said. "Mostly divorces. Estate settlement."

"Has he ever received threats on his life?" I said.

The widow spoke. "My husband was a very nice man. Nobody would want to kill him."

"Who knew he had that kind of money lying around?" I said.

Zoe turned sharply, her face anxious. "It wasn't lying around."

"Still, somebody must've known you could get your hands on a million dollars with ease," I said.

"Could be anybody," Chancellor said. "My father was well known. He gave money to a lot of causes. He gave money to the NAACP. To churches. To museums. To local civic organizations in the area. People knew he had money."

"What do you remember about the kidnappers? Anything distinctive about their voices? Any strange mannerisms?" I said.

Zoe shook her head. So did Mrs. Foder.

"They were black men," said Chancellor.

I turned to look at him.

Chancellor continued, "Their voices. I could tell by their voices."

Noah spoke up in a strained voice. "C'mon, Chancellor. You can't say that."

"Why not?" Chancellor said. "I was here, you weren't."

I shrugged, "Ok. So you think they were black."

"Yes," Chancellor said. "They called each other cuz."

"Is that why you think they were black?" I said to Chancellor.

He hesitated. "I know what you're thinking. But it's not a racial thing. I'm around a lot of black people. I could tell by their voices."

"Did anyone else hear this?" I asked.

Nobody answered.

I turned to Zoe, my tone facetious. "What about the man who phoned you? Did he sound black to you?"

"I couldn't tell," she said.

The widow rubbed the cloth against her face, letting out a barely audible, strangulated soprano note. "Why did they have to kill him?"

4

Negus introduced me to his new girlfriend that night in Voodoo. I could see why he was smitten with her. If there were any flaws in her skin there were none in her game. Like few women, she had mastered the skill of making a man feel as if he was King Midas. Every word that fell from Negus' mouth Komi picked up, dusted off and slipped right back down his throat with the ease of a conjure woman. She had obviously conjured up some magic for my DJ friend. The last time I saw Negus act like such a schoolboy around a woman, he ended up in the hospital with a collapsed lung from a bullet meant for that woman. Her name was River Paris.

Being a radio personality, Negus had no shortage of eager women vying for his attention. Every Saturday night women of all types and shapes—from hoochie-mama street girls, to virginal repressed homebodies—mesmerized by Negus' growl-deep radio voice, flocked to the club to get a glimpse of the "Caribbean Man." The bolder ones expected even more. A touch. A kiss on the cheek. His home phone number. What they got in Negus was an eyeful. Standing over six-two with lumberjack shoulders and a glistening bald head, Negus personified that bold black image hawked by Madison Avenue and other purveyors of American sexual fantasy.

Thanks to Negus, Voodoo was the place to be in Brooklyn for dancing. His live simulcast on WXES from the club every Saturday night didn't hurt. By 11 o'clock Voodoo was overrun by eager revelers intent of discarding last week's troubles in one night of drinking and uninhibited dancing to the latest soca and dancehall tunes.

Just before midnight Negus left me alone with Komi in his booth near the DJ's position to go begin his broadcast. She was sipping champagne; I was settling into my third Courvoisier.

"How long you and Negus been in business?" she asked.

I looked at her, wondering how she'd managed to squeeze herself into the bright orange dress, her plump butt making her look as close to an overripe mango as one could get. She was striking without being beautiful, round in the right places, with a nose too big for her face and a full laughing mouth.

"Two years. What do you do?" I asked.

"Real estate."

"Sales?"

Her smile covered her entire face. "Chasing the paper."

"Who do you work for?"

"Got my own company."

"That's gotta feel good," I said.

"Wanna go outside and smoke a joint?"

"Naw. I don't do that stuff."

She seemed surprised. "Yeah?"

"Just this." I tapped the cognac glass.

"Be right back," she said and got up.

I watched her wend her way through the thick crowd, her legs and ass straining for release from the skin-tight dress. When she had disappeared in the swamp of bodies I got up and went to the bathroom wondering how long it would take Komi to break Negus' heart.

I dropped my aching head on my pillow after 4 that morning, having crept into the bedroom as quietly as I could so as not to wake Anais. Once again sleep hid from me. Instead I lay awake pondering the stink and lust of city life, where danger lurked around every silhouetted garbage can. Every trembling shape in the dark, every shadow that twitched in misty night fog could be someone waiting to bring harm to you.

I thought about the Foder family and their suffering. I remembered the widow's wet, shiny eyes and the way she held that piece of cloth as if she would disintegrate if she released it. What was she doing now? Was she up, like me, unable to sleep, pondering fate?

I didn't like Chancellor Foder. I wanted to like him. After all, Noah thought enough of him to want to help him. Under most circumstances that would've been good enough for me. His assertion that the men who kidnapped his father were black founded on his natural talent at identifying a black man by voice alone was dubious at best. I didn't know what to make of it. Did he really believe what he was saying? And did that make him racist?

I tried to put those thoughts aside, to think of pleasanter things, lobbing my mind across the Atlantic to the silver sands of Barbados, hoping to find relaxation and sleep. Recently, I'd bought some sleep-aid tapes with wood-wind mood music and a female instructor talking in the monotone of a hypnotist. She mentioned this technique called visualization, which was supposed to help you relax. Visualizing something peaceful that promoted feelings of joy and happiness was supposed to bring on relaxation and sleep.

I tried to picture swelling waves breaking into silky surf. Birds sailing below a stretch of drifting clouds. But my mind would not stay there. Instead of bright sunlight my mind saw artificial light from street lamps drift-ing over a dark foggy New York street, and the swollen faces of destitute women crying, faces ravaged by time, by fear, by abuse. Faces from my past.

Someone once told me that a mind sinks to the level of its load. If that were so, what was I carrying? Half an island?

I got out of bed and went downstairs where I made a cup of mint tea. Sitting in the darkened den drinking my tea I heard the purr of footsteps across the floor. I suspected it was Anais though I didn't turn around to see.

"What's the matter, Blades?" she said, from behind me.

I held the hot mug in my hand not knowing what to say.

She came around to face me, stooping eye-level to cup my chin in her warm hands. I could see her eyes bright and intense in the dark.

"When are you going to tell me what's been bothering you?" Anais pleaded. "I know you haven't been sleeping well for days now."

I tried to avert my gaze.

She held my face steady in her hands forcing me to take her eyes. "I'm leaving tomorrow. I'm worried. I can't cancel my trip to take care of you."

"I'll be fine."

"Blades, we've been down this road before."

"What road?"

"You not leveling with me. And then your implosion which almost destroyed our marriage."

I could not shrink away from her good sense. "I've been having some terrible dreams lately."

"About what?"

"All sorts of things."

Anais stood and backed into the leather armchair. "Don't you trust me?"

"I keep having these dreams about my mother and father. Except..."

"Except what?"

"I'm not sure they're dreams. I think I may be remembering things that I've kept hidden for a long time."

"What kind of things?"

"Fights between my parents. I think my father was physically abusing my mother and I just blotted it out."

"What makes you so sure it's memory?"

"It just feels so real."

"There's a strange relationship between you and your father, Blades. You need to sort it out. Don't answer right now. Just think about it. But..." She paused, squeezing my hand hard. "Maybe you need to go talk to a professional, honey."

Anais got up and left the room. I bowed my head and must've drifted off to sleep because the next thing I saw was dawn's gray eye creeping past the scarlet window blinds. I sat there suspended in stillness, feeling a surge of energy flow through me. I got up and drew the blinds back exposing the mist bending under the weight of daylight.

At 3 o'clock, Flatbush Avenue was as busy that Sunday afternoon as if it had been Saturday. The sidewalk had been turned into an open-air bazaar lined with itinerant merchants hawking baseball caps, cheap watches bought for pennies on Canal Street, knock-off designer colognes and fake Fendi bags.

I tiptoed around a large woman standing at the edge of the street contemplating whether to plunk her money down on a fake Gucci sweater. Luckily, my destination on Fulton Street was one block away.

I entered the building next to African Heritage bookstore to be greeted by a bracing sour smell which scraped my nasal passages dry.

What the hell!

I had agreed to meet River Paris in her office. She did warn me not to expect a suite in Rockefeller Plaza. But this stinkaroo?

River's office was on the second floor. There, the sour smell gave way to the odor of old tires. I thought for a moment of calling her and telling her to meet me in the restaurant across the street.

I rang the bell. Dressed in tight black jeans and dark blue sweater, she was at the door in seconds, her muscled arms bulging with complete arrogance, her dark face smiling.

"Were you standing at the door?" I said.

"Come inside." Her voice as always, laced with wit and pride.

I stepped through the door into a cubbyhole that smelled as badly as the hallway.

She closed the door behind me. "Don't say anything about the smell. It didn't smell like this when I moved in. The landlord assured me he'll have it fixed by tomorrow. Else I'm gone."

She stood beside me fiddling with her earring.

"I just bought them on the street," she said. "What do you think?"

They were hoops made of some kind of brightly painted wood.

"There're nice."

"Made in Zimbabwe. I've never bought anything made in Zimbabwe before."

"Neither have I."

She laughed. "Want me to get you a pair?"

I'd forgotten how sparkling her voice was, how well she could command your attention, like a leopard leaping out of the dark. She had that rare combination of beauty and power, the kind that left you swaying long after she'd departed your company, as if you'd just listened to a Bob Marley song, and were waiting, hoping to get a reprise.

"Sit down, Blades."

I settled into a gray office chair and she squeezed behind the desk and sat down in a leather sway back. There was little else in the room because there was room for little else. The grayish walls were blank. One window. Shade pulled down. One of those combination fax machine-printers sat on the desk. A laptop hummed quietly.

"You just missed Tris," she said.

"Who's Tris?"

"Young woman from the Marcy Houses. Works for me part-time. Taking care of filing and billing and that sort of thing. She's studying criminal justice at John Jay. Wants to become a cop. Figure a few weeks with me and she'd come to her senses."

"How're things going otherwise?" I said.

"If I tell you the truth you'd laugh."

"I love a good laugh."

She chuckled. "Some other time. I have a question for you. Noah came to me, said you turned him down the other morning. What made you change your mind?"

"I don't like bad people," I said. "I don't like hearing about people being kidnapped and murdered. Makes me want to break things."

"We've always had that one thing in common."

"Just that one thing?"

Her eyes sparkled. "Wanna work together?"

"Makes sense."

A lazy half-grin. "Excellent. Shall we drink to celebrate our team?"

"Thanks, but too early for me."

"How's Chesney?"

"She's fine. You should drop by and see her."

She leaned forward and cleared her throat. "Your wife hates me."

"That's in the past. She knows I love her more than anything."

Eyebrows arched. "I bet."

"What do you make of the Foder family?" I said.

"I like Zoe. She's honest. The rest? Meh!"

"I don't like Chancellor."

"You think he's racist?"

I paused. "I don't know. I trust Noah's judgment. If Chancellor was racist Noah would've outed him a long time ago. I just don't like him. None of them to be honest."

"The police pulled the surveillance tape from the mall. They interviewed most of the drivers of the cars which entered before or followed Zoe into the mall during a half hour span. No suspects. They're going to have the Foders review the tape to see if they recognize anyone."

"How'd you get this information?"

"Detective Raymond Grant. The lead detective I told you about. He's a brother. He's not happy about our involvement but I got him to loosen up and he promised to share what he's got if we do the same."

"What did you do to loosen him up?"

Her eyes steadied on mine. "I told him I was single and bored. He felt sorry for my situation."

I smiled, knowing she was toying with me. "So they have nothing at all?"

"Nada. They interviewed all of the neighbors already. Canvassed the neighborhood. Nothing. Nobody saw a thing. Seems to have been a well-executed plan. And they picked a great night. Cold and foggy. Great cover."

"Compounded by the Foders' stupidity. They should've called the police the moment those gangsters left with the judge."

"Detective Grant invited me down to the precinct to look at some stills from the murder scene. Then he's gonna drive me out to that abandoned warehouse so I could take a look around."

"He must really pity your lonely situation," I said.

"He ain't my type, though."

"Maybe he'll grow on you."

"Like you did?"

"Is that what I did?"

"Not really. It was an instantaneous thing with you."

"Shouldn't we talk about how we're gonna catch these killers?" I said.

River grinned. "You're right."

"I say we give the Foders a day or so to catch themselves. Then talk to them again. Stress can make you very forgetful. I know the police talked to the neighbors, but you should have a go with them. Some people don't like talking to the police."

"I doubt that's the case in this neighborhood. These kinds of people have a great relationship with cops. After all, it's them the cops are really protecting. I'll see what I can find out about the judge's movements the past few weeks. I know he was only civil, but even they have enemies."

"And skeletons," I added.

"We need to talk to the housekeeper."

I got up and went to the door. I turned, leaning on the doorjamb.

"Blades." She walked toward me gesturing with her hand as if trying to articulate a thought with sign language. She hugged me, somewhat tentatively, her body leaning softly into my chest. Her hair smelled like sandalwood. "Thanks for coming."

5

The next day I drove Anais to the airport. Her father in Atlanta was sick. Apparently the prognosis wasn't good. Mother wanted her down for some moral support. Her sister was also flying in from North Carolina. I was hoping she wouldn't be gone too long.

Leaving LaGuardia airport I survived the dense 18-wheeler traffic on the BQE, before turning off at Exit 9A and cruising down Flatbush to Prospect Heights. I parked on a block of well-tended brownstones.

My destination was the corner of Underhill and Park, where I hoped to get some information from someone whose nose never left New York's underbelly for fear that he might miss the rumbling of revolt he knew would one day take down his drug empire.

Along with the one I was heading to in Brooklyn, Toni Monday owned another salon in Manhattan where he catered to some of New York's elite entertainers; but the salons were really an elaborate cover, somewhere to launder money from his drug business.

Last time I spoke to Toni he'd been forced to abandon—at least for the time being—an operation he'd always dreamed of having. Toni was a six-foot transgender who was born a man but identified as female. After successful hormone therapy to develop breasts, he was close to going under the knife to remove his testicles and penis when the doctor told Toni that he wasn't ready, that he needed more psychological therapy.

At the time I'd felt sorry for Toni. I should've reserved my sympathy for the doctor. I later discovered that Toni blinked out on the surgeon. Almost choked the poor man to death. Spent a night in jail and was released after the doctor refused to cooperate with police.

My knowledge of Toni's tendencies led me to believe that he had one of his wreckers whisper sweet nothings into the doctor's ears, scaring the man into silence. Toni was now back in psychotherapy.

I walked into the salon at the height of the business day. Was hot inside. Every chair in the joint was occupied. Outfitted with muted track lighting and wood-framed mirrors and leather stools at each station, this was one of the classiest joints anywhere in Brooklyn, or Manhattan for that matter.

Women with their heads trapped under huge devices read magazines; some appeared to be sleeping. Toni was busy applying makeup to a spike-haired woman's face.

Since I last saw him he'd dropped about 50 pounds. Not that he was now svelte by any means. Normally he loaded a solid 300 pounds.

Still dressed in the same flamboyant manner, though. Today it was hip-hugging purple pants and sequined black shirt. But there was something new. Large black-framed glasses.

He didn't see me until one of the stylists, a dark-skinned young woman with an awkward smile, came up to me and asked if she could help. I said I was looking for Toni. On hearing his name he turned in my direction.

"Blades, don't tell me. You're here for a haircut." His laughter was a bright thunder clap.

"I need to talk to you."

"What about?" He batted his eyes, playfully.

"Business. I need a favor."

"I should know better than to think this was a social visit. I'll be done in ten. How about I meet you across the street at Black Pearl?"

Half hour passed before Toni sashayed into the sparsely furnished joint across from his salon. With its shiny aluminum furniture and black and white pictures on chalk walls, the place had the feel of one of those pretentious East Village cafes. But that's the kind of joint you'd expect in this neighborhood whose residents—many of them transplanted Manhattanites running from high rents—wanted to pretend they were still living in the shadow of the Empire State Building. Get real.

I ordered coffee and posted myself at a street-side table taking in the traffic on the block. A group of kids playing touch football.

The tragedies I'd witnessed on this street could fill a dossier. Just a few blocks away I once watched an addict drown in his own puke before an ambulance could arrive to take him to the hospital.

Toni's entrance jangled the bells at the door. He ordered something from the waiter and then sat opposite me as noise built outside where the action in the football game was getting heated.

"You look like shit, Cuz," Toni said.

"Gee, why don't you tell me something I don't know?"

He laughed. "Wife troubles?"

"Things are fine with me and Anais."

"The fact that that woman is still married to you is more shocking than Michael Jackson being a father." He put his hands to his mouth mockingly. "Oh, did I just crack on Mike?"

The waiter brought a bowl of what looked like split-pea soup and set it down in front of Toni. Steam swirled above the large bowl.

"When I was a kid my grandmother used to make split-pea soup every freakin' Saturday. Best thing about it was the dumplings. She used to make these huge-ass, fluffy cornmeal dumplings. The soup used to be so thick you could use it for face mask. And she used to flavor that shit with pigtails. You know how them West Indians love their salted pork. Split pea soup is the only thing I get when I come in here. It reminds me of my granny." Toni dipped the spoon into the soup and stirred slowly. "Do you ever think about shit like that, Blades? You know, things you used to do when you were young? Things you used to eat. Things you used to hate. How fucked up things were around you but you were too cranked to notice?"

Toni looked at me expecting me to say something. Before the pause dissolved I had a flash of my grandmother making fish cakes in her Crown Heights apartment.

He tasted his soup, nodding approvingly. "So what can I do for you, Blades? I realize you don't come to see me unless you want something. You haven't even said anything about the way I look."

"I'm amazed."

"By what?"

"You've lost a lot of weight."

"Asshole! That was the objective of the operation."

"What operation?"

"Do you ever listen to anything I tell you?"

"What did you tell me? The only operation I know anything about was the one to snip your balls and you didn't have that, did you?"

"No, I didn't have that. But I had my stomach stapled."

"When was this?"

"It doesn't freakin' matter."

"Good for you. I mean, you look good. The weight loss."

"Whatever, Blades. You don't have to sound so patronizing. It wasn't easy, you know. After the surgery there's this desire to heave every time something passes your throat. I still have trouble keepin' shit in my stomach."

"A judge was kidnapped from his home in Queens a few days ago. He was later found dead in an abandoned warehouse in Long Island City after the kidnappers took a mil off his daughter in Kings County Mall."

"I saw that on the news."

"Heard anything on the street?"

Toni scooped a spoonful of soup and blew on it to cool it. He let the spoon fall back into the bowl. "All I know is what I saw on the news."

"Any 'fetti flowing from unlikely sources?"

"Not in my backyard. That's big game hunting, though. Sounds like pros."

"If you hear of anything, I'd appreciate you letting me know."

"So do you want to know what's going on in my life now?"

"Not particularly."

"I'm throwing a party next week," he said.

"You throw a party every week, Toni."

"Well, this one is special. It's a going away party."

"Going away? Who? You?"

"Yes, I'm going away."

"Where?"

His gravelly laughter floated above the silky steam. "Me and my boyfriend are going up to Canada to get married."

"Congratulations," I said.

He cocked his head. "You don't really mean that. I can tell."

"How can you tell?"

"I don't know. It doesn't sound sincere. Do you believe gays should be allowed to get married?"

"Toni, I really don't care what you do with your life. If you wanna get married, what difference does it make to me?"

"Then you'll come?"

"If I'm not busy."

He scowled and stirred his soup.

6

Next morning I called my friend Semin Gupta, a prize-winning reporter from the New York Times. The brightness in her voice made me feel like an old man. With a spry laugh she hinted that the source of her cheerfulness was a new outlook on life, and told me she was doing her morning exercises and would call back. Fifteen minutes later I greeted her breathless hello with a mouth full of coffee.

"Sorry, Semin," I said. "Trying to wake up."

"What's the matter, Blades? Your crowing days are gone?"

"Never one to crow very hard, you know that, Semin."

She breathed heavily. "You sound terrible. Cold?"

"Lack of sleep."

"Well, I can't help you with that."

"What can you can tell me about judge Rupert Foder."

"Are you investigating his murder?"

"Helping out a friend."

"What do you want to know?"

"Anything you can dig up. Enemies. Skeletons."

"I'll get back to you. In the meantime…"

"I know. Sleep. So, what's this new outlook you're professing?"

She laughed out loud. "Another time, Blades. I gotta run."

Later that day I drove Chesney to New Jersey. She and my mom would be leaving the next morning for Florida. I took Anais' SUV because of its state-of-the-art sound system. Anais had bought me a bunch of CDs recently, including Diane Reeves', which I brought along for company knowing that as soon as we got into the car Chez would attach herself to her precious IPod. My mom was chopping bell peppers and garlic to cook jambalaya when we arrived. After the round of greetings I sent Chez with a bag of Tostitos to watch TV in the living room. I needed to speak to my mother alone.

I sat at the small kitchen table while she bustled around. I made a mental note to ask her what new diet was giving her this youthful vigor.

"You know, Carmen, I didn't expect you until later tonight. And I thought of cooking gumbo after you called, but I'd already promised my friend I would cook him jambalaya for lunch. Are you going to join us?"

My mother, my sister and my father were the only people who still called me by my given name: Carmen. It is a name I shed when I was old enough to join the marines, elevating my last name to be my first name.

"Who's this friend you're cooking lunch for?"

She stopped what she was doing. "Do I detect a note of disapproval in your voice?"

"No. Curiosity maybe."

She flung her head back and laughed. "I know you well, my son."

"And I know you well, mother. I don't remember the last time I saw you this wound up and excited."

"Oh my! That's not good. He'll think I'm too eager."

"Too eager for what?"

She shunned my question. "What's wrong? I hear it in your voice."

"I've been having trouble sleeping."

She dropped oil into a hot skillet and tossed chicken thighs. "You and Anais okay?"

"Yes. No fires there."

"Then what's the problem?"

"It's these dreams I've been having. Can't seem to shake them. They leave me agitated and confused."

She began to cut up Andouille sausage. "There's an old Cajun saying: Dreams are your way to the truth."

"Did my father ever hit you?" I blurted out.

My mother's face crumpled. She put the knife down. "What's wrong with you, Carmen?"

"What do you mean what's wrong with me?"

"Is this what you've been dreaming about?"

"For a month now."

"You need to take a break. Get away. Take Anais on a cruise."

"What kind of answer is that?"

She wiped her hands on a towel before sitting at the table across from me. "Look Carmen, I've recently met someone. A very nice man. He's a visiting professor at the college. After twenty years of waiting to find out what happened to your father, I was finally able to close that chapter of my life when he reappeared last year and I was able to get a divorce. You knew where he was for a long time and never told me. I knew that you knew but I respected whatever bond you thought you were preserving by not asking you anything."

"If you did I would've told you. I wouldn't have lied to you."

She got up to check the chicken in the skillet. "That's not the point."

"What's the point?"

She turned to face me, her eyes watery. "You did lie to me, Carmen. You lied in your heart. But the point is that it's all in the past. You can't change the past."

"I'm not trying to change the past. I just want to understand what's happening to me now. In the present. I keep having these dreams... these nightmares... and they all involve you and dad and I'm wondering if it isn't because I saw something years ago that I couldn't deal with."

"It's just dreams, Carmen."

"You guys fought a lot. I remember that. And Melanie said she saw him hit you."

"I don't want to talk about this anymore. It's too negative. You need help, Carmen."

I stood staring at her realizing I was shaking. A strange feeling came over me, and I sat down closing my eyes to collect myself. When I opened them again I was alone in the kitchen. My mother had walked away.

"Blades?"

I lowered the volume on the car stereo. "Whaddup River?"

"You sound like you've just seen a wild beast prowling your back yard."

I laughed. "Maybe I was just thinking about you."

"I'm glad you think so fondly of me. Where are you?"

"Just escaped the Holland tunnel."

"New York side?"

"I'm on Chambers."

"Had a thirst for gumbo and a little motherly advice?"

I wasn't in the mood for witty banter. "What do you want?"

"I just called the Foder house. They told me the housekeeper quit."

"Do you blame her?"

"Under the circumstances, I suppose not. I'm going out to talk to her. Wanna come along?"

"I'll meet you there."

"Do you know where she lives?"

"That was gonna be my next question."

"Six-seventy-two Livonia. If you take…"

"I was born in Brooklyn, Mamita."

"See you in half an hour."

I flipped the phone onto the seat next to me and turned the volume on the stereo as loud as it would go. Solomon Burke was going *Down in the Valley*.

The colorful mural on Blake street depicted the history of East New York with style and humor. Named by John Pitkin who bought land north of New Lots in 1835 and called it East New York because it was east of Manhattan, it was once a neighborhood of German, Italian and Polish immigrants until African-Americans moved in during the '50s. That sent white people scurrying like rats for the suburbs of Long Island and New Jersey. Following the riots in the fucked up '60s East New York hit the skids and nobody wanted to live there.

In the '80s, new immigrants from the Caribbean and South America took over, transforming the main commercial areas of New Lots and Pennsylvania Avenue into strips for Caribbean and Latin restaurants and stores. Recently community groups and religious leaders have been banding together to rebuild the area.

Surrounded by the impenetrable smell of fear and neglect, Lourdes Calderon lived in a dented walk-up apartment building on Livonia on the edge of a park, and only a few blocks away from darkened warehouses.

Young men in hoodies prowled street corners spitting at each other's feet as if playing some street game of spit-bocce, their breath flying in free-forming circles of condensation. Sunlight bled through dingy clouds and even in daylight, the neighborhood seemed halved in darkness.

River was sitting in her jeep across the street from Lourdes' building when I pulled up. I curbed a few feet away from a garage attached to the building.

She approached my car, puffing on a cancer stick, her knee-length black leather jacket flapping open. I could see the gun butt peeking out of its holster. She flicked the cigarette away as she reached me and smiled. "I thought you'd gotten lost."

"You probably just got here," I said.

She zipped up her jacket. "She's expecting us."

Lourdes buzzed us in. We climbed the rickety stairs and knocked on her second floor apartment. A dark face creased with exhaustion peeked from behind the door.

River spoke. "Hi. River Paris. I called earlier."

Delight surfaced in the woman's eyes and I thought then that she would've been happy to see just about anyone other than the IRS.

"Si. Si. I'm Lourdes," she said.

"This is Blades Overstreet," River continued the introductions.

"Nice to meet you both," Lourdes said. "Come in. I was just cooking."

We entered and immediately surrendered our senses to a mixture of pungent aromas, a potent combination of pepper and onion and garlic.

"Whatever you're cooking, it smells wonderful," said River.

Lourdes smiled and her puffy cheeks rose like dough. "Thank you. It's just a little something for my daughter before she runs off to school. The girl loves to eat. I tell her this is America and boys no like girls who are fat, but she doesn't listen."

"What is it?" I asked.

"Oxtail stew. Would you like some?"

I declined politely. I'd stopped eating red meat not long ago.

"If it's not too much trouble," River said.

"Oh, no," Lourdes said. "I just finished. I fix you a plate."

She led us into the living room. Low ceilings along with poor ventilation and inadequate light gave the apartment a claustrophobic air. There was a stack of books in the middle of the floor, leaving little room to walk.

"Sit down," Lourdes said. "How many times I told that girl not to leave these books in the middle of the room like that?"

I grabbed a drab-looking chair which might've started out scarlet but had been bled of its luster and was now tongue-colored. River squeezed around the stack of books and settled into a sofa under the yellow-curtained window.

Lourdes turned to me. "I bought that chair you're sitting in at a flea-market on Atlantic Avenue. It was the very first thing I bought after I came to America. I know it's old but I can't seem to part with it."

"How long have you been living here?" I asked.

"Here, in this apartment?"

"In America?"

"Ten years. Oh, look at me. Forgetting my manners. Can I get you something to drink?"

"A glass of water, thank you," I said.

She turned to River.

With a hopeful shrug, River said. "Beer?"

"I only have Dos Equis?" Lourdes asked.

"My favorite," said River.

Lourdes smiled and left.

"That smell is making me hungry," I growled.

"Then have some. What do you have against red meat, anyway?"

Lourdes returned with a woven basket tray which she set on a circular table near a hanging flower pot. On the tray were two glasses, a bottle of Dos Equis and a blue earthenware bowl of food and a plate with tortillas. Lourdes handed me the water in a frosted blue glass. River picked up the beer, declining the glass offered.

"So why did you quit the Foders?" I said.

When Lourdes spoke her voice stayed low in her throat, her accent layering her English with bounce and rhythm. "I couldn't take it no more."

River dipped a tortilla into the bowl. "Couldn't take what?"

"Not so easy place to work. All of them tough. The wife. Daughter. Son. Everybody. Cruel family. No love in that house. Don't let all them tears fool you. He the one brought me there to that house. Now he's gone. I can't stay no more."

River paused her chewing. "This is so good."

Lourdes beamed. "Thank you."

I said. "If you hated it so much why didn't you leave before?"

"I had my reasons," Lourdes said without flinching.

I said, "The two men who broke in. Do you remember anything about them that you might not have told the police?"

Nervous laughter. "I was so scared. I don't mind telling you I peed myself. Right there in the middle of the room. On Mister Foder's beautiful floor."

"Fear can do that to you. Chancellor said he heard them calling each other cuz. Nobody else seemed to have heard it. Did you?"

Her eyes fell to the ground. "Yes. One of them said something like that."

River mumbled through a mouthful of food. "Who said? Only one of them said it?"

"Yes," Lourdes, replied. "The small one called the other cuz."

"Are you sure it was cuz?" I said.

"Sounded like it. He whispered it so I can't be one hundred percent."

"Could it have been Gus, or something like that?" River said.

"I suppose," Lourdes said.

"Did you hear anything else?" I said.

"That's all I heard," Lourdes replied.

"How long have you worked for the judge?"

"Eleven years. Since I come to this country in nineteen ninety-four. He helped me get my papers."

"That doesn't sound like such a cruel man to me," River said.

"He had a good side."

"Did the judge talk to you a lot?" River said.

"Yes. He say I listen to him good." Lourdes smiled.

"Did he ever mention any threats on his life?" said River.

"All the time. He say people call him on the phone. Tell him he going to die. He think it funny."

"He didn't take them seriously?" I said.

Lourdes said. "No. He would laugh. Even when the young man come to the house. That time I was scared."

"What young man?" River asked.

"Very angry, young man. He come one day. Say the judge is a thief. Rob him of his grandmother's money. Tell the judge he will kill him if he don't pay."

River said, "When was this?"

"Last year sometime. I don't remember exactly."

"How did the judge respond?" I said.

"He laugh. Tell the young boy to get a job."

"Did this young man have a weapon, a gun?" River said.

"No, I see nothing in his hand."

"What did he look like?" I asked.

"Not too big. Dark. He wearing sunglasses so I no see his eyes."

I said, "By dark, do you mean a black man?"

"Yes. Black."

"Did anyone else hear him threaten the judge?" River said.

"Zoe was upstairs," Lourdes said.

"Did she hear the threat?" I said.

Lourdes was thoughtful. "I don't know. Maybe."

River wiped her mouth with a paper napkin. "I have to tell you, Lourdes, you're an amazing cook. You know, I've had oxtails before. But this is the best."

"Thank you. If you want I give you recipe."

A figure appeared at the entrance to the room. Plump girl with big friendly eyes and a strong stance. She stood smiling, thick black hair cascading around her face.

Lourdes got up. "Elena, this is Mister Overstreet and Miss Paris. This is my daughter Elena."

River said. "Call me River."

"Nice to meet you both," Elena said in a smooth lilting voice.

Lourdes came to take the glass from my hand as I got up.

"Thank you for your time, Lourdes," I said.

"Any time you want to drop by please do. I always love to have company."

Elena said, "She means that too."

"So what will you do now?" I asked.

"I don't know. Maybe I'll take a cruise," Lourdes said.

"I've been trying to get her to take a trip for a long time," Elena said.

"I told her I will take trip when she graduates." Her laugh was filled with pride. "She graduates from Columbia this year. It will make me so proud. That is why I come to this country. For her. So she could come here and get a good education. She wants to be a lawyer. And then I can go back and tell all my family and they can be proud too."

Elena looked at her mother and the love brimmed in her eyes.

7

"I know you don't respect me very much, but you should have some respect for your mother."

I looked at my father stunned by the sudden attack. We had hardly settled into our seats at the counter of the tiny restaurant in the Village. Late last night he'd called saying he wanted to talk to me. "What about," I'd asked him. He'd refused to go into details. Face to face, he said. Man to man.

His phone call did not come as a complete surprise. I knew my mother's tendencies in some things. She hated change, and avoided confrontation wherever possible. That she might've called my father to tell him of our conversation the other day would not have shocked me.

"What are you talking about?" I said.

His eyes narrowed. "Don't bullshit me, Carmen."

"I'd really prefer if you call me Blades."

"Cut the crap, okay. This is not about your fucking name."

"Then tell me what it's about. Or did you bring me here just to show Manhattan what a blowhard you are?"

His jaws locked, his brown eyes flushed with anger. A waiter within earshot glanced quietly in our direction. And then like a referee in a boxing ring intending to separate two fighters from a clinch, she slid over to offer us menus. We declined the menus and ordered coffee.

Her eyes nimbly searched each of our faces, as if she was trying to determine which one of us needed help, a chance to escape. "That's all?"

"That's it." My father's voice was as stiff as a beam.

Still, she seemed intent on lingering. "The muffins are baked fresh."

"Just leave us alone," my father snapped.

Grinning self-consciously she shrugged and left.

My father unbuttoned his blue waist-length down jacket. "For crissakes, Carmen. What's wrong with you? Your mother's very upset."

I said nothing. We stared at each other for some time.

Bearing two cups and a coffee pot aloft, the waiter maneuvered the tight spaces between tables back to us. She poured coffee and left promptly this time.

My father grabbed a handful of sugar packets. "You know this is very childish."

I picked up the milk, poured a drop in my coffee and stirred. I remained silent though anger steeped in my gut. But I wasn't sure if I was angry at him or at my mother for calling him.

My father took a sip then rattled the cup back into the saucer. "She said you came over there raising Cain about some dreams you were having."

"Is that what she said? Or is that your interpretation?"

"Drop the smug attitude, Carmen."

"I told you before. I'd rather that you call me Blades."

"I don't really care right now what you'd rather I do. You asked me a year ago if I ever hit your mother. I told you no. If you didn't believe me then you should've said so. To my face. Not be a punk about it and go running to your mother, getting her all upset. You have a beautiful wife. And a sweet little girl in Chesney. You should enjoy your life more, son. Stop worrying about the past. Your life could be a lot worse."

"I wish you hadn't come back here." I said.

My words found their intended target. His heart. A scowl ripped across his face. Then he dropped his eyes to disguise the pain. He stroked his shaven scalp, breathing like a man weary of the world.

The door cracked open and cool air drafted through the tiny restaurant. I got up and buttoned my jacket. I could feel my father's eyes boring into the back of my head as I went out the door.

I fell asleep on the couch around 4 o'clock. Was a deep sleep too, until I was rousted by the phone ringing. Groggy, I picked up and mumbled something that was probably unintelligible to whoever was on the other end.

"Blades?"

"What?"

"It's River."

"What do you want?"

"Are you okay?"

"Nothing that a bullet to my head can't fix."

"Are you drunk?"

I detected genuine concern in her voice. "Just a joke…"

"Listen, Blades, I just got a call from Zoe Foder. Her mother tried to commit suicide last night."

I sat up trying to clear the mold from my head, which was looping like I'd just gotten off a rollercoaster.

"Where are you?" I said.

"At the hospital."

"She gonna make it?"

"They think so. Frankly, I'm beginning to get a little concerned about you."

"I'm not your concern, River."

"You'd like to think you're nobody's concern."

"Call me tomorrow."

"Wait. I have a present for you."

"What?"

"The police report from the murder scene."

"Give me the bullet points. No pun intended."

"Don't you want to read it yourself?"

"I trust your skills. Schools in Cuba are some of the best in the world."

"Whatever, Blades."

"Read it to me before I fall back to sleep."

"Two shots to the head. Point blank. Forty caliber. Same as the bullet in the Foder's ceiling. No finger prints at the scene. But they got two bloody boot prints."

"Make?"

"Tims. Sizes twelve and ten."

"Aren't you a size ten?"

"You're a regular comedian, Blades. You should try out for Caroline's."

I laughed. "Keep me updated on Mrs. Foder's condition."

"What're you doing for dinner?"

"Haven't thought about it yet. What time is it?"

"Six fifteen. Wanna meet for sushi?"

"I'm off fish for a while."

She laughed. "Liar."

My two-day-old leftover chicken and baked potato actually tasted better than when I first made it. In the background, Coltrane's Quartet was blasting through *Crescent*. Generally, good music not only soothes the soul, it helps digestion. But tonight Coltrane was going to need some help soothing me and I knew exactly what that would be. I opened a bottle of inexpensive Merlot and killed that by the time Coltrane's CD was done. It was Ramsey Lewis' turn to try his luck talking me down. *Sky Islands* kicked off with *Julia*, a Lennon, McCartney joint. By the time Ramsay Lewis was done I'd finished another bottle of wine, had hardly touched my food and was still as restless as a caged tiger.

Time to try something else. I opened another bottle of wine, taking it with me into the den where I flicked through television stations before settling on the History Channel. A dramatization of the flight of the Enola Gay was playing. It wasn't the first time I'd seen that program but as always I watched in fascination and horror. Finished the third bottle by the time the program was done. My skin pulsed with warmth from the wine and I began to float away remembering warm family smells and playing games with my siblings.

I was back in our kitchen helping Mom polish the silver after a dinner party. My mom grew up in the South where polishing the silver was something of a family ritual. She took us down to Louisiana when I was about ten. There, I met my maternal grandmother who had the strangest eyes I'd ever seen. They were a silvery-green and darted about her small face like little fish in a clear bowl. And she always smelled of gardenias. We stayed there for three months. My brother, Jason, and I used to run through the rippling spears of sugar cane looking for snakes, and hunt fish in the lake a few hundred yards from the house.

Somewhat drunk, I sat in the crackling bluish glow of the television, subdued and relaxed.

Very drunk, to tell the truth.

By now I'd forgotten everything that had transpired that day. And it felt good. Forgetting one thing and remembering another. My memory of Louisiana became so fresh and clear I felt as if I was looking into a healing eye. The wind was blowing soft and steadfast on my cheeks.

Then I remembered the night of rage that precipitated that long stay in Louisiana with my grandparents.

My mother screaming. My father cursing. Terrible shouts. Shattering glass.

And then the neon world of police cars. My father screaming at the police trying to handcuff him. Angry cops threatening to break his arm if he didn't stop resisting. Seeing my father forced into the squad car. The car driving off with my father in the back.

The next day we were on a plane bound for Louisiana.

8

Sometime after midnight I passed out in front of the television. I woke around 8:30 next morning with a frightening sense of loss. As if something in my heart had died. My throat was parched and my mouth felt as if it had been filled with blood.

I took a shower, washed my hair and brushed my teeth. My left eye began to twitch.

Stress. Used to happen to me when I was a cop after a steady diet of stakeouts where I would go for long stretches without sleep. It was as annoying now as it was then.

I decided to go out for breakfast. Dressed in army fatigues that Anais had bought for me as a prank, I stepped out into a depressing New York morning robbed of color by dark clouds. A gull, fat on junk like the rest of us, sat on my fence. I watched fascinated for no reason I could fathom, as it was joined by two others who were even larger. They proceeded to hop around on the fence like dancers rehearsing new steps. It made me smile as I got into my car and backed into the street.

Took me ten minutes to get to my destination, a small coffee shop on 7th Avenue in Park Slope. A long time ago, after pulling an all-nighter at the club, Negus and I ate there. I remembered that the pancakes were served with lavish amounts of blueberries. I was in a mood for blueberries.

As I parked my phone rang.

Semin, sounding excited and out of breath. "You seen the newspaper?"

"Morning, Semin. Working out again?"

"Just finished."

"Which newspaper?"

"Is that a serious question?"

I laughed. "Not really. What's shaking?"

"Your judge had some skeletons, all right. I'd say dinosaur sized. He was about to be hit with a major federal indictment for his part in a bride-for-hire ring."

"Bride for hire?"

"Read the article."

"Give me a synopsis."

"Don't have time. You asked me to do some digging. This article has a lot of stuff that you might find interesting."

"OK. Where're you rushing off too?"

"Who said I was rushing off?"

"Why're you being so mysterious?"

She laughed. "Only you would think that, Blades."

"I'm about to have breakfast in your backyard. Wanna join me?"

"Sorry, not today. I do have to run. Bye Blades."

"Goodbye, Semin."

Before entering the restaurant I bought the New York Times from the vendor on the corner, an Arab dressed in a green army surplus jacket. He looked at my uniform and gave a knowing nod of comradeship. I walked away smiling at the irony.

The breakfast crowd was just arriving and I had to wait a few minutes before I got a table in the back of the room near the kitchen. I didn't mind. It was in a corner, perfect for eating alone.

I ordered blueberry pancakes and coffee. After the waiter walked away I opened the newspaper searching for the article on Judge Foder.

The front page was taken up by terror in the Middle East and threats of terror in the United States. Our government had raised America's antiter-rorism alert status from yellow to orange. Again. It was occurring with such frequency people were beginning to take the warnings in stride. Another attack on American soil was coming, the experts believed. Would we be ready?

Coffee came shortly followed by my large stack of blueberry pancakes. I found the article on Judge Foder in the metro section which I pulled out, dropping the rest of the paper on the floor.

In between bites I skimmed the article. The Brooklyn District Attorney had charged a woman with setting up and running a bride-for-hire organi-zation to help undocumented immigrants get green cards. The men hailed mostly from Latin America, the Middle East and the Caribbean. According to the article Judge Rupert Foder performed many of the civil ceremonies at his home. The woman charged with procuring the clientele was one of Brooklyn's most intriguing personalities.

Odessa Rose was a popular Brooklyn activist who attended more community events in a month than most politicians did in a year. You could find her at christenings, funerals, fundraising cake sales, dances, church luncheons and dinners. Though it was rumored that she owned several businesses, and was wealthy enough to live anywhere in New York, she continued to live in the projects where she grew up.

Her flair for drama was well documented. Painting her body red, Odessa Rose once stopped traffic by dancing naked in the middle of Flatbush Avenue to bring attention to the plight of women being abused in shelters. A few months back she cut down a twenty-year-old oak in Prospect Park to protest the treatment meted out to Pakistani immigrants arrested by the government after 9/11 who were kept in detention for months without access to lawyers.

The New York Times ran a feature on her life in their Sunday Magazine not too long ago. Fascinating story. A high school dropout, she was arrested but not charged with attempting to kill an abusive husband whom she later divorced. This all happened before she was twenty. She remarried, but that husband died in what was ruled an accident after some kind of confrontation with police. She raised three children on her own and went on to get a GED and a degree in business from Brooklyn College where, along with some other survivors of abusive husbands, she formed a group called WAAM (Women Against Abusive Men).

Judge Foder and Odessa Rose: what strange bedfellows capitalism made.

After I finished eating, I called River and told her to read the story in the Times then I drove out to East New York, to the Louis H. Pink Houses where Odessa lived.

The day remained overcast. I left my car on the outskirts of the housing project—a rowdy shabby expanse of tall buildings stretching for ten blocks from Autumn Avenue to Eldert Lane—and walked through a basketball court taken over by a gang of indigent pigeons waiting on welfare, their feathers sullied with New York soot and each other's shit.

Much has been written about the plight or blight of housing projects. Conservatives claimed that housing projects, along with failed welfare policies and the reluctance by authorities to tackle crime, forced many whites to flee to the suburbs, ruining Brooklyn's once-thriving middleclass neighborhoods. I've always wondered why is it that when whites move out of a neighborhood, it was suddenly considered ruined?

Residents in the projects were generally wary of nosy strangers. You may as well wave a badge in the air. Cops were as welcome to them as someone selling used condoms. But for the right price you could always find somebody to talk.

The first person I met was a string bean crawling along the edge of the complex. She walked with a pronounced limp and wore enough paint to be a walking ad for Benjamin Moore. Shiny scarlet parka zipped up to the neck. A small camera in one hand and a bottle of soda in the other.

"Excuse me," I greeted from about two feet away.

She hesitated for a second and then kept walking without replying, her pockets jingling with what sounded like coins. After she'd passed she stopped abruptly and turned around.

I walked back, coming abreast. "Where I can find Odessa Rose?"

She squeezed her scorched sleepless eyes. "That why you stopped me, muthafucker? Thought you wanted something. I don't know no Odessa Rose."

"Thanks," I said and walked away.

Some men piled near the entrance of one of the towers were passing a cigarette between them. Drops of rain began to litter the concrete walkway.

I reached the group and stopped. In their eyes and in their faded jackets I saw repackaged misery. But I wasn't here to do social work.

"I'm looking for Odessa Rose," I said to the group.

Each one looked at me. Their expressions ranged from disinterest to fascination. It was possible they'd assumed I was a cop. Dressed the way I was that would've been a reasonable assumption.

"Who're you?" one man said. He twirled a piece of tissue in his hand and his face was as tight as a plate of steel.

"Not a cop."

"I didn't ask you that."

"Name's Blades Overstreet."

His back straightened. "You used to be a cop, though. You still got that walk."

I deflected his cold ass stare with a sub-zero one of my own.

He sneered. "Yeah, you know what the fuck I'm talking about, right? That straight-up walk like you own the air and shit. Like you can walk up to a group of grown men and open a conversation without saying hello."

"Odessa lives in the building across the street," the man with the cigarette said.

"Don't tell him shit," said steel-plated face.

The cigarette smoker sneered at him. "Shut the fuck up, Carter. Who the hell you think you talking to?" Then he turned to me. "Apartment thirty-four D. But you ain't gonna get in to see her. She's on lock down."

"By whom?"

"Self-imposed. She got her boys checking anybody who goes into that building."

"Her boys?"

He smiled and passed the cigarette from his big paw to one of the other men. "You got any cigarettes on you?"

"No, I quit."

"Smart."

"So who're her boys?"

"You'll see. This place been crawling with reporters since that story broke in the news. Ain't one of them got up there to see 'Dessa. You won't neither."

"Thanks," I said and walked off.

"Hey," he called out to me.

I turned around.

"Can you help me out with a pack of cigarettes?"

I walked back and handed him ten bucks. "It's cheaper if you quit."

He grinned. "Sure. Been trying for twenty-five years. Watch out for 'Dessa's boys. They some mean muthas."

I thanked him again and crossed the street, advancing to the building he'd pointed to as rain began to pelt. Four beefy black men, two on each side of the walkway, stood under the canopy at the prison-green entrance door. All four were dressed in black sweaters with black wool caps on their heads, and looked like they could easily have been borrowed off the New York Jets defensive line.

As I approached the door two of them stepped in front of me.

"Excuse me," I said.

"What's your business here?" one of them said. His head was as big as a basketball. He was well groomed, pencil thin mustache and sideburns.

"My own."

He said. "Do you live in this building?"

Another one of the men began whispering into a walkie-talkie.

"You the police?" I said.

Two of them laughed and it sounded like donkeys had suddenly decided to offer their critique of the weather.

The one with the walkie-talkie remained serious. "We protect this building. That's all you need to know."

A slender man of light complexion came out of the building zipping up his black leather bomber. He had a walkie-talkie; his proud eyes appeared agitated. He stepped toward the other walkie-talkie carrier and they whispered to each other for a few moments.

He turned to me, mouth twisted. "Can you go into a residential building on Fifth Avenue without explaining why you're there? No. So why you wanna do it here?"

I contemplated what he said and realized there was no point being stubborn any longer. "Name's Blades Overstreet. I'm here to see Odessa Rose."

He came toward me. "Miss Rose ain't seeing nobody today."

"How about if you let her tell me that?"

His face reddened. "I'm telling you that."

"Are you her spokesman?"

"Does she know you?"

"Yes. I'm a friend of her hairdresser. Toni Monday. We met at a party Toni threw at my club, Voodoo, about six months ago."

The men glanced at each other and I had an image of them on a football field huddling up to decide what play to call. The spokesman walked away toward the entrance of the building. I couldn't tell what he was saying but he spoke into his walkie-talkie.

Moments later he was back with a smile of satisfaction on his face. "Miss Rose wants to know what's your business with her?"

"I'm investigating the murder of Judge Rupert Foder."

"Miss Rose don't know nothing 'bout no murder."

"How about you? Do you know anything about a murder?"

His eyes coarsened. "Are you stupid or something?"

"Not stupid," I said. "Must be something."

"You must be stupid to try and insult me."

"Sorry to disappoint you, my friend. If I wanted to insult you I would. Just trying to find the truth. No insult intended."

"Take my advice and bounce."

I looked at him, then at the other four and decided it would be suicide to try to force my way past them. I turned and strode easily through the rain to my car.

9

That Judge Foder might've been corrupt didn't shock me. New York City was embedded in me like a plant in soil, but my passion for this city didn't blind me to its blights: the lack of decent affordable housing for people who didn't make six figure salaries; inept schools in Black and Latino districts; a network of self-serving, corrupt elected officials which left New Yorkers dazed and jaded.

Judge Foder had been appointed through the powerful Democratic Party machine in Queens. An organization tainted over the years by unbridled top-down corruption. Years ago their political boss had committed suicide after it was leaked that he was being investigated for taking bribes and payoffs. Investigations into the shenanigans of local politicians were conducted almost as frequently as the INS made sweeps in Sunset Park.

Did Mrs. Foder's attempted suicide have anything to do with revelations about her husband?

I arrived at Long Island Jewish Medical Center around four, passing through an emergency room filled with old women and children, most of them black or Hispanic. In America, people with no health insurance found refuge from the high cost of medicine in hospital emergency rooms. I asked the receptionist for directions to in-patient wards. She pointed me to the south side of the building.

Maria Foder occupied a private room on the seventh floor. I got my pass from the attendant stationed at a desk and boarded the elevator. Her room was the middle one in the block of rooms along the brightly-lit antiseptic hallway.

I knocked. A voice from inside invited me in. The patient was sitting up, alert and smiling when I pushed the door. The presence of a good-looking man with neatly trimmed silvery hair might've had something to do with her bubbly spirit. Or perhaps the wonderful arrangement of flowers on the bedside table coupled with the box of well-abused Ghirardelli chocolates opened on her bed. Whatever it was, she didn't fit the cliché of a recently attempted suicide.

"How are you, Mrs. Foder?" I greeted.

"Oh, Mr. Overstreet, how nice to see you."

"Are you as well as you look?"

She smiled. "I don't know what the fret was all about. I took a few pills to get some sleep and everybody is saying I tried to kill myself."

"Sometimes it's better to err on the side of caution," I said.

"But I didn't try to kill myself, Mr. Overstreet. My step-daughter came into my room and saw the empty pill bottle next to my bed and I don't know what got into her."

"They tried to wake you and couldn't," I said, repeating what I was told.

"Is that what they told you? Goodness! I admit I may've taken more than I should've, but I was just fast asleep. I hadn't slept in three days. I couldn't go on without sleep."

"I know that feeling," I said.

"I can promise you she isn't the kind of woman who'd attempt suicide," the silver-haired man said.

Mrs. Foder giggled self-consciously. "My apologies to you both. I've lost my manners. Mr. Overstreet, this is Diego Ercolo."

He looked to be in his early fifties, with a loose but pleasant smile and the appearance of a man who spent an inordinate amount of time putting himself together. Tie and shirt matching. Silvery blue. The four-buttoned gray suit was European. Italian, I'd say. Expensive. He was cleanly shaven, no nicks.

He extended his hand. "It's a pleasure to meet you, Mr. Overstreet."

I took his hand, absorbing his strong handshake. "Good to meet you."

His hands were cottony soft and his penny-colored eyes had an air of supercilious arrogance.

"Are you a family friend?" He said.

"Mr. Overstreet is investigating my husband's murder," Mrs. Foder said.

"Oh, a cop?" Diego said.

"Ex-cop," I said.

"Have you found out anything so far?" he said.

"Nothing," I said, perhaps too curtly.

He grunted with boredom and held Mrs. Foder's hand in both of his. "Maria, you must excuse me. I have to rush back to the gallery. I will call you tomorrow. I expect you should be out of here by then."

"Gracias por venir, Diego."

"De nada."

He turned to me and extended his hand again. "The next time we meet I hope your disposition would be much improved, Mr... ."

I suspected he was deliberately pretending to have forgotten my name. I took his hand in the spirit it was offered. "Nothing wrong with my disposition. But I hope by then your memory would be much improved."

Silence floated over the room. He held onto my hand as if he was trying to make up his mind whether to wring it or massage it. Then he smiled and released me, took a black wool coat off a chair back and went out with the coat slung over his arm.

Mrs. Foder said, "Would you like a mint chocolate, Mr. Overstreet?"

I sat in the chair vacated by Mr. Ercolo's coat. "No thank you. And please, call me Blades."

"Diego is an old friend. He's a lawyer but would rather be an artist, I think."

I looked around the room. It was larger than she needed. Blinds were drawn at the two large windows. Two chairs jammed against the wall. A table with magazines.

I drew the chair close to her bed. "Mrs. Foder..."

"Ah..." She shook her head and waggled her index finger playfully. "Maria."

I smiled. "I have to ask you some questions."

"Okay."

"Has anyone told you about the article in today's newspaper about your husband."

She looked puzzled. "That's not surprising. He was just murdered."

"It's not altogether about his murder."

"What's it about?"

"Your husband's involvement with a bride-for-hire organization?"

"What on earth is that?"

"According to the article he took money to perform marriages between American citizens and undocumented immigrants."

"What's wrong with that?"

"Nothing if you ask me. But the government doesn't like marriages performed solely for the purpose of getting someone a green card."

Her nostrils fluted. "What are you saying?"

"That had he not been killed, he would've been arrested."

Her face stiffened. "Please go away. I'm not feeling well."

"I'm sorry, I didn't mean to upset you."

"Oh really? What did you expect? Leave me alone. Please."

I got up and took one last look at the room. I hated hospitals but if I ever had to stay in a hospital again I'd want a room like this.

I walked out wishing I'd taken that mint chocolate.

That evening I turned up at the Foder residence around twilight. The fog was so fat I could barely see two feet in front of me.

I rang the golden heart-shaped bell and waited. A few minutes later Zoe opened the door peering into my face as if she had difficulty seeing me or remembering who I was. Her eyes were red and unfocused.

"It's Blades," I said.

"What do you want?"

Narrow-hipped and flat-chested, her petite body swam in overalls a couple sizes too large. One could certainly understand her being surly. Under the circumstances who wouldn't be. Father murdered. Mother suicidal. But it was cold and ugly outside and I'd hoped for a friendlier reception.

I said. "Did your father have an office here?"

"Of course he did."

"I'd like to look around."

She grimaced and swallowed hard. "This is not a convenient time."

"It's a long way from Brooklyn."

"You should've called first."

I wanted to curse but shorted it. She continued to stare at me, her expression as cloudy as the soup I'd just driven through.

Sometimes reality itself is an illusion but there was something not right about the way her eyes hazed. Could be drugs. Could be the grief. Nothing distorts like grief.

I said, "Please, can I come in?"

She stepped aside for me to enter. We stood facing each other in silence. A silence that smelled of ripened fruit. Pineapples. And alcohol. She was half drunk.

"The FBI got to my father's office first," she said. "They took everything. So you are more than welcome to take out the trash they left behind."

"What were they looking for?"

"How should I know?" She took a deep breath. "Why do you want to search my father's office?"

"In case you forgot, I am trying to help find your father's killers."

"And you think you're going to find them in his office? I told you, there's nothing there. When I said they took everything, I meant everything. Desks. Chairs. Files. Computer. Everything. But since you seem to be one of those men who have to see the blood to believe there is a wound, follow me."

I tagged along as she walked around the stairwell and through what looked like a library stopping in front of a thick oak door. In one smooth motion, she twisted the knob, pushed the door open and flicked the switch on the wall.

"This was my father's office."

Except for a few scraps of paper on the floor and dust in the corners, the room was bare. Paper clips here and there. I could see dust particles swirling near the light. The walls, too, were bare.

She closed the door. "Someone broke into it two weeks ago. Then the FBI walks off with the whole shebang."

The large room in which we were now standing boasted ceiling-high bookshelves of shiny dark wood. The shelves themselves were packed with leather-bound law books. There was a stylish wooden armchair and ottoman next to a fireplace. I liked the way the room smelled, of books.

"What was stolen?"

She leaned away from me. "My father said nothing was missing."

"Did you know about the indictment that was about to come down on his head?"

Eyebrows raised, she side-stepped the question. "Do you want a drink? I'm in a drinking mood today."

"I can see that."

"Don't you think it's a good day to get drunk? I'd bet you half of New York is getting drunk right now."

"And the other half?"

She started to giggle but caught herself and like a trained puppy set her mouth in a tight twist. "What do you think? Your life must be pretty lonely to be driving through this fog to search my father's office. Don't you have anything fun to do? Does it make you feel like a big man, riding to the rescue, playing the big hero?"

I couldn't reply. She had a point. I had a beautiful wife, a wonderful daughter, a going concern in Voodoo, yet I lived as if my life wasn't complete. Like I was missing some important ingredient needed for fulfillment.

She said, "So what will it be? Scotch?"

"Nothing. Thanks."

"Well, sit down. If you're going to watch me get drunk, you should get comfortable. I don't want to appear inhospitable."

She leaned against the fireplace, her eyes empty and forlorn. I touched her arm in a reassuring way. She thrust my arm aside and I saw distrust in her eyes, a distrust that didn't come from grief. It was the kind of distrust I used to see in the eyes of beamed-up prostitutes and abused runaways.

I sat on a coffee-colored leather sofa and watched as she opened a finely-polished cabinet at the other end of the room, took out a short glass and a decanter of what looked like whisky and poured.

"I asked you earlier if you knew about the indictment against your father," I said.

She drained the glass and cleared her throat. Then she wiped her mouth with the back of her hand like a pro. "I knew about the indictment. I think it's what sent my mother over the edge."

She poured again. The same amount. I was tempted to ask her why bother with the ritual of pouring the drink into a glass. Why not plunder the entire decanter at one swoop? Get the whole mess over while I was there to drive her to the hospital to join her mother.

"Sure you don't want a hit?" she said.

Her eyes had found a thin spark. Half a glass of whisky at one shot could spark just about every nerve in your body. That much I knew. Especially somebody who was already gassed.

"No, thank you." I said. "Is there anybody else in the house?"

An easy blunt laugh. "Please don't do that paternalistic macho shit and tell me you're worried about me."

"I am."

"It's so corny."

"I'm a corny guy."

"I can forgive corny but don't get boring. That I have no patience for."

"I'll remember that. So your mother knew about the indictment?"

"Of course. Why?"

"Didn't seem that way when I spoke to her earlier. Anyway, she said she didn't try to commit suicide. That it was an accident."

Zoe shrugged and brushed back a strand of hair. "Yeah, well, the pills in the bottle didn't evaporate."

"She said there were only a few in the bottle."

"A few?" She gave a little laugh. "To my mother a few is twenty. Let's not talk about that. You're beginning to bore me."

"Has she done this before?"

Her voice turned frigid. "Drop it."

"Why're you trying to get drunk?" I said.

"Are you an idiot?"

She looked at me with unapologetic disdain. Then she broke into passionate sobs, swaying as if she would fall. I got up and went to hold her vibrating body.

After her sobs had bottomed out I took her into the kitchen for a glass of water. Pared pineapple sat on a plate on the table, the discarded skins curled in alphabetical-looking shapes near the edge of the granite countertop.

She wrapped pink bony hands around the glass of water, tipped it to her lips and didn't stop guzzling until the glass was empty.

"When did they come?" I asked, refilling her glass. "The agents?"

"This morning. At dawn. I hadn't slept. They came like an army. Guns drawn. The whole fucking cliché. I felt like I was watching a James Cameron movie being filmed in my own house." She gulped a mouthful of water. "Want some pineapple?"

"No thanks."

"It's very good. Honor brought it back from Hawaii."

"When was she in Hawaii?"

"She came back the day after father was kidnapped. Or was it that same night? I forgot. But she brought the pineapple. It really does taste different to the one you get in stores."

"The FBI claims he performed many of the marriages in his office here. Did you know about them?"

"It's a bunch of lies. The FBI isn't a bunch of priests, you know. That bunch is a swastika short of a Gestapo outfit."

"Did you know about your father's involvement with Odessa Rose?"

"I don't know anything about Odessa Rose. I just wish all of you would go away and leave us alone. I feel like I'm in the middle of a potato patch. Everybody digging and digging around me. The police. The FBI. You and that woman. Everybody digging. My father's dead. All this digging is not going to bring him back."

"You came to us."

"Well, I'm sorry I did that."

"What're you afraid of, Zoe?"

She looked at the glass of water in her hand. "I'm afraid of being sober. I need a damn drink."

She left me in the kitchen and lurched unsteadily back toward the study. I pondered whether to follow. I decided it wasn't my place. She was a big girl with a bigger mouth. I didn't think she'd miss me.

Chancellor had said that his sister had an acid tongue. What I just experienced was something else. And it didn't make sense. Yes, she was grieving. But that was fear I heard in her voice. She was running from something.

As I made my way down the driveway I imagined her drunk and asleep on the floor.

10

The fog had thinned a bit by the time I drove away from the grotesque sorrow of the Foder house. The prismatic light from fog lamps seemed to be dancing in space. I crept along, thankfully encountering little traffic. Approaching the Williamsburg Bridge old warehouses on my right sprang out of the watery mist. It was strange but beautiful to see.

River called as I turned off the bridge.

"Where're you?"

"On my way home," I said. "Just got ambushed by Zoe."

"Have dinner with me, tonight. You can tell me about it."

"I'm kinda tired, actually."

"Come on, Blades. You hate eating alone. That much I know."

"Where're we having dinner?"

"My place."

I laughed. "What's for dinner?"

"You ain't all that, Blades."

"I'll be there in an hour."

I went on home, showered and changed into black slacks and dark blue shirt. I had three messages on my answering machine. The only one of importance came from Anais. I wondered why she hadn't called my cell. I dialed hers and got voice mail. I left a message and went out the door.

Fifteen minutes later, I rang the bell of River's second-floor loft in Williamsburg. River came down to the door in a black dress which revealed far more than it hid. Earrings jangling as she walked.

"You look… great," I stuttered.

Her eyes shone like water in the dark. "You said that like there's a gun to your head."

"I'm sorry. You look stunning."

"Thank you."

We embraced. Her scent reminded me of the sea, a hint of wildness and exuberance.

She pressed her pelvis into me. "Come on upstairs. I don't want the rice to burn."

I followed her urgent steps up the stairs. The entrance opened onto a wide dining room.

"Sit down." She hurried into the kitchen beyond red French doors.

I sat at a square walnut table on a raised platform. One avocado rested in a bowl in the middle of the table. I looked around at the white-washed walls. The floor had been stained ebony and a large red urn guarded one corner like a forlorn Roman sentry.

River returned smiling. "I helped a woman locate her missing husband and she gave me a case of Fox Creek Cabernet Sauvignon Reserve. Wanna try it? She said it's excellent."

"Sounds good to me. Where'd you find her husband?"

"Under a football player. Looked like they were having a ball." River opened the wine. "Is Anais coming back soon?"

"I don't know. Why?"

She poured two glasses and with a relaxed gaze offered she offered me one. "Just asking."

I sipped and held the wine in my mouth a touch before swallowing. "Nice flavor."

She was smiling. "Yes, just right for the occasion."

I liked her large, red-accented apartment. Red dining chairs and red curtains. A chunky African stool had been turned into a coffee table.

"Very bold." I said.

"The wine?"

"This apartment. The color. Everything. It's you."

She laughed. "Whatever. Guess who I had lunch with today?"

"Your pastor."

"Hmmm. What's a pastor?"

I laughed.

"Detective Grant," she said.

"Oh, the one who finds your loneliness pitiful? Zoe told me the FBI moved in this morning. Carted away the contents of the judge's office. Did your detective friend give an angle?"

"I think he knew, but he wouldn't say."

"Did he say if the police reviewed the security tape from the cinema with the Folders?"

"Unfortunately, the computers were down that day. No recording." She pause. "Do you know this Odessa Rose? The more I read the more I like her."

"I tried to see her this morning."

"What happened?"

"She sent an entire NFL defensive line to block me."

"You probably weren't polite enough."

"Well, I didn't get down on my knees, if that's what you mean."

"It always works, Blades. Take it from a woman. Nothing more moving than a man on his knees soliciting our help."

"The judge's office was broken into two weeks ago. I have a hunch it was Odessa trying to dispose of her garbage before the indictment came down."

"If you're right, she had motive to crash the judge's party."

"And the means, judging from the size of her crew."

"Grant told me something interesting about Honor Foder. She's an ex-cop."

"Really?"

"She was forced to resign. Got tapped shaking down drug dealers along with her partner. One Bartholomew Temple."

"She did time?"

"They flipped on their supervisor. Cut a deal."

"Zoe was acting really strange today."

"Strange? How?"

"Can't really put my finger on it. Something about her manner. Her eyes. Her look. Wasn't right."

"Excuse me Blades, but it's not like you know the woman intimately."

"I'm good with eyes."

"Is that right?"

"That's right."

"So what are my eyes saying right now?'

"That you're hungry."

She laughed. "Then let's eat."

The cocked bass of Bob Marley's *Catch Afire* album playing in the background had us both tapping our feet as we sat on the sofa after dinner. Gripped in the coppery intensity of Bob's voice, we killed another bottle of that Australian Cabernet. I felt comfortable in River's place. Totally. I didn't want to leave.

River tilted her head toward me as if to ask what was I thinking.

"You wanna know what I'm thinking, right?"

A quick smile, with a dash of mischief. "No. I know what you're thinking."

"Oh, you do, ah? What am I thinking?"

She stretched her legs out like a cat unfurling. "You're comfortable here. This is a comfortable place. That's what you're thinking."

I smiled in submission to her wisdom and finished the wine in my glass.

She stood up, balancing herself on one leg like a dancer. "Should I open another bottle?"

Her voice had a strange echo, and seemed to be traveling through an underbrush, winding around me like a hunter's net. I was getting drunk. She was standing over me, smiling, spraying her draughty beauty all over me.

"You trying to get me drunk?" I said.

"Why not?"

"I gotta drive."

Lifting my hand to her mouth, she moving her lips along the length of each finger.

I breathed deeply to bolster my resistance. The blood in my veins was perilously close to submission. I imagined caressing her, feeling the brightening and darkening of her voice in my ear, the roughness of her breath on my neck.

I stood up, just a head taller than she was. She leaned into me, the fullness of her breasts lighting a fire in my chest. The bulge in my pants was full grown.

"Don't leave, Blades. I want you to stay. I want you to fuck me."

Can't say I was shocked by her bluntness. For as long as I knew River-and I admit it hadn't been quite that long-she'd never been one to hide her feelings behind virginal modesty.

She leaned deeper into my body and kissed me. It was a small kiss, exalted in its plainness. No locking of lips. But it was a kiss. A miraculous moment that made my spirit soar. Perhaps I was just feeling terribly lonesome.

I'm not one to meditate on the irresolute nature of passion, or the bravery or cruelty, if you will, of denial. But I was devoted to my wife. And determined to stay that way. Forever. Still, if there was a woman who could break the lock on that loyalty it might be River.

Her honesty, her wide-eyed fury when crossed and her unrestrained sexuality were enough to make her irresistible. But she was also unswervingly loyal and steadfast in the face of danger.

Our paths first crossed about a year and a half ago when I hired her to manage my club. That pact didn't last long. Six months later we parted company. And not on good terms either. At that time River held a secret that would set our two worlds on a collision course which almost cost one of us our lives.

Her real name was Regina Peterson. Many years ago, when we were both kids, my father had ratted out her father. Both were members of the Brooklyn chapter of the Black Panthers at that time. The information my father gave police about her father's involvement in the murder of two cops got him a life sentence. He escaped from prison and ultimately to Cuba taking River and her brother. But not before a shootout with police in which River's mom was killed. Having sworn death on my father, her dad bred in her the same hate.

Many years later her father returned to the States determined to kill my father. I got to him first and shot him dead. A few years later River arrived in New York seeking revenge.

How she and I overcame that history without killing each is a wonder. We grew to respect each other and this sexual energy that right now threatened to shatter my marriage had always been present, though I tried to pretend otherwise.

River continued to press her damp lips to mine. And for a moment I thought of the original sin. The taking of that fruit, which, according to the Bible, changed mankind's trajectory forever. A part of me wanted to let go. What is salvation without sin?

"I know you want me, Blades," she whispered into my mouth.

I could only shudder. I was in a cold stormy sea. And I was sinking. Fast.

"I can feel it." She licked my lips; her breath hot and sweet, her tongue sharp as a scalpel on my mouth. "I can feel it through your skin."

"I can't do it, River."

Still clutching my hand, she guided it under her dress. Passion rode on the edge of her breath. "Touch it. Can be yours. This door is open to you, Blades. Right now. Tonight. It might not be later."

I felt her wetness and did nothing to take my hand away.

"Go then, if you want," she said, and turned her back to me.

11

I should've stayed with River.

Halfway home snow began to dust. I drove thinking about River and the irony of our lives, both of us sired by revolutionary-minded fathers, both of us doing stints protecting the status-quo as police officers. As was much the case lately, my mind wandered too far from my body. It made me careless.

I drove through my gate and got out to open the garage door.

What was that figure swooping through the air on my left?

Fear and instinct jolted my mind from its trance. Crouched, I spun ready for action.

I avoided the first blow, but that attacker was only a decoy. Someone else hit me hard from behind with a solid phlunk.

A bolt of pain shot through me. For an instant I was blinded by the sheer weight of it. Then it exploded down through the hollow of my spine and my legs crumbled beneath me.

Miraculously, I was still conscious. Barely. My nipples tingled; was the only sensation I could collect.

Scabs of snow furling out of the blackness, settling gently on my face. Lights reverberating in my head. Was that the moon bursting through clouds? Or was that the lamp which illuminated my yard?

A dark shape blotting out the light. Losing consciousness.

Spit flew in my face. "This is a warning. Stay away from Odessa."

I awoke coughing. Buried in snow. How much time had passed I couldn't be sure, but it had been enough time for the snow to tie me into a white bundle. I thought of brushing snow from my face but my hands wouldn't move. Tried to raise my head from the ground and couldn't. Panic took me for a quick wild ride into lunacy. Was I paralyzed?

Then I opened my eyes and looked around. I was in my bed. A dream.

I sat up and let my gaze feast on the scene outside my window. My head ached to insanity but I could still appreciate the picture before me. Say what you like about snow, there was nothing more ethereally beautiful than fresh snow dazzling under the blue blaze of morning sunshine.

I tried to recall my encounter with Odessa's thugs last night. The edges of the memory were rough, half of it lost in the cavern of my burning headache.

I remembered pulling myself off the ground and dragging myself inside where I called Toni Monday. Told him what had happened to me. I hadn't seen any faces but the voice was familiar. Belonged to the small dude with the thin mustache and marshmallow-white eyes I'd spoken to at the Pink Houses. He had a strange smell too, like rancid milk.

"That'd be Mallet," Toni said.

"Mallet? First name or last name?"

"Who cares? He goes by the name of Mallet."

"Who's he?" I said.

"Controls Odessa's crew of bodyguards. I understand he's guarding more than her body these days, but that's only gossip and you know I don't listen to that shit."

"Of course not."

He chuckled mightily into the phone. "You always go playing with the wrong people, Blades. Didn't you have any friends when you were a kid?"

The spot where I'd been hit was buzzing like a cluster of bees. I touched it. A polyp of inflammation conceived by the blow was pushing its way out into the world.

"Gotta go put some ice on this shit," I said.

"Stay away from Odessa, Blades. She's too fat for you anyway."

"You shouldn't talk about your elders like that."

He laughed.

"When's her next hair appointment?" I said.

"In two days. She's due in for a wash. Why?"

"I gotta talk to her."

"Don't tangle with Mallet, Blades. He'll will eat your balls for lunch. And wash it down with your spleen."

"No wonder he smells like a sewage plant."

"You're not taking me seriously. The guy's a flipper. Just last week he put a man in the hospital. Took a pliers to the man's nuts. Turned them into mash potatoes."

"Is he in the closet or something? Maybe you should have a talk with him."

"I bet you won't find it so funny when he's got your nuts in his mouth."

"Do you think Odessa would've sent her jocks after a judge?"

"Personally, I don't think she would retire a judge."

"What if she wanted to shut him down before the FBI got to him?"

"Odessa can scam that charge with her high-priced lawyers. She's got one of the best firms in the city. Blacker, Peterkin and Cummins."

"That's a white firm. Thought she hated white people?"

"You're juvenile, Blades. You of all people should know not to buy the hype. You know the game. Everybody's got a hustle. Even the President. Remember his great speech about welfare reform? What a joke! Acting like there would be jobs available to everyone. You wanna hear a secret. No jobs. That's the bottom line. He hoodwinked everyone. The old bait and switch."

"Whoa! Toni? You're getting all socially conscious on me. What's the deal? When'd your conscience start peeping out of the ground?"

"In case you don't know, all the people working for me were once on welfare. I paid for them to go to beauty school. Got them trained and licensed. They're people all over this country going hungry. Can't find jobs. Can't afford to feed their families. I do what I can."

"Is that why your drug business is booming?"

"You know what? Fuck you, Blades. I try to enlighten you. Try to have a serious conversation with you and you always gotta act like you got somebody's fist up your ass."

That's when he hung up on me.

I called Anais but she didn't answer her cell and the phone at her family's house just kept ringing. I gave up after seven ticks.

I went out to clear the driveway and the sidewalk and to dig my car out of the snow. A ridge of crystals had accumulated on the bumper. Snow covered the hedges and the walls and had plotted its way up to the back door of the house.

My neighbors had already swept their driveways and sidewalks clear. The street was another matter. Sanitation hadn't made it to Maple Street.

I worked diligently for half an hour, the exertion bracing my spirits and kindling a fire in my muscles. Sweating and tired though I was at the end, I was actually sorry that the task did not take longer.

After a conventional breakfast of eggs, coffee and toast with jam, I went upstairs to shower. I took my time, still not convinced that I shouldn't just spend the rest of the day in bed nurturing the numbing loneliness I was beginning to feel. The prospects ahead of me weren't at all appealing. I wasn't dealing with Anais' absence very well. Witness that Pandora's box I opened last night in River's apartment. Though I'm glad I didn't let it go any farther, the temptation had been great. Too great.

And I was not looking forward to locking horns with this Mallet, who by Toni Monday's account, was one fuse short of a complete burnout.

But life, as the saying goes, stops for no man. And my clock was still humming. Which meant I had to keep moving.

Feeling much better after my shower, I called Anais again. Luck was sitting on my shoulder this time.

"I can't figure out why I'm only getting some of my calls," she said. "I'll have to call the company."

"How's your mom handling the situation?"

"Better than I. Can you come down?" she said.

"I guess that means you won't be coming back anytime soon."

"I don't know. I need your strength. If only for a day. Can you come?"

"How much longer will you stay?"

"You haven't answered me. Surely, New York can do without you for a day," she asserted.

"I'll try to get a flight out as soon as I can."

"Thank you, darling."

I got my travel agent to book me on a flight to Atlanta for 2 o'clock the next day.

As I got into the Volvo to head for the club where I was expecting delivery of some new sound equipment, River called. I bluetoothed and spoke to her as I backed out of the driveway.

"I've found our jailbird."

"Our jailbird? Who's that?" I said.

"The guy whose grandmother got taken by the judge."

"He's a convict?"

"Paroled a year ago. Goes by the name of Shaka."

"Shaka? Nice name."

"Incarcerated as Graylin Wright and came out as Shaka."

"Walked into jail a convict and came out a prince. I admire a man with a sense of history. "Where is he? Have you spoken to him?"

"Heading there right now. You wanna make the play with me?"

"Is he expecting you?"

"I thought I'd surprise him."

"Why was he in jail?"

"Drug possession. A gun charge against him was dropped."

"What else you got?"

"I started checking into estates the judge probated over the past five years. Only came up with one black case. Shaka's grandmother. Shaka actually hired a lawyer to go after the trustee who was put in charge of his grandmother's estate." The judge was never named in any of the affidavits filed by Shaka's lawyer. But he was the one who appointed the trustee. Shaka dropped the case after beating the trustee bloody. I talked to the Trustee. He denies taking any money from the old woman's estate that wasn't covered by the trustee agreement."

"Meaning he bled the estate dry with all kinds of ancillary fees."

"Exactly. But after Shaka attacked him, the trustee then put the screws to our warrior and his lawyer. Forced them to drop the case."

I merged into traffic on Flatbush. "I'll holler later. You can tell me how it went."

"You're not coming?"

"No. I'll let you handle this, baby."

"Hey Blades... about last night..."

I sensed that she was about to apologize. "Last night was great. Except after I left you."

"What happened after you left?"

"Odessa's bullies thumped me pretty good. I guess they didn't like me showing my pale face in the projects."

"You okay?"

"I'm fine. But I think I smell smoke coming from under Odessa's dress."

"Don't go putting your hands in fires you can't control, Blades."

I laughed and hung up.

12

Anais met me at Hartsfield Atlanta airport where I arrived minutes after 4 PM. I saw her standing motionless, dressed in gray baggy jeans and light blue cotton sweater, her hair falling on her face like ragged vines. She seemed so naked, vulnerable, as if she was on the edge of tears.

I strode up to her in the sprawling Delta terminal and took her hand. She smiled weakly and turned her face up to kiss me. She smelled of lavender.

Then she threw her arms around my neck, clinging to me. Her voice was breathy and low as she told me how glad she was to see me. She backed away wiping tears from her cheeks.

On the way to the car she asked about Chesney and my mother. I told her Chez was having a good time in Florida, but I was more concerned about her.

Dusk gathered around Atlanta as we drove along the highway. The air was balmy, but dusty; grit flew from the highway where construction was under-way.

"We don't know if he's gonna make it," Anais said. "One of his lungs collapsed."

She was referring to her father. He'd suffered with emphysema for some time and recently had contracted severe pneumonia.

I felt like I had to say something. "I'm sure he'll pull through."

I leaned back in the seat contemplating how fortunate her father was in having his family at his side. The mere idea of being alone at a time of crisis can be frightening. I remembered the time I was shot accidentally by a fellow cop and the fear of death that came with it. Anais spent days and nights by my bedside, nursing me back from death.

Anais was born in northwest Atlanta near Vine City, a black enclave during segregation. Her father, a professor at Morris Brown college, had moved the family from Bessemer, Alabama. The family moved to Loganville after the integrationists prevailed and Vine City became run down.

Approaching their house, I breathed air rich with the aroma of ripe peaches. They didn't call this the Peachtree state for nothing. The large two-story house itself sat on a quiet leafy street set way back from the drive. We entered through the dining room. Tons of family mementos lined the walls: pictures, plaques, certificates. There was a picture of Anais' father with Malcolm X on the steps of Morehouse.

Anais' mother, Gloria, was in the living room along with a number of other women. It wasn't until our wedding that I met Anais' mom for the first time and saw where Anais got her lively eyes and full blossomy lips from. Tonight Gloria's eyes were quiet.

After hugging me Mrs. Machel introduced me to the other women. Greetings out of the way, the women returned to their conversation.

I followed Anais upstairs to her room nestled in the back of the house. Voices echoed downstairs.

I showered and we went down to eat.

The women continued their animated discussion at dinner. Most of the talk centered around their church, which I gathered was about to hire a new pastor. They cruised down memory lane past marriages and divorces, to marching in the civil rights movement of the '60s, to their arrival in Georgia from other states in the South.

Anais and I stepped off the trip at the arrival in Georgia and returned to her room upstairs. There, we shared a bottle of port which I'd brought with me. For the first time that day I saw a semblance of relaxation creep into her smile.

"I have so many memories of this place."

From her widening smile I could tell that memories were coming in a long steady stream.

"In the summers we used to go to the pool at the Ollie Street Y. That's where I learned to swim. And right outside there was this jolly fat guy who used to sell ice-cream. His name was Mr. Dutton. Every day after my swim I would stop to have an ice-cream at Mr. Dutton's cart. There was this boy, I'd never see him in the Y but he was always out there sitting on his bike whenever I came out. He was very dark, with very intense eyes. But he'd never say anything. One day when I came out he was standing at the ice-cream cart. Before I could pay for my ice-cream he handed Mr. Dutton ten cents. Said that was for my ice-cream. I tried to tell him I couldn't let him buy me ice-cream, but he said he had to. I asked him why. He said that he'd saved all week to buy me ice-cream. He was skinny but so gallant and hand-some. And then he walked me all the way home. When we got here he kissed me. My father was looking out through the window and came running out screaming at the boy. Poor Peter Samuels. He ran away so fast."

"I'm jealous," I said in an artificially boyish voice.

"Oh, don't be, sweetie. I never saw him again."

I drew her into my arms. She surrendered to my embrace, her body slack and quivering with sobs. Unexpectedly she kissed me passionately draining her pain into my mouth. I waited for her to stop. But her tongue was rough, insisting on finding refuge in me.

I didn't know what to do; I'd never seen her like this before. Needy and blistered with doubt and pain; at the same time overripe with desire.

She snaked out of her dress and panties. Naked, she lay over me. Anais was coming at me from some dark place. A place I'd never visited. A place for which I had no eye. I decided to relax and go with it, seeing it as a continued validation of our connectedness.

We made love slowly, as if disassembling each other, patiently consuming each other, particle by particle, transfiguring, transforming, becoming one again. Her skin was damp and smooth; I felt as if I was touching it for the first time. Nipples hard as knuckles. I sucked each one with a rapture that made me dizzy. We rolled this way and that way on the tiny bed. I lapped adoringly at her soft belly, obsessed with the sogginess between her thighs. And when she rose to get on top of me there was the purest gleam I've ever seen in her eyes. I imagined I could feel every corpuscle of blood inside her, as if I were possessing her for the first time and all things I'd ever dreamed of seemed infinitely possible.

Next day I went with Anais to the Atlanta Medical Center. Her father was hooked up to machines with so many wires, he looked like a college lab experiment. Anais rubbed his hands and using a Q-tip, cleaned dirt from beneath his fingernails. She talked to him and sang him a Sarah Vaughn song. Her father loved Sarah.

Leaving the hospital three hours later, we walked around for a while before going home. She held my hand and tried to smile, but her eyes remained sad. We had lunch on the porch as squirrels played among the dogwood. Anais ate very little, picking at the fried chicken with a stricken expression which she kept for most of the afternoon. That evening as Anais' mother pared excess from her rose garden, I bade farewell to Atlanta.

We drove in silence until we got to the airport. The sun had climbed to the top of the mountain showering the valley with light.

"Blades, I feel as if I've got a piece of the sun in my bosom. It's so hot in there. I can't stand it."

"Do you want me to stay?"

"I do appreciate the offer, darling, but go on. You've got work to do."

I arrived in New York at 7:55 PM, and called River as I was getting into a yellow cab. Her phone rang a number of times before she picked up saying hello in a voice that throbbed with impatience.

"Did you hold court with Shaka?"

She sounded tipsy. "Shaka is still running across the plains of Brooklyn, I suspect."

I laughed. "What happened?"

"Shaka heard my voice and had a flashback to one of his battles."

"Did you chase him?"

"History had taught me that you don't chase Shaka. Could be an ambush. Did you know he had twelve hundred concubines?"

"Who, Shaka?"

"Yes, the real Shaka. But he didn't like sex. Never really fucked any of them."

"Where did you read that?"

"In Cuba. History is big there."

"We like history, too. But too often we discover it's somebody else's fiction."

"I managed to convince his neighbor who's a retired cop that Shaka's a menace to society. He's gonna tip me whenever our warrior shows up again."

"What're you up to now?"

"I have company, if you must know."

"Male company?"

"You jealous?"

"No reason for me to be jealous. I'm a happily married man."

"Whatever."

New York after a snowfall is as elusive as memory. The peaks and rifts of snow piled up in front of houses, beside highways, on housetops, covering hedges and even some roadways, robs you of that sense of familiarity, that sense of home, even though you've only been gone one day.

My block had still not been plowed. Snow had been compacted by moving vehicles leaving dark mounds on the edge of the roadway.

There were several messages on my machine: My mother had called to say they were having fun in Orlando. There was a frantic message from Lourdes' daughter which I could hardly understand because she was crying so hard.

I called the number she left. A man picked up. Moments later Elena came to the phone. She broke into tears no sooner than she said hello. I made out this much through her sobs. After a date with her boyfriend she woke up this morning to find her mother hanging by her stockings from an exposed pipe in the ceiling of the shower. She was as cold as the February morning.

13

Our phone conversation lasted about ten minutes. She wanted to see me. I offered to come over but she insisted on meeting in public. Something to do with wanting to get out of the house. We agreed on Junior's because of its central location.

I arrived at the restaurant first. Five minutes later she showed up holding hands with a young man. Dressed in a fur-trimmed brown coat, her thick hair pulled up and piled under a Yankees baseball cap, her eyes were swollen the size of lemons. From crying, I presumed.

The stocky youth's long blond hair was obviously bleached. Underneath his white bubble jacket he wore a T-shirt, revealing a tattoo of a snake on his forearm. He helped her out of the faux sheepskin and they sat together opposite me.

"Are you hungry?" I asked.

She shook her head and tried to smile but only succeeded in crinkling her brow.

The young man said nothing. I sensed he was rubbing her hands under the table. I ordered a round of coffee. Cheesecake was tempting but I opted for roast chicken salad as I was quite famished.

Elena took off her cap, releasing her hair which cascaded down her back like fresh silk. Her eyes fell off me onto the surface of the table. I realized by the quiet tremor of her shoulders that she was crying.

After a while her shoulders became still.

She lifted her face up and the tears seemed to have refreshed her smile. "I'm sorry."

"Don't be. I can only imagine how you feel. Who's this?"

"This is Javier. My boyfriend."

The youngster nodded. I presume that was his way of saying hello. He didn't extend his hand for a grip. Neither did I.

I said. "When did you last see your mother alive?"

"Yesterday afternoon. She was very happy. Excited. She'd been talking non-stop about going back to Nicaragua. My older sister in Managua just had a baby. My mother's first grandchild. She was so looking forward to seeing her granddaughter. She had all kinds of plans. She managed to save up quite a bit of money and wanted to travel."

The waiter returned with the order.

Javier looked at his coffee with disinterest. Elena poured milk into hers and stirred it with a tarnished spoon.

I asked Elena if she wanted half of my salad. She shook her head. After pouring dressing on, I took a fork full.

"She didn't kill herself, Mr. Overstreet."

"Call me Blades."

"The police say she committed suicide. They're wrong."

"Was there a note?"

Elena bowed her head. Her boyfriend caressed her back like a paid masseuse.

I said. "What did it say?"

She looked at me, her eyes wet. "My baby, Misa. I'm sorry."

"That's all? My baby, Misa. I'm sorry?"

"That all."

"Who's Misa?"

"My father used to call me that when I was little. My mother and I, we both hated it."

"She's been under a lot of strain the last couple of days. Did she appear despondent at any time?" I asked.

Sipping coffee, Elena contemplated my question. Then she set the cup down. "No, not really. The whole thing with Mr. Foder upset her as you can imagine. But she was happy to get away from that house."

"Was anything of value missing?"

"Not that I could tell."

"And everything looked normal when you got home that night?"

"Yes."

"What time did you find the body?"

"It wasn't until the morning. I got home about midnight. I'd drank so much and was so tired I passed out on the couch. The TV was on in the living room and I sat down for a moment and didn't move until the next morning about six o'clock. I got up to go to the bathroom. I saw this thing through the shower curtain. I couldn't imagine what it was. I pulled back the curtain to get a better look. That's when I saw her."

"Naked?"

She nodded.

"Any reason the pipes in the ceiling were exposed?"

"We had a leak the day before. Plumbers had started fixing it, but hadn't finished.

She buried her head in Javier's neck and quietly sobbed for a while. He was nice about it, gently rubbing her neck and shoulder until she'd gathered herself.

I said. "Perhaps we should talk some other time, when you're more up to it."

She wiped tears with the back of her hand. "No, I'm fine."

"Where's your father?"

"Died in a fire in a Sandinista jail. That's why my mother left Nicaragua."

"You said your mother had money saved up. Is it enough for you to finish school?"

Her smile was heavy with sadness. "I think half a million dollars is more than enough."

I stopped chewing and swallowed. "You're kidding, right?"

"No."

"Did she win the Lotto?"

"I don't think so."

"Did she gamble?"

"Not really. She told me Raoul liked to bet on horses and sometimes she went with him to the track. But that's all."

"Who's Raoul?"

"Her ex-husband."

I looked at Elena but didn't see the need to voice the question forming in my mind. Did she really think her mother saved half a million dollars on her salary?

"She remarried when she got here, but it didn't last long. They divorced before I came. I don't think she has talked about him in years."

"Where's Raoul now?"

"I don't know really. She said he was a musician. He's from Cuba." She sipped her coffee and her hands shook. "I know she didn't kill herself, Mr. Overstreet. I believe that in my heart. I know my mother. I'm telling you she wouldn't do that."

I leaned back in my chair. "That leaves murder."

"Yes, that leaves murder."

"What about the note?"

"I don't care what that note said."

"Did it look like her handwriting?"

"Yes, it was, I think. Looked like it. But she didn't write that note voluntarily, Mr. Overstreet. That's why she used a name I hated. She was trying to tell me she was murdered. I want you to find out who killed my mother. I can pay you."

I'd lost my appetite. I felt tired and wanted nothing to do with death or any conversation about the subject. "I'll see what I can do."

She sighed and made the sign of a cross on her chest. "Thank you."

I offered them a ride but her boyfriend had a car. I drove along Brooklyn's bleak white streets with the radio tuned to WFUV which was doing a day of blues. During the 10 minutes it took to get home I managed to hear two of my favorites: Lightning Hopkins thwanging guitar on *California Mudslide* and Buddy Guy's dark, enigmatic *Night Flight*.

I called River. Told her everything Elena had told me. She was on her way out but said she'd call me the next day.

Even after downing half a bottle of wine I was unable to find sleep. I thrashed like a demented person, replaying distorted images of past events, exceedingly ugly memories of incidents from my life as an undercover drug cop, things I thought I'd forgotten.

In undercover life there was never a moment when you felt safe. Never a moment when you thought you could let your guard down. Seldom did you live to regret such a mistake.

Once, I got caught in the middle of a domestic dispute between a dealer named Big Stone and his woman. I'd gotten close to Big Stone and had discovered that he was fronting for the leader of a deadly Crips gang out of Chicago. Their mules were exclusively women who used just about every trick in the book to transport coke from Chicago to New York.

Big Stone suspected that his woman, Bilal, was two-timing him and also stealing his supply. He wanted to use Bilal to teach the other women a lesson. And he tapped me to do the bodywork. He brought Bilal up to the roof of a building in the Jacob Riis houses and told me to shoot her.

When I worked this deep undercover I normally carried two guns. One gun was rigged to jam in the event I was asked to shoot anyone. I knew the game. Gang-bangers were fond of asking initiates to shoot somebody to prove their loyalty. I pulled out my gun, pointed it at Bilal, and pulled the trigger. Those few seconds were the most frightening of my life. What if the gun didn't jam?

My gun did jam. You can appreciate my relief. But Bilal's fate had long been sealed. Big Stone pulled out his own piece and shot her dead. Then he looked at me with a wily smile. I knew I was marked for death at that moment. Why he didn't kill me then I could only guess at. Perhaps he suspected I was a cop and figured it'd be best to outsource such a job. He didn't get a second chance. I dropped out of sight that night. The next time he saw me was from the defendant's chair in court.

14

Noah showed up at my house at nine o'clock the next morning after dropping his wife off at a women's shelter in Cobble Hill. Ever since her son was killed a year ago she'd kept herself busy with volunteer work throughout the city. Noah still had his job as a theater professor though he was more focused now on writing and producing a musical about Duke Ellington.

For a long time I stared at him standing at my doorstep.

"Are you gonna let me in, guy?"

"Forgive me, Noah, but I'm not sure if I'm awake or dreaming." I opened the door wider so he could come in.

He shucked his shoes at the door and took off his coat. "You look like Polyphemus used you as his bitch last night. What's the matter? Still not sleeping well?"

"I'm going crazy, Noah."

"Can I suggest something?"

"What?"

"You and Anais should get your asses to the Caribbean. Get away."

"She's in Atlanta."

"Well, maybe you should join her."

"I was about to make some coffee. You want some?"

"Sure. Put a little of that spiced Bajan rum in it, too."

"Come on into the kitchen."

Noah sat on a high stool around the island in the kitchen as I poured beans and water into the coffee maker. He was dressed in a thick black wool sweater and his trademark threaded corduroy pants. Olive. He kept cracking his knuckles. Something was bothering him.

"Looks like I'm not the only one with a big rock in their gut," I said.

He heaved a smile at me and his thoughts started to spill out. "I feel like giving the shit up, you understand? I'm tired of the bullshit."

"What's that you gonna give up?"

"My backers, they pulled out on me."

"Backers?"

"For the Ellington musical. All of a sudden they have concerns. What concerns I asked. They wouldn't even give me the courtesy of telling me what these so-called concerns are."

"Who're these people?"

"Who do you think? White muthafuckers from downtown."

"You say white like it's shit in your mouth."

"Don't try to out me, Blades. I'm mad as hell. I shouldn't have to go to white people to get money to do a musical about Duke Ellington. He's our black prince of swing. That's what's got me so fucking mad. I mean, when're black people in this country gonna wake up?"

"Maybe your white backers are iffy because of the way you talk. Maybe they want to hear you say he's America's prince of swing."

"He's our prince. Black America's prince. And we should be the ones financing and producing his work. Remember when Spike Lee was doing that movie about Malcolm X and ran out of studio money and had to run to Oprah and Michael Jordan and Magic Johnson for money? It should never have come to that."

"Why not?"

"He never should've been in hock to the studios in the first place. Black people should've been producing that movie from day one. It's all about control, Blades."

"What difference does it make? He made his movie."

"The difference is this, Blades. As if you didn't know. The only entertainer out there who seems to know what the fuck is going on is Prince. There's a battle going on out there, Blades, and you better get hip to it."

"Which battle is that?"

"For control of information in America. And black people better wake up and smell the coffee. We're being swept aside. A few people will soon control all of the radio stations, television stations, recording and movie companies in this country. And when that happens they will dictate what and who gets seen or heard on radio and TV. And if we don't try to get control of some of this shit we will have no recourse but to beg for scraps. Remember the bullshit debate over hip-hop a few years ago? The pants wearing low, the hat backwards? That was really about control. Now that

Hip-hop music and paraphernalia is the biggest seller who's complaining? Only black people. You know why? They lost control of the shit. All that craziness is okay now that corporate America controls the record companies and the magazines which promote it."

I poured two cups of coffee. "I don't listen to Hip-hop."

Noah took his cup and raised it to his lips. He put it down again without taking a sip. "Where's the rum?"

"In the cabinet behind you."

"What, I gotta get it myself?"

I laughed. "Your foot ain't broke."

He chuckled and got up to walk to the cabinet. "You're right not to listen to that music. It's toxic music from a toxic environment. Look at what's happening to the environment. That music is doing the same thing to our kids' minds."

He returned with a bottle of spiced rum, pouring about two knuckles into his cup. He took a sip without stirring the mixture. Licking his lips. "If you listen carefully to the message in that music you'd see that we've bought into this corrupt society. We're become the schizophrenic beast that raised us. Make no bones about it. We're their children. We eat and feast on ourselves, and a lot of this anger comes from not being able to attain the materialism that they have. We've accepted that all there is to this country is buying and selling. Turning a profit on every muthafucking thing you do. That's all these rappers sing about. Death and guns and mayhem. Money and bitches. What happened to singing about love and peace, or passion and desire. Things like that? And I can't get anybody to put some money into a musical about Duke Ellington's music."

"You know, you should write a book."

He sat back and poured more rum into his coffee. "What are you trying to say?"

"Or maybe run for political office."

"I know you're not trying to insult me, Blades."

"Do you rant like this to all your friends or just to me?"

His eyes hardened. "You know what, Blades? I came here to tell you something, so I'll say it and get the fuck out your house."

"What is it?"

"Zoe Foder called last night. You and River are fired. I left River a message and since I was in your backyard I thought I'd stop by and tell you in person."

"Why didn't Zoe call me herself?"

"She didn't wanna talk to you. She doesn't like you, Blades. She said something about the way you treated her some time when you came to the house. What did you do to her?"

"Nothing. I went over there. She was drunk. Acting like a real bitch."

"You said something nasty to her?"

"Would I do that?"

"You probably did."

"I was doing this as a favor to you, Noah. Not for the money. But there's something weird with that family. Ever since this story about the judge and the bride-for-hire ring broke everyone in that house has been acting like they swallowed tarantulas."

He toyed with the cup. "Maybe that's just the kind of family they are."

"What're you saying?"

"I've read some of Chancellor's plays. Not for the faint of heart."

"Why?"

"Lots of messy family relations in his plays. Violence. Domineering fathers. Obsessive children. Incest. A lot of cruelty."

"The housekeeper did say there was a lot of cruelty in that house."

"I wouldn't doubt it."

"Their housekeeper was found hanging in her shower two nights ago."

"Suicide?"

"That's what the police think. The daughter has doubts."

"Hanging is a pretty ghastly way to snuff your own candle." Noah got up and looked at me with a tough-guy smile. "I gotta talk to one more muthafucker downtown. If he says no I'm just gonna dump the shit."

"It's not like you to give up so easily."

He left the kitchen and strode to the closet to get his coat. "I'm getting older. Wiser."

"Maybe you're just getting older."

He slipped on his navy blue down coat. At the door he said, "By the way, I am writing a book."

He went through the door with a smirk on his face.

Whether Zoe Foder wanted to keep me on the case made no difference to me that morning. I had a beef to settle with Odessa's boys.

Toni had said that Odessa would be coming for her wash at 3 PM. I had a little time to convene my welcoming committee.

I couldn't get River on the phone so I decided to swing by her place.

River's truck was parked on the street, cocked on a mound of ice. I rang her bell several times but got no response.

Movement in the studio downstairs caught my eye so I rang that bell. At the sound of the electronic bzzz I pushed the door. It opened onto a cluttered and dusty room thick with the smell of paint and turpentine. A slender man with the bright eyes of a child greeted me. Thick mustache and beard. Dreadlocks wrapped neatly in a black tam.

"Can I help you?"

"Are you Kerry?"

"Yes, I am."

I smiled, pleased that I'd remembered the name River had given me of her downstairs neighbor and landlord. "My name's Blades. I was looking for River. Your tenant upstairs. We're old friends. Her car's on the street, but she's not answering her door."

Stroking his dense beard. "You tried her phone?"

"She isn't picking up."

His manner was loose and friendly and he spoke with a diluted Trinidadian accent. "Sorry, Blades. I don't know where she is."

"Seen her today?"

He hesitated. "Early this morning."

"What time?"

"Five-thirty."

"Going out?" I asked.

Eyebrows raised suspiciously, he hesitated. "Coming in."

I said thank you and went back to my car where I dialed River's number again. Still no answer. I left a detailed message, telling her where I was going and what I planned to do. Told her to meet me there if she could. It was about half past one when I drove away. Looked like I was going to have to handle Odessa's boys on my own.

Black Pearl. 2:30 P.M. The joint was practically empty. Myself and the young woman who served me were the only ones in the place. I ordered latte and settled at a table by the floor-to-ceiling glass front. From here I could see anyone entering or leaving Toni's place. Some kind of Celtic-sounding music echoed softly from ceiling-mounted speakers.

Odessa and her tribe rolled up at 2:55. I watched the black Explorer with tinted-windows double-park outside Toni's. Mallet stepped out wearing one of those long dark wool coats TV mafia guys wear. Looking around in four directions. I had to laugh. Who the hell did this dude think he was guarding? The President?

Odessa tumbled out in a purple lambskin quickly followed by one of her lumberjacks.

The Explorer scratched off leaving Odessa and the two men on the sidewalk. They waited for an old man and the nurse pushing his wheelchair to pass before disappearing into Toni's. How polite.

Ten minutes later I buttoned my leather jacket to the neck and went out into the bright afternoon. I walked one block in both directions to see if the Explorer was parked anywhere in sight. No sign of it. I doubled back to the salon.

To burnish a reputation carved out of privacy and exclusivity, Toni's salon sported yellow blinds at the door and the windows. Impossible to see inside from the street. On the other hand, it was also impossible to see outside without pulling the blinds back.

Odessa was a diva. Toni had told me that hers was the last appointment that day; this was normal for any of her visits. And all other customers had to be out of the salon by the time Odessa arrived. In addition, she booked the entire salon for the block of time she would be there, willing to pay whatever Toni charged for this absolute privacy. And this woman lived in the projects. Go figure.

As I reached Park and Underhill the black Explorer pulled up outside Toni's. I quickly flattened myself against the side of the building, cursing under my breath.

I waited to see if anyone got out. Nobody did.

My phone rang. It was River.

"Where are you?" I asked.

"Coming up on the salon. One block away."

"Come in softly," I said.

"I just passed a parking spot. I'll swing around. I got your message. Sounds like you're ready to set it off."

"Odessa's about to have a bad hair day."

"You sure you wanna do this?"

"Somebody's gotta save the ozone."

"OK. How can I help?"

"I'm about to bum rush Toni's joint. There's a black Explorer out front. Some of Odessa's pups are in there. Probably feeding. Whip's got tinted windows."

"Diversion?"

"Yes. Don't let any of them get out of the Explorer until you see me come out."

"What if I can't spit without soiling somebody?"

"Just leave 'em breathing and call an ambulance."

"I'm parking now. I'll do the rest on foot. You should see me in about two minutes."

Two minutes later I spotted River across the street dressed in tight black jeans and waist-length jacket. She walked casually, but with purpose, her strides long and graceful. When she came abreast of the Explorer she crossed the street. I lost sight of her, but waited a few seconds more to make sure no one was getting out of the truck.

Gun drawn, I quickly turned the corner and buzzed the door to Toni's.

Mallet opened. I stuck the Glock between his eyes and pushed him backwards, closing the door behind me.

Mallet's eyes jerked to the left. Out of the corner of my eye I saw Steroid Man reach into his jacket. I spun and snapped a hard kick to his nuts. He let out a pitiful cry. A cow bellowing from hunger. Limbs scattering in all directions as he fell. His gun clattered to the hardwood floor with an amplified clack. I took two steps and kicked it as far across the room as I could. Steroids Man was bringing up his lunch all over Toni's shiny floor.

"Don't even swallow," I said to Mallet.

He smirked, sticking out his tongue like a lizard.

I got closer. "You're a coward."

"Your mama!"

I broke his nose with the gun butt. He collapsed sputtering blood. With my knee on his neck I bent and tossed him, removing a shiny .45 caliber automatic Ruger from his waist. I dumped the clip, stuffing the gun in my waist and went over to toss Mr. Steroids laying flat as a deflated blimp. The bile from his stomach looked and smelled like dog poop.

No other weapons on him. He was no longer a threat to do anything more than continue to stink up Toni's joint. I turned my attention to Queen Odessa.

She sat with a quiet preoccupied look on her face, seemingly unmoved by the events that had just taken place.. "Who're you?"

"Name's Blades Overstreet."

She turned to Toni. "He a friend of yours?"

Toni said, "Never seen him in my life. Looking at him it's clear he's one fucked up nigga. That much is obvious."

Toni stepped behind me and I swiveled Odessa's chair around so she could face me, at the same time I was able to keep an eye on Mallet and his partner near the door. "Did you kill Judge Foder?"

She tried to get up. I pushed her back down.

"Keep your hands off me, muthafucker! Do you know who I am?"

"Relax. I'm not here to hurt you."

"You wouldn't be so stupid. You know, you better kill Mallet before you leave here. He ain't one to let go of a beef until you got a tag on your toe."

"Right now his throat is filling up with his own blood. If he likes the taste of it then I'll be happy to tap some more for him. But I'd just a soon break his neck if he prefers."

"That's the talk of a scared man."

"You know what they say. A man scared is as dangerous as a wounded lion. But I didn't come here for small talk. I wanna hear about you and the judge. Heard the Feds hauled away his office. Does that concern you? Or did you get the incriminating evidence when you broke in two weeks ago?"

"You know, I have a theory about people like you."

"What's so special about people like me?"

"Nothing, that's the point. Nothing special happened in your childhood. In fact you obviously had a deprived childhood, my friend. That's what I mean by people like you. People who get pleasure snooping around in shit that's none of their business. Why don't you get a life?"

I refused to take her bait. I could hear Toni snickering behind me.

Odessa grabbed her purse from the chair next to her and stood up. "Toni, I'm leaving your establishment. If this man puts his hands on me to stop me I expect you to take action against him."

We squared off eye to eye. I go about a buck ninety-five after a big lunch. Odessa outweighed me by about 200 pounds and could've probably pancaked me if she wanted to. But I got the feeling she was measuring me.

I moved out of her way.

She wobbled past and out the door. Mallet stared at me with hate-filled eyes before helping his shriveled pal to his feet. I tossed Mallet's gun across the floor. He picked up and limped after his mistress.

I went to the door to alert River. She came around the back of the truck as Odessa and her two embarrassed bodyguards got inside. Together we watched as the Explorer was gunned into traffic.

"That wasn't too hard," River said. "Nothing like the threat of some pussy to immobilize a man."

I laughed.

We went back inside the salon where Toni was sitting on a stool dragging on a cigarette, snorting smoke through his nose like an angry dragon.

"River, I'd like you to meet an old friend. This is Toni Monday."

She stretched out her hand to Toni. "I've heard a lot about you, Toni. Nice to finally meet you."

Toni took her hand and bared white teeth. "Forgive me if I'm not my usual sociable self. But I'm real mad right now. And no matter what he tells you, I'm no friend of his. Have no fucking idea where he got that impression."

River chuckled. "He can be delusional at times. I know that."

"I'm really sorry, Toni…" I began.

He shot to his feet, shoving the cigarette two inches from my nose. "No, you're not. You're not sorry, Blades. You think you could fuck with me anyway you like."

My skin was beginning to tingle from the heat of the cigarette. I sat on a bench under a set of bright lights. "It's not that big a deal, Toni."

Toni remained standing over me. "What if I walked into your club and pull that shit?"

"You wouldn't be able to get into my club with a piece, you know that."

"Fuck you, Blades. Get outta my joint." He turned to River, "I'm sorry you have to see my bitchy side on our first meeting, but I don't want to see his face in my place."

I said, "Does this mean I can't come to your party?"

The look on his face told me my jokes were as flat as my manners. What I'd done was arrogant and stupid. My only salvation was the knowledge that Toni was, after all, a drug dealer and probably should be in jail.

River and I stood on the sidewalk watching pedestrians bustle along in both directions. She dipped a hand into her jacket and came up with a pack of Marlboro's. She popped one between purple-painted lips and then pointed the box at me.

"No thanks."

"You really pissed off your friend," she said

"He'll get over it."

We walked two blocks to her car.

"You don't respect anybody, do you?"

I ignored the question, which was more a remark than a question, and turned up the collar of my jacket against the cold. "You heard from Noah?"

"He left a message. We're off the case."

"We have another client. Elena's convinced her mother was murdered. I told her we'd do some digging."

River got into her rig. "How's she gonna pay?"

"Apparently her mother was a very frugal woman. Lourdes was worth about half a mil. Not bad for the housekeeper, huh?"

"Not bad. Who knew sleeping in could be so rewarding."

"I want you to canvas Lourdes' building. It's a small building. One of the residents might've seen something odd."

"What're you gonna do?"

"Find out if Zoe's mind was changed for her."

"Is that what you suspect?"

"It wouldn't surprise me if Odessa sent her wolf-pack to scare her."

"You don't like her do you?"

"Who Zoe?"

"Odessa."

"All I know about the woman is that she's a legend in some parts of Brooklyn."

"And you like bringing down legends, is that it?"

"What's with all the probing?" I said, annoyed. "You trying to build a psychological profile on me?"

"Just trying to get under your skin. I can't seem to get anywhere else with you."

"I'll see you later."

I turned and walked away. The vroom of the big Ford's engine disturbed the quiet of the block but I didn't look back.

15

Next day the cold broke. By nine o'clock the temperature had climbed to a whopping 35 degrees. Whoopee! I'd gotten about three hours sleep. Not nearly enough to bolster my kinder, gentler side, but enough to keep hope alive. I took a long hot shower, hoping the heat would wake me up. Two cups of coffee and toast later, I still felt edgy and disoriented. A constant buzz in my head. It wasn't a sound, but a sensation of things vibrating. Best to keep moving. The faster I moved the easier it would be to ignore the buzz.

Around 11 A.M., I got into my car. Between the ever-present road repairs and construction and the crazy lane-changing truckers who all seemed to drive as if they only had one good eye, getting to Queens was always a high-stress affair. I made it to Northern Boulevard without getting the finger from anyone, which was an accomplishment and a relief. The way I felt this morning, a finger—any finger for any reason—might've provoked a road-rage incident.

I cruised through Douglaston Manor, taking in the beautiful homes. Arriving at the Foders, I decided that a brisk walk up the incline might just wake me up. I parked on the street and locked the Volvo. As I climbed the hill I unwrapped a stick of Big Red. Anais has been trying to get me to switch to sugarless for the longest time. Tried it for a while too. No dice. Tasted like shit. Yeah, I know, Big Red was bad for my teeth. But I had a connection with Big Red. Kept my company on many stakeouts. How could I desert her for sugarless?

I arrived at the front door feeling less panicky, though not yet ready to sing "We Are the World". The walk in the sunshine had indeed given me a lift.

I rang the bell, and sat on the head of one of the stone lions to wait.

When I called last night to talk to Zoe her sister-in-law had answered the phone. Sounding like a warden, she rudely informed me that Zoe was unavailable. Early this morning I called again. Honor was still on duty. And Zoe was still engaged.

She must be feeding New York's homeless, I said.

Honor didn't see the humor.

The door opened and Honor stood there dressed in thick black sweat pants and gray T-shirt. She was a big woman; thick-waisted and heavy-chested. She appeared to be braless. Not a pretty sight.

"What are you doing here?" she asked.

"Can I come in?"

Her voice had the snap of a Rottweiler's bark. "I was about to get into the shower."

"That's okay. I'll try to resist the urge to rub your back."

She cocked her head like a fox who'd smelled a predator. "Save the wise cracks for your friends."

"Zoe still occupied?"

"You just missed her. She went to the hospital. Maria is coming home today."

"Do you mind if I come in and wait?"

Her eyes hardened. "I do actually."

"What's your objection to my waiting?"

"I just do. I don't have to explain it to you."

"You think I'm gonna rob you? What?"

That question caught her off guard and she rocked back. A dark smile broke over her spatula-thin lips. She quickly reigned it in and stepped back. Why she changed her mind I don't know but I slipped past her and she closed the door.

Her steps were heavy on the polished floor as I followed her into the living room. Without the cloud of woe generated by anguished crying, the room sparkled in the sunlight, its air of extravagance more pronounced. Sunlight brightened the pale walls. The creamy furniture had the bloomy shine of newness.

"You can wait in here, I suppose." Honor said.

The bark had left her voice. Not that it had become inviting by any stretch. Just less glacial. Made little difference to me. She didn't have to like me and I certainly didn't have to like her. Besides, I was chewing Big Red. I could handle anything on Big Red.

"Can I ask you a question?" I said.

"I can't promise you I'll answer."

Hers was a deep voice, like her appearance, more manly than feminine. I suspected it worked to her advantage when she was in the NYPD.

"I suppose you heard about Lourdes."

Her expression softened the way a Doberman's eyes filled with pity before it made you his lunch. "Her daughter called. Lourdes didn't seem the type to commit suicide."

I said, "Why wouldn't you let me speak to Zoe on the phone?"

Laughter. Hers. Carefree and arrogant. She was the only one getting the jokes right now. But that was okay.

"I don't like people like you," she said. "I thought your name was familiar when you first showed up here. But I couldn't recall where I knew it from. I mentioned it to a friend the other day and he refreshed my memory. I was still a recruit when that shit with you and that white cop went down. It split the whole class right down the middle. Blacks on your side. Whites on the other side. We thought it was an accident. That the cop who shot you just made a judgment call. We thought you played it like a nigger. Hiding behind race. The black recruits didn't openly come out and say they believed you, but we knew they thought it. Whenever there was a discussion about it they kept silent."

"That was long time ago. Me and that guy, we had it out. It was a mistake. He just wasn't a good cop."

"Did you know he committed suicide?"

"I heard."

"Do you feel any responsibility?"

"I'm not responsible for his weakness."

"You're living scum, you know that."

"That's just one opinion. And it doesn't really count in my world."

"Your world?" She snorted. "What the fuck is your world? Low-life niggers like yourself?"

Without thinking I punched her.

She stumbled back, then fell to the floor holding the left side of her face. Her dark eyes filled with fire. "Just like a nigger. Beating up on women."

"Nobody calls me that. I don't give a fuck who you are."

Her cheeks reddened. "What're you going to do, nigger? Hit me again?"

Blood rattled around in my head. Or was that the buzz from this morning? I felt like strangling her. I was so angry I was having a problem focusing on her face. My vision was fogged and my head throbbed with a vicious pain.

"You'd better leave now. Else I'm going upstairs for my gun and I might just use it to wipe your nigger ass."

I staggered from the room toward the exit.

She screamed after me. "And if I ever see you again I might just kill you."

I ran down the driveway, angry at myself for reacting so violently.

Hitting the woman! You must be crazy! That was no way to deal with the situation.

Behind the shame over my loss of control came a dark recklessness. I hit the Douglaston Parkway with the needle kissing 75 and by the time I merged onto the Cross Island I was doing 95, not caring if I saw berries flashing or heard sirens blasting behind me.

As I whistled along the Grand Central my spirits got a needed reprieve. A phone call from Semin who wanted to meet for lunch. She was in the mood for a burger. I felt more like slitting my wrists, but agreed to meet her at noon Downtown Brooklyn where she was covering a story at the Brooklyn Supreme Court.

Slowing down to speak to Semin might've saved my life, too. Moments later I passed a car flipped over in one of the tight corners of the Jackie Robinson Parkway.

I walked into the restaurant on Remsen five short of noon. Semin was already there, sitting at the bar sipping a drink. Petite with a dark handsome face, she was simply a good looking woman, her charcoal pantsuit snug in the right areas. Her warm embrace and bright smile lifted my spirits immediately.

"So how have you been?" I said, taking a seat next to her.

"Working my ass off."

A tall Asian woman came over, handed out menus and placed glasses of water in front of us. I pushed mine away and ordered a dry martini.

"How're you?" Semin said.

"Craving sleep like an addict."

Semin opened her menu. "I never figured you for a man who'd carry around a lot of demons."

I perused the menu before I looked up. "I don't see how you wouldn't, Semin. I was a damn cop for longer than I care to remember. That alone is more of a burden than most people will ever have to carry. If I were to describe some of the things I did or some of the things I saw you wouldn't be able to eat lunch. One thing I learned first hand. Not from books. Not from the newspaper. From dealing with people. There's a lot of pain out there. A lot of fucked up people walking around who don't care who they hurt. The depravity in some people's hearts is frightening. And some of the worst of it can be found in families. Wasn't a good life, Semin. The scary thing is, until I got shot, I'd convinced myself that I loved it. That it was my mission. That my life was on the street bagging bad guys."

"You're still out there bagging bad guy, Blades. What has changed?"

"It's not my life anymore."

"But hunting bad guys still gives you a rush."

"I don't know what it is, Semin."

"When you find out let me know. It might make a great magazine piece."

"You're mocking me."

"Not at all, Blades. You're quite a fascinating man. Scary at times but fascinating."

My martini was deliciously primed with gin. The alcohol fired the correct node in my brain and I felt myself smiling.

Semin got a burger with fries. I wasn't hungry.

"You like taking chances, don't you?" Semin said. "Perhaps there's something about danger, about taking chances, about the prospect of violence that awakens a hunger in you."

"That doesn't sound too complimentary."

She smiled self-consciously. "I'm sorry. I'm through playing amateur psychologist for today."

"Thanks for sharing it anyway."

"I suspect that you're being disingenuous with me."

"What do you mean?"

"That you know yourself much better than you pretend. You're crafty, Blades. You abound with self-confidence. Perhaps, too much of it. You're searching for something. The question is: what."

I did not answer. Instead I looked away through the glass window, letting my eyes linger on the street outside. I could see feet turning over rapidly along the sidewalk but no faces.

"Do you think we become free by accepting the worst in ourselves?"

"I'm not sure I understand the question."

"I'm not a very nice person, Semin. I've done a lot bad things. I've killed. I've beaten suspects just because I had the power to do it. I've lied to put men in jail and justified it by telling myself they were bad men. That they deserved it. I'm a married man, yet I lust after another woman. I just punched a woman no more than an hour ago for saying something I didn't like. Perhaps I'm searching for the good in me and before I can find it I must find out how much evil there is."

"That sounds a little scary, to me. Who did you punch?"

"The judge's step-daughter."

"What did she say to you?"

"I should've been man enough to walk away."

Semin's burger came and I watched her eat in silence.

After a while Semin looked at me. "I still want to know what she said."

"What she said doesn't justify what I did."

"If it were a man would you've punched him?"

I pondered. "I would've broken something on his body."

Semin paused her chewing. "And that doesn't bother you?"

"Not in the least," I said.

Semin chewed and sipped water. Her voice was noticeably tensed when she spoke again. "I went to the doctor today."

"Checkup?"

"Sort of. I'm pregnant."

I straightened up. "You kidding me?"

She laughed, her eyes lit up. "I'm serious."

"Congratulations. I didn't even know you were seeing someone seriously."

"I'm not."

"Oh, one of those."

"Yeah, one of those. I was unprepared. Totally. Sounds silly, but it's the truth."

"What're you going to do?"

"I'm keeping it."

"You and the father? Anything serious?"

"Not really. I mean, we like each other. But... No. I don't know if anything can happen there. But it's not him that I'm concerned about right now. It's my parents. They're coming from India to stay with me in about three months. It's going to be hell."

"Call me if you need a referee."

She looked at me for a moment as if I'd punched her in the gut then burst out laughing. "You just can't help, can you, Blades?"

"Wouldn't know what to do with myself."

"I've got some information for you. That is if you still want it."

"Is it about the judge?"

"The FBI took all his files under this new homeland security act."

"For what reason?"

"I thought you read the article."

"I did."

"Apparently many of the people who got green cards through this marriage ring were from the Middle East. The buzz is that one of them was connected to Al Qaeda."

"That wasn't in the article."

"Are you sure?"

"I'd remember something like that."

"I thought it was. Perhaps I got it from the author of the article. Probably didn't print it because he couldn't confirm."

"You think it's true? This Al Qaeda link?"

"No. We checked it out. It's simply FBI posturing for the media. I'm writing a piece about Pakistani and Indian Muslims arrested and detained and sent home in chains without ever seeing a judge for nothing more than overstaying their visa. The FBI flips up a possible Al Qaeda link and INS sends them packing."

"Did they put any heat on Odessa?"

"They questioned her. Raided her house and offices, too. If they had anything she'd be in jail. Don't let her public antics fool you. She's got connections. She gave quite a lot of money to President Clinton's campaigns and I've heard that he still takes her calls."

"Impressive."

"This ring was very sophisticated, Blades. Wasn't a moms and pops operation. Apparently, the women were using many aliases to go undetected.

They had fake names and had access to social security numbers and fake birth certificates so that the same women were getting married under many aliases that appeared to be quite legitimate."

"How'd they bust it?"

"Under questioning the suspected terrorist revealed that he was married to a US citizen. When the FBI tried to find her they found that she existed only on paper. She had no record of employment. Never paid any income tax. No bank records. No credit records. They traced the birth certificate back to a clerk in the County Record Office who may've ratted out Odessa. He hanged himself a few days later."

"Wait a minute. You saying this clerk hanged himself?"

"Flipped a rope over a branch and went for a swing."

"How common is suicide by hanging in this town?"

"I don't know. Why do you ask?"

The judge's housekeeper was found hanging in her shower a few days ago. Police say it was suicide."

"Strange coincidence."

"I'd say. Anyway this guy wasn't a suicide?"

"No, he was definitely suicide. A neighbor saw him tying the rope. Didn't think anything of it. Saw him stick his head in the noose, too. She called 9-1-1, but they were to late."

"How much cash was flowing through Odessa's pockets?"

"The police claims she was charging between ten and fifteen grand for each marriage. Cash. Up front. According to them over a ten year span they may've been over five thousand such arranged marriages."

"A thirty million dollar business?"

"More. If only Cupid knew this match-making thing would turn out to be such a lucrative enterprise."

"With that kinda silk why is this woman still living in the projects?"

"What better cover. Her money was put to good use, though. She's got two children who've both donned Ivy League colors. And she owns several printing businesses across Brooklyn. This is one shrewd woman."

"Sounds to me like they got her cold, though."

"I'm not so sure. Word I'm getting is that they don't really have a case against her without this guy who necktied himself to a tree."

"What do you mean?"

"Apparently all the money went through him. He took the money from the prospects though Odessa was pulling the strings. But there's no paper trail from him to Odessa. Nothing but his word."

"That's worth little more than toilet paper now."

"The only person who had real contact with Odessa was the judge. And he's dead too.

"None of the people getting married ever met Odessa?"

"The police can't establish a direct link."

"She must've had recruiters. How about them?"

"Hard to locate. They never used their real names. None of the names given to police have turned up a real person."

"What's the FBI saying about the judge's death? Any Al Qaeda link there?"

"Not that I've heard. But don't give up on that just yet. The FBI has a way of tying things together that would make Houdini's head spin."

"Can you dig up that clerk's name and address? The suicide. Was he married?"

"Have it right here. Figured you'd ask." She took a notebook out of her purse and flipped it open. "Name was Justice Malveaux. Lived in Suffolk. 324 Padmore Lane. He was from Haiti. His wife is from Nigeria. No kids."

I smiled and finished my martini.

16

I spoke briefly with Anais that evening. No change in her father's condition but her sister had arrived with news that she was pregnant. If nothing else it broke the cloud of gloom and gave them much needed distraction.

My brother called to tell me that our sister, Melanie, was in New York. She'd arrived earlier that day from L.A.

I was caught off guard at my own disappointed that Melanie hadn't called to tell me she was coming. But why would I even expect her to do that?

"Where's Melanie staying?" I asked

"Park Avenue Hotel. She's got some kind of conference tomorrow."

"When is she going back?"

"I don't know. I better warn you if you speak to her. She's angry."

"About?"

"She wouldn't tell me. I suspect it's got something to do with Mom's new boyfriend."

"What about Mom's new boyfriend?"

"She said she didn't want to meet him."

"Have you?"

"Yes, I was over there two weeks ago and met him."

"Is he black?"

"Yes."

My sister was a piece of work. Only Melanie would be so presumptuous to express dislike for a man she hadn't met. Good thing Melanie was a corporate attorney and didn't work in a DA's office somewhere. Beginning with my father, my sister has had issues with black men as far back as I could remember.

Melanie never shied away from admitting that she hated my father. Not because he was black, she'd reason, but for the way he treated our mother and the rest of us. I'd never really believed her. I knew her hatred had been fueled by her own father who couldn't accept losing his young wife to a black man and filled Melanie's head with the rhetoric of racial hatred. But why his machinations worked on Melanie and not Jason was a puzzle. Jason was far more open-minded than our high IQ sister.

I called the Park Avenue Hotel. Melanie was not in her room so I left a message. In spite of everything I was always eager to talk to my sister.

River called as I walked to Flatbush to get jerk chicken for dinner.

"I spoke to two women in Lourdes' building. A Mrs. Eversley and an old woman from Barbados who I could hardly understand."

"Anything?" I asked.

"Nada. Mrs. Eversley lives on the first floor. She spent the night watching TV. She had smothered pork chops for dinner and drank a little whisky around eight-thirty to put her to sleep. Slept like a lamb in heaven, she said. Saw no evil. Heard no evil. But dreamed of the devil. The lady from Barbados, she also lives on the first floor. In the back. She's wheelchair bound and don't get out much."

"Who lives on the second floor besides Lourdes?"

"Unoccupied."

"Can you get a copy of the coroner's report on Lourdes?"

"Sure thing."

"I found out something interesting today."

"What?"

"One of Odessa's elves was found hanging by his collar a few days ago."

"Who was he?"

"Magician from the County Clerk's office. Created women out of paper."

"Suicide?"

"Apparently Name's Justice Malveaux. Check him out."

I gave River the address in Suffolk County.

"One last thing," I said.

"What?"

"Can I come over?"

"I got a date."

"Oh."

"You had your shot, Blades."

"Just needed some company, that's all."

"Too bad."

After hanging up from River, I called Elena and told her I was coming over in half an hour to look around the apartment. Her passion and conviction had rubbed off on me and her explanation of the suicide note made sense. My instincts were leading me down the path to foul play.

I called River back. "Meet me at Lourdes' apartment in half an hour?"

"What for?"

"I wanna take a look around."

"You can do that without me."

"I thought we were working this case together."

"You just wanna block my flow, Blades."

"I'll pick you up in half an hour."

"Forget that. I'm driving my own rig."

"Suit yourself."

The temperature dipped again below freezing. As I curbed outside the tenement building I saw River's SUV parked under a burnt-out street lamp half a block in front of me.

The street was empty and quiet; many of the buildings around were dark and looked abandoned. No lights shining in the tiny park across the street either, but in the shadowy space I could make out a dark figure on a bench.

I got out, locked the car and stared into the darkness across the street, weighing in my mind if I should investigate. It was too damn cold for anyone to be sitting in the park. I crossed the wide road for a better look.

Couldn't tell the gender but it was indeed a person. He or she had their face secured to their chest, their body curled into a C, a blanket wrapped tightly around them. I moved closer, bending down for a better look.

"Hey, it's kinda cold out here. You okay?"

No response. No movement either. I tapped the blanket.

The person swayed back, then forward. He raised his head and our eyes made four.

"Aren't you cold?" I said.

His face looked stiff and frozen.

"You got any food?"

"Aren't you cold?" I repeated.

"I ain't cold. But I'm hungry."

"It's very cold. You gotta be cold."

"I say I ain't cold. If you ain't got no food leave me alone."

"I'm gonna get you into a shelter. You should be able to get some food there."

"Mind your own damn business. I ain't going to no shelter."

I took out my cell phone and dialed 4-1-1. Got the number for the nearest police precinct and spoke to the sergeant at the desk. He said he'd send someone out to take a look.

"Somebody's coming to get you," I said.

He growled. "I told you I ain't going to no shelter. Scat."

I took ten dollars from my wallet and handed it to him.

He looked at the money in the dim light then he raised his body so that he was now sitting erect for the first time. "I ain't say I want money."

"You can buy yourself some food."

He yanked the money from my hand and curved his body back into a C. I left him and crossed the street.

When I rapped Elena's apartment door upstairs River opened.

"What took you so long?"

"Traffic. Where's Elena?"

"In the bedroom. I found her crying."

I shucked my jacket as I followed River down the narrow hall to the bedroom. Music. From somewhere in the apartment. Marvin Gaye's inflamed voice wailing. Trouble Man.

Whoever said young people didn't have good taste?

Elena was sitting on the edge of the bed no longer crying but her face was pulpy. She looked at me with red irritated eyes and smiled weakly. A thread of gray smoke rose from the cigarette in her hand.

"How're you doing?" I said.

Puffing the cigarette. Perhaps for courage. "I'm okay."

"Where's Javier?"

Another drag. Deep and long. She exhaled then waited before she spoke. "He had to work."

"Where does he work?"

A sharp glance. "Why do you want to know that?"

"No reason. Just conversation. Where's your mother's bedroom?"

"Down the hall."

I left her there and walked along the hallway. The switch for the light was outside on the wall. Flicked it on. Her mother's room was much bigger, fitting a king-size sleigh bed, a dresser in matching bald wood, a full length mirror on the wall.

On top of a covered wicker laundry basket sat a box of cheap chocolates. Four kernels missing. The bed had been made up with a gold bedspread with red dancing bears. Neat room. Nothing out of place. No clothes on the floor. No books or papers lying around.

Plenty of framed photographs on the dresser and walls. Vivid portraits of Lourdes' life in Nicaragua. Pictures of her with two little children. Pictures of her with other women, and an old man whose eyes were as keen as fire. Pictures of her with Elena wearing a white dress in front of a church.

Leaving the bedroom I peeked into Elena's room on my way to the kitchen. River hugged the edge of the bed next to the grieving young woman now prone, her thick legs extending off the bed.

In one hand River held Elena's fingers by the tips; a smoldering cigarette in the other.

The kitchen was another vision of neatness. The empty sink was shiny clean. A stainless steel dish rack held one glass.

I opened the fridge. It was well stocked with the heart-clogging staples of our diet: ground beef, pork, bacon, eggs. Vegetable bin was full too. The cupboards were stuffed with tins and cartons. Looked as if Lourdes had been paying close attention to the Homeland Security Office's red alerts and had stocked up for a terrorist attack.

I trotted back to Elena's room. Now she was sitting up, her eyes wet and constricted, her face the color of apricots.

"Was the house this neat that night?"

"No, I cleaned up," said Elena

"Was there anything different about the way it appeared?"

"Different how?" asked Elena.

I said. "Like there might've been a struggle?"

She shrugged. "Hard to say. My mother worked as a housekeeper but she didn't keep this house very neat. It was always messy."

River said, "Did you eat today?"

"I haven't eaten anything in days," Elena said.

"Why don't we take you out to eat?" River said.

Rubbing her knuckles, Elena said. "I'll be okay."

"Are you sure?" River said, squeezing the girl's hand. "You gotta eat."

Elena sucked on her lower lip. "I can't eat."

I looked at Elena and her eyes appeared to be floating in darkness. She'd been dispossessed of someone very important to her, leaving an absence deeper than darkness in her soul. There was no shelter against that kind of hunger; no quilt soft enough to comfort her. And there wouldn't be for a long time.

17

The air outside was soft, the night thick with the illusion of quiet. My eyes swept the park. The man I'd seen sitting there earlier was gone.

"I believe Elena," I said to River as we walked to her car. "I believe her mother was murdered."

"You're crazy, Blades. Where's the proof? She's a Catholic. She's in denial. She can't believe her mother took her own life. I saw in many times in Cuba."

"There's something not right. I can feel it. Something about that note. Why would she use a name her daughter hated?"

"I don't know. Maybe she was angry with Elena about something."

"It was too short."

"Long suicide notes is a Hollywood cliché."

We reached River's truck.

She unlocked the door. Pulling herself into the cab, she said. "Why'd you drag me over here, Blades? You sure as hell didn't need me to wipe Elena's nose."

"Is your hot date still waiting for you, or he already flossed?"

"Why you wanna dip on me like that, Blades? I thought you were my friend."

"Maybe I saved you from a night of disappointment."

She laughed. "There's somebody I want you to meet." River kicked the ignition and gunned the engine.

I held the door open. "Who? Where? What for?"

"My house. Follow me."

River drove off, her cool lights slicing through the shadows.

Fifteen minutes later I was following River up the stairs to her apartment. She opened the door and the sharp smell of burning incense cut through the air. River closed the door and threw her keys into a basket on the floor.

"Komi, we've got company, honey," River said.

A female rapper shrieked from the stereo. I couldn't understand the lyrics but the beat was catchy, the bouncy bass line balancing out the piercing horns and histrionic vocals. I was feeling the song. My body began to dip to the sway of the bass.

"Well, look at you," River sang out, flinging her arms into the air. Hips swiveling in tight circles.

Dressed in a tight body suit Komi came out of the kitchen, a glass of wine held aloft in her hand. Dancing her way over to River. They locked lips.

I stood, hypnotized, watching their display.

River was the first to pull away. "Do you know Komi?"

"We've met," I said.

Komi's eyes lifted provocatively. "Hello Blades. Nice to see you again."

I didn't know what to make of the situation. When Negus introduced me to Komi at the club I got the impression she was his new Shorty. Judging from that saliva-swap she just performed with River this was no sister act.

"Komi's staying with me for a few days. I met her a few nights ago and we really clicked."

"I can see that."

Komi rubbed River's arm. "Are you hungry? I cooked."

River took the glass from Komi's hand. They kissed again.

"You hungry, Blades?" River said.

I didn't trust that enigmatic smile plastered on her face. "No, gonna bounce right now."

"Blades, there's more than enough for all of us. Isn't that right Komi?"

Komi's head swayed lazily in my direction. Too much to drink.

She said, "Come on. Stay and eat. Don't be shy."

I walked to the door and opened it. "Some other time."

River came toward me, a frothy smile on her face. I did not wait. As I went down the stairs I heard the door close behind me.

Perhaps the sight of Odessa's overgrown boys getting in and out of black Explorers had made me wary of all black trucks with darkened windows. One was parked in front of my house when I got home. I cruised past it, and circled the block once, my eyes probing the dark for anything odd. Call me paranoid but the tightness in my gut told me something wasn't right. Deciding not to pull into my driveway, I coasted in behind the black truck and killed the engine.

Lifting my 9 mm Glock from my waist holster I released the safety and racked it. I liked the way it felt in my hand. Solid and heavy. I immediately felt more at ease.

Setting the gun on my lap I turned the heat on in the Volvo and reached for a stick of Big Red from the glove compartment.

Five. Ten. Fifteen minutes passed. Half an hour. Nothing.

I safetied the Glock and stuck in back into my holster. But the feeling that something was amiss hadn't left me. I opened the door and stepped into the street, drawing several deep breaths to chill my jumpy nerves. The frozen air burned my nostrils.

Bright headlights flooded the night. A car hurtling toward me.

Blinded by the blazing fog lamps charging at me I forgot all about the Explorer.

Big mistake.

As I leapt over the front of the Volvo to escape the car, three men jumped from the truck with guns drawn. I grabbed for my gun but they were on me too soon. I understand now what it feels like to be tackled by the Dallas Cowboys linebacker corp.

Somebody grabbed my neck. A shoulder slammed into my gut knocking me to the ground. The force of the blow snatching the air from my lungs.

Arrgh! Pain ripped through my back. My arms flopped at my side. I looked up. Three guns pointed at my head. The broadest of the linebackers reached down and dragged me to my feet.

The car had come to a stop a few yards away. Engine still revving. The reverb echoed through the night. Mallet got out and walked toward me. An empty fear ignited in my chest. Wild thoughts raced through my head. What kind of torture was I in store for? Was he as sadistic as Toni had said?

He appeared smaller than I remembered. Close to me now, drawing himself erect as if trying to match my height. His broken nose was swollen the size of a cucumber. With a leather-gloved hand he reached out and caressed my face, his eyeballs as murky as uncooked blood sausage. He lit up a big black and mild; it was a stinker too. You'd think he'd be able to afford a better quality cigar. He sucked on it, staring into my face with sickening menace.

There was no nuance in his voice, which was deeply nasal, the voice of a man who had trouble breathing.

"Blades, you done gone and diced with the wrong nigga. I'm going to fuck you up so bad you gonna wish you was born in Afghanistan. But for right now I got somebody who wanna talk to you."

I wanted to ask him if he knew where Afghanistan was, but I said nothing. The pain in my back had grown so intense I just wanted to sink to my knees.

Two pairs of powerful arms yanked me into motion, leading me to the Explorer. Someone opened the back door. I was lifted off my feet. A sack of rice. They flung me inside the smoke-filled truck. Two of the three men joined me, one on each side. Two others already inside, occupying the front seats, were blowing trees. Before the door could close the big body screeched away from the curb.

A stomach-turning odor hung inside the truck; a mixture of musk-scented air freshener and chronic. Only someone who'd had their olfactory organs ripped out could stand that mixture for more than five seconds. Smelled like a skunk had given birth inside their rig. I tried to hold my breath, but how long did I really expect to do that.

Collectively these guys had the class of a bucket of imprisoned lobsters. I asked the banger sitting to my left to crack the window so I could get some fresh air. He looked at me as if I was an Iraqi prisoner and he was my jailor. I directed the same question to the driver. All he did was turn the stereo up full blast. As the Explorer sharked through Brooklyn's sooty streets the four of them blew smoke rings and prattled away about football. What a surprise!

Why did Odessa want to speak to me? And why was it so urgent that she sent her cubs to escort me to her lair.

And what a lair it was.

Situated on the top floor of the building, Odessa's joint appeared to be two or three apartments combined. No way apartments in the projects came this super-sized.

That she managed to commandeer such a large space for herself in a building meant for low-income wage earners only underscored the corruptness of the system. What else was new? No doubt she paid off someone in the Housing Department or used some other manner of trickery to get control of this huge space. The upshot of it all was that high up above the welfare moms, struggling office workers and factory day-workers, Odessa was living larger than Donald Trump.

For its size the sunken living room still had a cozy earth-cool feel. The artifacts on pedestals, and the paintings on the walls might've had something to do with that. Grand piano facing the window. Extra-wide glass windows affording an expansive view of Brooklyn's tangle of lighted buildings. A dazzling scene. Thousands of lights crashing together across New York's largest borough.

She sat at a grand piano facing the window playing some kind of classical tune. I don't know much about classical music but the piece seemed weighty and dull. She must've known I was there, but she kept her face in the sheet of music.

I stood on the landing and continued to look around at the framed black and white pictures on walls, wondering how long she was going to let me twist in the wind.

Odessa stopped playing finally, and hauled herself upright. Walking toward me with a relaxed bearing. Gone was the undistinguished wobble that characterized her departure from Toni's salon the other day.

Her head was wrapped in a multicolored cloth and she wore an olive knee-length dress, exposing the thickest calves and ankles I'd ever seen on a woman. They blended well with the rest of her, however: the rhinoceros legs that rubbed together when she walked and the fleshy arms. I made a mental not to ask if exercise was part of her regimen.

"Mr. Overstreet. How nice of you to accept my invitation."

"I wasn't aware I had a choice in the matter."

I looked behind me. My escorts had left. My legs were so stiff I felt as if I was standing on a broken chair that would come crashing down if I moved.

"There's always choice," she said. "Never forget that. Even death is a choice." She dumped herself in a blue-trimmed cream sofa facing the window and beckoned me with thick fingers. "Come. Sit down. Let's chat."

"I'm in the directory, you know. You could've called."

"Ah, but if we'd had this chat on the phone you wouldn'ta had a chance to hear me play, would you?"

I was tempted to fog her glasses by saying something irreverent about her playing but the stiffness in my legs reminded me that I was in no shape to throw stones.

Toddling to a brown armchair opposite her, I sat down. I tried to look at her but her eyes had a sickening energy, like the eyes of a voodoo woman.

"Do you like classical music, Mr. Overstreet?"

"Am I going to get out of here alive if I say no?"

She laughed. "Who do you think I am?"

"Why did you bring me here?"

"You didn't answer my question?"

I paused. "Some."

"What do you like?"

"I don't know. Mozart, I guess."

"Good choice. Great composer. The symphonies? The operas? The concertos? What do you like best?"

"I'm sure you didn't bring me here to quiz me on my musical taste."

"I started playing the piano at forty-five. How long ago do you think that was?"

"I have no idea."

"Five. And today I can play many of Mozart's concertos from my head."

"If I knew more about music I might be impressed," I said.

She ignored my attempt at sarcasm. "Bought me a piano, hired a tutor and everyday I practiced for nine hours. Five in the morning. Four in the evening. You know why?"

"That was going to be my next question."

"When I was a little girl, somewhere around seven or eight, I had a teacher, this woman named Mrs. Lundee. She had the nicest smile, I thought. Prettiest teeth. And she held herself like she was made of glass. So perfect. I told her I wanted to become a concert pianist. She asked me where did I get such a silly idea. I told her I saw two men on TV playing the piano. One a white man. The other a black man. The white man was playing classical music. The black man was playing the blues. And they were going at it. One would play. Then the other would play his tune. The audience was mostly white people. And they were applauding the white man every time he played and booing the black man when he finished. Until the end. The black man walked offstage and came back with several pages of sheet music. And he announced he was going to play something from Bach. I thought he was saying that he was going to play behind his back. The audience sat in shock when he was finished. The room was silent. Then they all started clapping like crazy. I realized later it was all a fictitious set up by Hollywood. But I remember then it made me want to do something like that. Make white people shut up. That's why I wanted to be a concert pianist."

I didn't respond.

She heaved herself up and shuffled over to a portable bar against a wall. It was crowded with all kinds of liquor.

"Can I get you a drink?" She asked.

"No thank you," I said. "I just wanna know why I'm here."

She poured herself an inch of scotch in a short glass and turned with an arthritic smile on her face. "I have a lot of friends in the NYPD. Most of them are just lunching on the job. Drawing a check like most civil servants. But I was told you used to be a good cop."

"What's it to you?"

After a sip of her drink, she said. "The police are anxious to pin the judge on somebody and I seem to be the candidate of their choice."

"Did you kill him?"

"I'm not that stupid."

"Somebody snatched him. And it wasn't the tooth fairy."

She walked to the window. "Come here. I wanna show you something."

I followed her to the window, standing beside her, a few feet away.

"See those basketball courts down there? I got them built. Got them lights put in so the kids could play at night. Couldn't get a politician to put up a dime, so I went to the businesses around here. Got them to chip in. Told them, the kids would rather play basketball at night than do something stupid, like join gangs and rob their businesses. There's a childcare center in the basement of this building which is free to all residents of these houses. I got that started so that these women could go out and get an education or jobs. The city wouldn't help them. Wanted to put them on WEP. You know what WEP is?"

"Work Experience Program."

"But what kind of work experience? They put you to pick up trash in the park or in the subway. What is that preparing these people for?"

"First a music lesson, now a sociology lesson. What's next? History?"

Her head turned; we locked eyes. An indistinct glow of dissatisfaction bloomed in hers.

She walked back to the bar and refreshed her drink. "Sure you wanna stay dry?"

"Scotch," I said.

"That's more like it," she quipped.

She poured me a glass, returned to where I was standing and handed it to me. There was a ring on each finger of her left hand, including a wedding band on the appropriate finger.

She turned and trudged back to the sofa, sitting and crossing her thick legs with some difficulty. She sipped her drink. "I need to find out who killed the judge."

I tasted the scotch. Expensive. She watched me swallow.

"Black Label," she said. "My husband's favorite brand. He couldn't afford it often, but when he did." She tilted her head back and laughed. "Oh boy, was it ever on."

"Why do you care who did the judge if it wasn't you?"

"It's impacting the quality of my life. There are people in this town who hate me, you understand? Who'd love to see me eating off the pavement. I've pissed off a lot of people. Politicians. Lawyers. Police. They'd love to see me shut up. The FBI tried to link me and the judge to some fictional plot to help terrorists into the country. That failed. Now the police are trying to make the case that I killed the judge to shut him up."

"Why should I care?"

That mirthless smirk again. She really should consider breaking out Richard Pryor's old standup comedy tapes. It might restore her ability to smile with joy.

She said, "Two reasons. Because you're an honest man. You understand how unjust this country is. And that's something we have in common."

She paused.

"What's the other reason?"

"Mallet is looking for any excuse to tag you. The only reason he hasn't up to now is because I've convinced him that I need your help to find out who really killed the judge."

"You're asking me to work for you?"

"Yes. I want these badges off my back. They're bad for business."

"And if I refuse?"

"I didn't accomplish all that I have by accepting no from people."

"If I refuse you're going to sic your dog on me, is that it?"

"You wanna know what it's like to have dogs sicced on you? Try standing in my size nines for a few seconds. They've tapped all my phones.

Frozen all my accounts. Taken my passport. They've raided my apartment at least three times. Harassed my children. They think I don't understand what they're trying to do. But I ain't scared. I ain't scared of none of these muthafuckers. FBI. CIA. Homeland Security. Not even the president. I ain't scared of none of them. But I know what these muthafuckers are capable of. They'll persecute anyone who speaks out on behalf of black people. It's an old game. I'm just a new target."

"How'd you get the judge in your pocket?"

"In my pocket? I don't need anybody in my pocket."

"Why would a man like that jeopardize his reputation by getting involved in a scheme with you?"

"He made a choice, Mr. Overstreet. Like you and I do everyday."

"Even death is a choice. I remember. Is that the choice you offered him?"

She laughed. "What was so wrong about what we were doing?"

"It was illegal."

"So's prostitution. That don't stop the judges and cops and politicians from buying some pussy when necessary, does it?"

"The truth is I don't care one way or another."

"Well, you should."

"Why?"

"You used to be a cop and I'm sure you arrested your share of drug suspects. Probably beat up a lot of them too. What percentage of drug suspects you arrested were white, would you say?"

I didn't answer.

"Check the prisons. White people buy and use more crack cocaine than any other group, yet over seventy percent of drug convictions are Black and Hispanic. The percentages don't add up. Only one explanation for that. Racism. We get blamed for all of America's social problems and we get punished more than anyone else for our mistakes." She took a deliberate sip. "The people I decide to help are profiled carefully."

"Say what?"

"Yes, I used the dirty P-word. Profiled. Non-white. What you would call Third-World. White people aren't the only ones who can practice social engineering. It's not just marriages I arrange, Mr. Overstreet. I help to get them green cards. And I make sure they become citizens. And register to vote.

And I educate them to the conservative agenda which, if it got its way, would send them all back to the countries they came from. So that when they vote, they vote wisely."

"Meaning the way you'd like them to."

"I'm doing this country a favor."

"Then why charge them such high fees?"

"Propaganda. Don't let them trick you out."

"Tell me about Justice Malveaux... Clerk from Long Island who was found hanging."

"What else do you need to know about him?"

"Did he work for you?"

"I would say he was an independent contractor."

"Did you kill him?"

"From what I hear that was a suicide."

"His choice or yours?"

She watched hard, her eyes not flickering once. "Now you've asked a lot of questions but you haven't answered mine."

"I don't trust you"

"Would two hundred thousand dollars buy your trust?"

"I don't need your money."

"Oh, yes, I forgot. You had yourself quite a windfall a little while back. You shouldn't let yourself get too comfortable, Mr. Overstreet. Everybody could always use a little more money. Things have a way of shifting unexpectedly in this country."

"I'll keep that in mind. Is it okay if I leave now?"

"It'd be in your best interest to reconsider. What you did to Mallet the other day, nobody's ever done. He's embarrassed. Now you don't have to worry about the other fools who work for me. They're overgrown babies whose brains have been fried by steroids. Mallet's a very dangerous man because he still has a brain. If I tell him you've declined my offer, he's gonna take that as an excuse to turn you into his mouse."

"What if I apologize?"

She laughed. "Somehow I can't see you doing that. The choice is yours. Work for me or play with Mallet."

"Can I think it over."

"You do that."

"Now can I go?"

"I'll have one of my boys drive you home."

"Tell me one thing."

"What?"

"What were you looking for when you broke into the judge's office?"

"I don't know what you're talking about."

"I bet you don't. I also bet that hiring me to find the judge's killer is not what you really want. You want me to find something for you, don't you? The judge kept some kind of record of his dealings with you, didn't he?"

Her face registered cold silence. It was clear that our conversation was over.

18

I had no interest in working for Odessa Rose. The only reason I told her I'd consider her offer was so I could get out of her cave with my head still attached to the rest of me. With Mallet skulking somewhere on that compound like some underfed lioness, I would've been at a distinct disadvantage had she decided to give him the go ahead to satisfy his thirst for blood. Mine.

I was not long inside my house before the phone rang. Don't answer it. Let the damn machine do its job, was my first thought, then I remembered that both Anais and Chez were away. I grabbed the phone.

A nasal voice. "Miss Rose says she needs an answer by tomorrow."

Before I could respond the person rang off.

I poured myself a large whisky and went to turn on the TV. The phone rang again. I picked it up, speaking before I'd placed the receiver to my ear properly. "Listen, you worm. Why don't you go find somebody to put a baseball bat up your ass!"

"Blades, what's the matter with you?"

It was Melanie.

"Oh, Melanie. I'm sorry."

"What was that all about?"

"Nothing. Thought it was a prank call."

"How are you, Blades?"

"I'm fine. I understand you're in New York."

"Yes. I'm having dinner with Jason right now. I'd like to see you later. Is that okay?"

"Sure. What time?"

"Well, we're just about done here."

"Where're you?"

"Park Slope. I could be there in half an hour."

"Are you bringing Jason?"

"No. I'd like to see you alone."

"OK."

"See you in half an hour then."

I managed to shower and change into a gray flannel shirt and thick black sweatpants inside of twenty-five minutes. The hot water had soothed my nerves and I felt relaxed.

I'd just finished combing my hair when a car with a tired-sounding engine pulled into my driveway. The white Taurus' lights flashed and then burnt out, its engine whining to a stop. Melanie stepped out in a long brown lambskin coat. She was average in build, though she never got tired of throwing her above-average intellect about.

I greeted my sister at the door with a warm silent hug.

It had been several months since I last saw Melanie. She looked radiant and tanned as always. I hung her coat in the closet near the foyer and we moved to the living room where we stood smiling at each other. For some reason, I've always felt awkward around my sister.

I broke the silence. "You look good, Melanie. How are you?"

Melanie was still smiling. "Thank you, Blades. I'm well. It's good to see you looking so well yourself."

"It's been too long, sis."

She laughed. "Sis? Ooh!"

I wanted to laugh too, but I wasn't quite sure what the joke was about. My laughter would've been at the urge of nervousness.

"What?"

"I don't know. The way you said 'sis'. Just sounds strange. But good."

"Sit down. You're making me nervous."

She sat in the sofa near the fireplace. "Can a girl get a drink around here?"

"Sorry. What would you like?"

"A glass of Burgundy would be much appreciated. If you don't have Burgundy... But I know you have Burgundy."

I laughed. "But of course. I opened a nice bottle last night. I think you'll find it to your liking."

I got the bottle of wine from the kitchen and poured two glasses, leaving the bottle on the side table next to the window. Moonlight weaved behind a crack in the window blinds.

"Thank you," she said, taking the glass from me. After a quiet sip she tucked her lips before breaking into a smile. "I spoke to Chesney earlier this evening."

"Really?"

"Yes, I called Mom in Orlando and spoke to Chesney for a few minutes. She's so sweet. You're a lucky man, Blades."

"Yes, I feel blessed."

"How's Anais?"

"She's in Atlanta visiting family."

"Jason said her father isn't well."

"Yes, he's in the hospital."

"Is he going to be okay?"

"Nobody seems to know the answer to that question." I settled into the recliner opposite my sister. "So what brings you to New York?"

Her eyes brightened, but mockery tiptoed on the edge of her voice. "Can't a girl want to come home?"

"Depends on the girl," I said with a smile and just enough skepticism in my voice to let her know I was being playful.

"I was being serious."

A weighty pause. I watched as she sipped her wine. She was wearing a rich cream cashmere sweater and brown pants. Her eyes became resolute.

"I'm coming back east," she said. 'Maybe Jersey or Connecticut."

"What? New York's not good enough for you and Marty?"

She got up and walked to the window. She swiveled like a cadet on parade and walked back, sitting with a solid plop. She leaned over and rested her hand on my knee, her eyes coarse as sand. "Marty and I are splitting up."

I waited for the shock to leave my brain. "I'm sorry to hear that, sis."

"Don't be. I'm not."

"But moving back east, that's pretty drastic."

"Not as drastic as what I initially had in mind."

"Are you sure about this? I mean, have you given this a lot of thought? You can be very impulsive at times."

"He's cheating on me, Blades. Should I stay and give him a medal?"

"This is rather ironic, you know."

"What?"

"You coming here to announce that you're leaving your husband, and I thought you were coming to tell me what a mistake Mom was making getting hooked up with another black man."

"I don't want to discuss that, Blades."

"But you don't like it, I'm sure."

Her eyes moistened. "Blades, I'm not interested in a fight. I came here for your support. That's what I need right now."

There was a long pause. I took deep breaths choking on my urge to condemn her.

Melanie said, "We've had our differences to be sure. But I've always admired your strength, Blades. You've always been true to yourself. Done what your heart told you to do. Never bowing to pressure. Maybe that's what I've resented about you all these years. Of the three of us, you're probably the most self-sufficient, the most determined, the most..."

"Stubborn?"

She laughed and touched my arm gently. "I love you, Blades. You should know that. We're family. I realize now how important that is. I really have nobody else I can lean on but you. I want to change our relationship. Make it better."

"Somehow, that doesn't sound right coming out of your mouth."

"But I do. Our family is complicated, I know that."

"I think it's fucked up, that's what I think."

"We are who we are. As fucked up as we are, we're still family. And I do love you, Blades. I guess where there's love, there's always bitterness around the corner." She sighed. "Can I have some more wine?"

I retrieved the bottle from the kitchen and filled her glass. Silence floated in like winter's fog. We sat listening to the silence. I thought of putting some music on but couldn't think of anything appropriate for the mood. My mind began flipping through our history of fights and abusive behavior toward each other.

"I've been having these terrible dreams lately," I confessed. "They all involve Mom and Dad. I'm beginning to think they're not dreams at all, but pieces of buried memories. A year ago you told me that you witnessed my dad hitting our mom. Was that the truth?"

Her voice was soft and gauged. "I don't remember saying that."

"We were on the phone."

Her eyes hardened, "I don't remember, Blades."

"You don't remember seeing it, or you don't remember saying you saw it?"

Putting the glass on the side table. "I don't remember saying that."

"But you remember seeing it?"

"Jesus, Blades!" She jumped up. "I have to go."

I grabbed her hand. "No, Melanie. You said it to me on the phone."

"What do you want from me, Blades? I can't remember saying that. Leave me alone."

My grip tightened on her wrist. "Did you ever see him hit her?"

"You're hurting me."

I released her hand. "Did you?"

She sat down rubbing her right wrist. "To what end, Blades? Why is it so important?"

"My sanity."

"You know, the brain is a very interesting organ. I was reading one time that it protects you from trauma by forgetting. Whatever it is you've forgotten, perhaps it's best to leave it there."

"Please don't patronize me, Melanie."

She got up. "I really must go."

I tried to think of a way to keep her. "Why don't you stay here tonight?"

She smiled. "Thank you, Blades. But you and I under the same roof. We've got to work up to that. I'd like to keep what's left of our relationship."

"You reason that we have a relationship?"

"If you're trying to hurt me, Blades, you have. That cut like a knife."

"I'm sorry. I feel like I'm walking down this dark, lonely road. And I can't see what's around me. And I have no idea what's behind me. It's a scary feeling."

She took a step toward me and paused. "For what it's worth, I never saw your Dad hit Mom."

Then she hugged me and I felt the tears on my shoulder.

I wanted to believe Melanie so much, my gut hurt.

19

Sleep was a temporary diversion in a night spent tossing around my big bed. I was up before dawn and sat by the window to watch the sharp-edged morning light slice Brooklyn into segments.

As the bells of a distant church pealed for eight o'clock I layered a vinyl track suit over my sweats and jogged to Prospect Park where I ran twice around the paved track. I kept an even pace until the last 100 yards which I ran hard.

I walked home, tired and still on edge, churning the conversation I had last night with my sister over in my mind. Why was it so hard for me to let things go? To forget about the past, to move forward without the weight of regret. And why has my life seemed so disharmonious?

I grew up around political discourse and activism. Both my parents and most of their friends were Civil Rights-era activists and spent many nights in our living room drinking wine and arguing politics. Maybe because of that I became imbued with the idea that everyone had a obligation to try to make a difference.

But my home was just as disharmonious as the world outside. Perhaps even more so. And there was nothing I could've done about that. Given the prevailing social winds it's incredible to me that my parents even attempted the experiment they tried to pass off as a marriage. Sometimes I ask myself, what the hell could they've been thinking.

Geneticists say that race is biologically meaningless. Historians say that race is just an illusion created to justify enslavement of other people. Historians also say that the Africans who were dragged to the Americas did not see themselves as Black people, or Negroes. They had their own set of ethnic identities. We got caught in the trap of race and now we can't escape. To the average American, race has as much mythological power as the idea of the American Dream. We're all wrapped up in it in one way or another.

No matter how I feel about my father, I respect that he and my mother were willing to risk everything to follow the madness of their love at a time of such intense racial conflict in America. Hey, I'm the result.

For me, catching bad guys became one way of restoring order, of putting things back in harmony. And I was good at it. But for all my good intentions nothing much changed in the world. My own world just got more fucked up. I became angrier, more violent. I became as perverted as the bad guys.

You may not believe this, but I hate violence. I wish I never had to resort to it, and that we all lived in a non-violent world. But I also know that I am capable of bringing hurt to people who I deem to be bad. It is my arrogance, I suppose, my belief that I can protect good people from those who wish to do harm to the goodness in the world. But there've been times when I enjoyed too much the hurting I put on people I felt deserved it.

I've come to accept that the world will always be in turmoil. You can't eradicate greed. You can't wipe out materialism. There's no cure for envy. Maybe it's true that out of death and disorder come the thrust for regeneration. New ideas. Renewal. Maybe that's the energy driving human endeavor. Whether we are driven to live better, more virtuous lives, or driven to amass fortunes, this disorder is the energy which propels us. I get all that. Question is: when will I escape my own jungle? How do I make peace with myself?

I showered and had a light breakfast: bagel with cheddar cheese and coffee in the kitchen. From there I called Anais.

"I miss you, Blades."

"I miss you too, babe."

"I might be coming home soon."

"That's good news."

"How are you doing?"

"Keeping busy."

"Still working on that case?"

"Yes."

"How's it going?"

"You're asking me how the case is going?"

"Is that a problem?"

"No. You don't usually do that."

"Life is too short, Blades. I'm trying to work with what I got. Largely, that's you. And you can't help but try to change the world. So, what else can I do?"

The doorbell chimed.

"There's somebody at the door."

"I love you, Blades."

"I love you, too, babe."

River stood on my doorstep, a dark scowl on her face. I thought she would smile but she didn't. She stepped inside with a nod, impatience a steel cape around her shoulders.

"I just got a call from Shaka's neighbor. The one I told you about. He said Shaka showed up this morning with a girl. Wanna ride over there?"

"Shouldn't we give him some time to take care of business?"

"History says Shaka's not into sex. Let's go."

"I'm a trust your intimate knowledge of the brother. Gimme a minute."

I went upstairs to get my Glock from the drawer in the bedroom. I checked the magazine. Full clip.

From the closet downstairs I got a brown knee-length leather jacket. River was standing in the now open door smoking.

I said, "You heavy?"

She turned around. "Don't leave home without it."

"How do you hide that big ass gun? What's it called again?"

"You mean my FN-forty-nine?"

"Yeah. How do you hide that cannon in those tight clothes?"

She bent down, lifted her pants leg. "I don't. When I wanna travel light I use this Walther PPK thirty-eight."

In a black holster velcroed to her ankle was a compact black polymer-grip pistol.

I slipped my jacket on. "Your car or mine?"

"My truck definitely."

Along the way River almost came apart telling me about her tour of Justice Malveaux's house in Long Island.

"I tell you, Blades, you should've been there. This joint was smack out of that show with all them stupid rappers showing off their ugly ass homes. This guy wasn't hiding his lottery winnings under the bush, that's for damn sure. A Mercedes and a Lexus SUV were in the driveway. And that's only for starters. There was a Bentley and another Mercedes in the garage."

"Did you speak to Mrs. Malveaux?" I grunted.

"Shut up, Blades. Just let me break the shit down my way."

I glanced over and her smile was as sly as thief's.

"This house was ridiculous," River continued. "There's marble everywhere. The floors are chocolate marble. Looked like somebody smothered the floor in shit. The staircase was bone white marble. Fireplace. That was marble too. Somebody was towed down when they designed this place."

"But did you speak to Mrs. Malveaux?"

"Do you wanna hear what happened or not?"

I stared ahead in silence.

"The woman was a gracious host. Very dignified."

"Mrs. Malveaux?"

"Yes. Gave me a tour of the whole house. All twelve rooms. Including the master bedroom with its gold bathroom faucets. She was very proud of her husband. As are the people in Gonaives where he was born. Fifteen years ago, he swam to the mainland after being thrown off a raft some ten miles from shore. Was kept in detention for a year before he escaped and then he couldn't find work paying more than three dollars an hour. Worked as a barber, a dishwasher, a guard. Stayed in the basement of a cousin where he spent his free time watching television, practicing his English. You know what his favorite program was? Oprah. She inspired him. Anything was possible if you had a dream. He made it to New York, took night courses to improve his English, got into City College and got a degree in business."

"Did he hang himself?" I said.

"You don't get it, do you, Blades?"

"Get what? I ask you to go out there to find out what happened and you come back with a novel."

"He brought his mother and grandmother here, set them up in a house in Miami. Also his four sisters and a brother. Bought them all houses and cars. Sent money and clothes and food back to Gonaives on the regular."

"What is it that I don't get?"

"The man couldn't go to jail. He was like Robin Hood to the people of Gonaives."

"Robin Hood didn't live in a palace."

"Well, a modern-day Robin Hood might."

"Are you telling me he killed himself for a rep?"

"That's what his wife said."

"What does she know about Odessa?"

"Nothing."

"You believe her?"

"She's a princess. She didn't care where the money was coming from."

"Why didn't he run? He had all this money?"

"You can't get Odessa on this, Blades. The man notched his own belt."

20

Took us fifteen minutes maneuvering the clotted streets of Crown Heights to get to Shaka's. We curbed in the middle of the block behind a blue Honda, the only spot available, and got out, walking toward Nostrand.

River stopped when we reached a boarded up pre-war tenement building at the end of the block. She turned, pointing upward at apartments on the other side of the street. "That's the fire escape he bolted down."

A Laundromat at the corner seemed empty, but the McDonalds next to it was doing brisk business. A balding man wobbled out, his hands full of large McDonalds' bags. Three kids trailing, their faces lit up with glee anticipating all the fat they were about to consume.

River said, "Third floor. Apartment three-F. End of the hall facing the street."

"You stay here. Catch him if he falls. If he stays in the barn I'll wave once."

I stepped over a pike of snow and crossed behind a parked bus, moving casually up the warped stoop. The iron guard rail had been eaten away by rust. Front door lock busted.

I entered. Dark and smoky in the narrow stairwell. The building needed fixing. Exposed red bricks was a nice touch, though. Might've been pretty if all the bricks were in place. The empty spaces had been turned into ash trays.

I crept up the wooden stairs. Like sticks breaking they creaked with my every step. Made it to the third floor without the stairs giving way. Angled light streamed through the window at the end of the hall, glancing off the dark wall. I walked through the light.

A poster of Malcolm X was plastered over the black paint on Shaka's door. I paused a moment, taking in Malcolm's poetically tilted chin and steadfast, almost angry gaze. Now there was a man who should have a holiday named after him.

As I raised my fist to bang on the door I heard oohs and ahhs from inside. River had been wrong. This Shaka was no throw back. This Shaka loved sex and from the sound of things, took his time in the sauce. I listened to the tender whimpers and moans thinking perhaps I should go back downstairs and wait. Let the man have his moment of glory. Would I want somebody busting in on me while I'm in the mash?

Then I thought. Suppose the girl isn't having any fun? Suppose she was faking. She'd welcome the interruption, right?

The rationale worked for me. I pulled the 9mm from my waist and took two steps back. As hard as I could I drove the heel of my right foot into the lock. The door flew open.

Clad in black boxers, Shaka was on the bed, his head buried between the thick legs of a naked young woman. She screamed in shock, clamping her legs around Shaka's head. Poor guy. Looked like a dog with its head caught in a bucket. I closed the door and watched him flail to get free.

The girl kicked Shaka loose and grabbed the sheet to cover her body. Still screaming. Though not as loud now. Confident that she wouldn't drop dead from fright I cornered Shaka before he had time to recover.

My gun was pointed at the middle of his chest.

He tried to sit up. "What the fuck?"

"Don't move."

He sighed heavily before laying back down, stretching his legs out.

I looked at the young girl. Hoped she hadn't peed herself. Her eyes were open wide. Tears streamed down her face. She was shaking. I had to get her out of there quickly.

"Hey, calm down," I said to her. "You're not gonna get hurt."

One eye glued to Shaka, I moved quickly to the window. River stood on the edge of the sidewalk her eyes trained upward. I gave her the signal. She spat her cigarette to the ground and trotted across the street.

I eased back to the bed.

Shaka rolled his eyes. "You Five-O?"

"You keep quiet." I turned to the girl. "What's your name?"

She looked at me as if I was speaking to her in Russian, continuing to cry hysterically.

I heard River's boots chopping up the stairs. Seconds later she rushed through the door, slamming it closed behind her.

"Get her outta here," I said to River.

River went to the girl. "Get your clothes, honey. And stop crying. That's for boys."

Never underestimate the power of a woman. The girl stopped crying immediately and began scooping up her clothes from the bed and the floor.

"You the police?" she asked, struggling into black jeans.

"I'm an investigator," River said.

The girl lanced her eyes at me.

River said, "He's assisting me."

The girl looked at Shaka, her face weathered with concern.

"Don't worry about Shaka," River said. "We'll take good care of him."

"You ain't gonna hurt him, are you?" She said.

"No," River said, helping the girl into her coat.

The girl eyed me. "Then why he have a gun?"

"I heard voices," I said. "Thought I heard somebody crying. Look I'll put the gun away." I holstered the Glock. "We're just here to talk to Shaka, that's all."

The girl wasn't convinced. "You say you're investigators? That means you're the police, right?"

River pulled out her New York City private detective license. "Look, see. I'm a licensed investigator. Licensed in New York. Now you gotta get out of here let us do our job."

River led the girl to the door.

The young woman paused, taking on last glance at Shaka still prone on the bed. River gently nudged her over the threshold and closed the door locking the girl outside.

Shaka sat up. "Who the hell are you if you ain't Five-Oh?"

"We can be whoever you want us to be," River said, approaching the bed. "From your best friend to your worst nightmare. Take your pick."

Lips curled into a disdainful smile. "Be my bitch, then. Suck my dick."

River slapped his face. "Watch your language around me, son."

He sprang to his knees, flailing his arms in River's face. One lash caught the side of her head. Her eyes closed slightly, trapping a spark of anger which quickly spread like a hot wind over her entire face.

She knocked his arms aside, and locked her fingers around his neck.

Shaka was trembling. His eyes bulged and his mouth tightened into ferocious nothingness, because try as he might he could not dislodge River's claws from his throat. Fear scorched his face.

He fixed his eyes on me, imploring me to stop her. Like most men who'd made the mistake of misjudging River's strength, he was now pondering the frailties of his own mind: *How the fuck could I've made this mistake?*

I decided to let him ponder it a while longer. Nothing enlightens like a near-death experience. By the time the bright white light of his life rolled slowly before him, Shaka's swollen pride will lose its gristle. Talking to him will be a lot easier after that.

I waited until his eyes began to roll around in their sockets. I touched River's granite biceps to say "Ease up."

"The boy better learn some manners," she said.

Keeping one hand locked to Shaka's throat, River unhooked bracelets from her belt and clipped one hoop onto Shaka's right hand, the other onto the iron bed.

She stepped back, her body still tensed, breathing hard.

Shaka lay still, gaped-mouth, his face gripped in a weird expression, half self-satisfactory smirk, half relief. "She's a freak, man."

"You looked like you were about to bust a nut there," I said.

"What you here for, man?" His voice cracked at the last syllable.

"Like I said. Just wanna ask you some questions."

He swiveled his neck around. "You kick down my door. This here freak nearly chokes me to death. And you expect me to answer your freaking questions. Nigga please!"

River walked away from the bed, tilted her chin and laughed. "Ain't you the same track star who bounced at the sound of my voice two days ago? Now you wanna talk trash?"

"Why'd you run from her the other day?" I said

"Somebody banged on my door. Talking bout 'open up.' I thought it was the cops."

"You ran because you thought she was a cop? Why would you run from the cops?" I said. "What you got to hide?"

His face cracked. "I hate cops. Don't talk to them. Don't even wanna see them on the screen unless they dying. Wouldn't even piss on one if he on fire."

"You got a beef with the boys in blue?" I said.

"What black man ain't got a beef with them fags? All them conspired to put me in jail. The cops. The judge. The dyke D.A. All them fags. Treat me like I was obsolete."

"You talk like you're obsolete," River said.

"You need to peddle in my shoes before you step to me," Shaka said. "A young black man in this country, I was automatically a statistic before I spoke a sensible word."

"I wish you would speak a few sensible words," River said. "You're boring me. You all just need to stop complaining and stop killing each other out here on the streets. Stay the hell out of the system, that's what you all need to do."

"See what I mean. You think just like the Crackers. Every black man is out here committing crimes. That's so low grade."

I scanned the one-room apartment. TV in one corner. Sink, stove and fridge lumped together in another corner. A crib strictly for a man with no responsibilities, or a transient.

"What numbers you pulled?" I asked.

"Five to ten on possession with intent to distribute. Did three and a half. It was all bullshit. I was stopped by two Crackers on Atlantic one night. They tossed me because I refused to look in their face. Said I disrespected them. I told them to fuck off. Next thing, they're arresting me. Saying I had half a kilo in my knapsack and a gun."

"How much longer we gonna listen to his whining?" River snapped.

"Where'd you do time?" I said.

"Green Haven," Shaka said.

"That's a maximum hotel, ain't it?"

"Full lock down."

"For a first time offence?"

He smirked. "Believe it. That's how they try to break us down."

"I would've been scared." I said.

"At first I was. Big time. Ain't nothing as scary as your first day in the pen. Man, when you walk into prison you walk into a jungle. I was angry, man, 'cause I didn't belong there. I never thought that shit woulda happened to

me. Man, I had a job. A girlfriend. A nice apartment. I would've been crazy
to get into that drug game. I seen what it done to people. For me to deal with
the shit I told myself all white people are evil. All cops are evil. All judges were
evil. Can you imagine being locked every night in a cell with a toilet and a
man? Think about that. You got a bunch of men who've been snatched away
from women. That's some shit. You don't know how much shit that is until
a man looks at you like food. The way an animal would look at raw meat.
They want to bring all kinda harm on you. But I had to get my head straight.
You know what helped me? I started reading our history. That helped me
survive. I began to understand that we came from kings and queens. That this
here condition in America. We can overcome this."

River said, "So what'd you do with that discovery when you got out?"

"What you mean?" He said.

I said, "You went straight to a judge's house and threatened him. Not
very smart."

"That judge stole all my grandmother's money."

"Now he's dead," I said.

"And I'm alive."

"He was murdered," I said.

"Forgive me if I don't break down in tears," he said.

"Did you kill him?" I said.

"You must be crazy."

River said, "You threatened him."

"I was blitzed that day. Been drinking from the night before. The system
fucked me, and then it dry-fucked my granny too. You'd a done the same
freaking thing."

"Where were you the night he was kidnapped?" I said.

"When was that?"

"Friday night last. Around eight," River said.

"Right here."

"Alone?" I said.

"Yeah."

"Did you speak to anybody around that time?"

"Naw, I was tired."

"Yeah, laziness can make your ass real tired," River quipped.

I said, "So you have no alibi."

"Why do I need an alibi?"

"To keep your ass outta jail," River said.

"Can't you give that freak something to chew on?" His words had bravado but his voice shook with doubt. "Man, I'm innocent so I don't need to establish shit."

"Everybody in that fancy hotel claims they're virgins," I said. "You been there. You've heard the junk."

His eyelids twitched, and the muscles in his jaw tightened. He moved his legs up and down and drew his tongue in circles over his lips. "But those who really are walk with a sense of integrity. You can see it in their eyes. Look into my eyes. I'm innocent. See."

"Uncuff him," I said to River.

She moved quietly to the bed.

He contorted his body so she could release him without having to touch his legs. He grinned open-mouthed when he heard the clack. Rubbing his wrist, he shot his eyes at River's face. "Lemme see your dick. I bet you got a dick. You ain't no woman. Ain't no woman that strong."

She stood over him, her eyes quiet like a hunter's. Then she stepped back and drew a solid breath. "We done with this punk?"

"For now," I said.

River's steady eyes held him transfixed. Shoulders bowed, he said nothing, his chest moving quickly. He was breathing like a man scared.

21

There was a placeless sheen to the soiled buildings, many of them plastered with billboards over a year old, as we drove along Nostrand Avenue which quivered in the mid-morning light.

I glanced over at River. Her grille was fixed in a passionate scowl.

"Did you believe him?" I said.

She grunted and pumped gas to the big truck, powering through a yellow light at the intersection at Atlantic Avenue.

She turned to me, her eyes squeezed. "He's lying."

"That was no act back there, was it?" I said.

Her words crackled with an insane energy. "I really hate lying scumbags like him. We got too many of them out here on the streets. We ain't ever gonna get our neighborhoods cleaned up if we don't stop producing trash like him."

"You must've been some badass down in Miami."

We pulled up at the light next to a man in a matchbox of a car, one of those Korean jobs, eating fried chicken out of a paper bag.

River stared motionless out the windshield. "In Miami I pulled a tour in Overtown for two years. I've heard every lie ever told by mankind. Ain't a muthafucker who ain't got some game they wanna run on you when you collar them. They all bad and shit when they're selling drugs to children, but when you roll up on them they can't take the weight."

I touched her knee. "You would've been a helluva partner."

She glanced at me. "Not for you. Wouldn't have been able to keep this pussy outta your face."

I laughed. "What? You had sex with all your partners?"

We crawled away from the light, picking up speed after turning on Empire Boulevard.

"Only had two. Both white. I don't do vanilla."

"Whaddup with you and Negus' girl?"

"Komi? What's it look like?"

"You kicking it like that?"

"You disapprove?"

"That's Negus's girl. Haven't you messed up his head enough?"

"I met her at a sex club a few nights ago."

"A sex club? Did you say a sex club?"

"That's what I said. A sex club."

"Like in a sex club. Where you go to meet people to have sex?"

"Don't act like an F.O.B, Blades. You were born and raised right here in Gomorrah. Don't tell me you've never been to a sex club."

"I've never been to a sex club."

"You sound proud."

"I'm no prude, but..."

"But what?"

"If it's your thing, hey."

"It's not my thing, okay. The dude I was with suggested it. I went along. I didn't do anything at first. Just watched. It was fun, watching, though. Can't say I didn't enjoy that. Then somebody started to kiss my breasts. It felt nice. Then somebody started to touch me, you know, finger me. It felt good. He was gentle, so I just let it flow."

"What was your friend doing?"

"He was watching. That's his thing. Then a white dude tried to touch me. I shooed him away. After that a black guy came and put the tip of his dick in me. The brotha had me tripping. I don't know what the hell he was doing. I mean it was just the tip but he had me screaming. I must've had three or four orgasms by the time he was done. And the whole time he never put more than the tip in me. Changed my whole perspective on sex."

I looked at her; the shock must've been ripe on my face.

"Everybody wears condoms, so chill. After he pulled out I felt somebody's tongue. It felt different. More gentle and precise than anything I've ever had. I looked down. It was Komi."

"Did you know she was Negus' woman?"

"I'd seen her with him. He'd introduced us, but he never said she was his woman. Anyway, she told me she came with Negus to the club."

"Where was Negus?"

"I don't know. I didn't see him."

"I don't believe Negus went to no sex club with her."

"I don't care anyway. I dumped the dude and Komi and I came back to my place."

"To live happily ever after."

Before she could answer my phone rang. It was Elena. Raoul, her mother's ex-husband, had called to offer his condolences and had left his telephone number.

"Hold a sec." I turned to River. "You got a pen?"

"In the glove."

I opened the glove box and rifled through the junk she had stowed away in there, coming up with a felt-tip pen and a piece of paper.

"Go ahead," I said into the phone.

I jotted the number down and hung up.

River said, "I spoke to the detective investigating Lourdes' death. Name's Brady Pitter-something. Petersaw. Lourdes died around eleven or twelve. Got him to fax me a copy of the autopsy report."

"How did you manage that? Playing the lonely woman again?"

We pulled up outside my house.

River said, "You know Blades, sometimes you just know how to rub a girl the wrong way. Get the hell out my truck."

I opened the door. "The report?"

Her hand jerked up to the breast pocket of her jacket; she groped around inside and yanked out folded sheets of paper.

A smile floundered and died on her lips as she handed it over.

"Good work," I said.

"Screw you!"

According to the autopsy, Lourdes was five-four, 190 pounds and well-nourished. Very well nourished I would say.

There were deep impressions around her neck, apparently from the wire. No ecchymosis. From my limited experience of autopsies I remembered that meant bruising. Dislocation of the spine at C2. Her neck. Larynx also fractured. The vital organs were normal. No engorgement. All free of disease. Air passages clear. Recent sexual activity, but no evidence that it was forced.

Cause of death: Asphyxia due to ligature strangulation.

But who did Lourdes have sex with before she died?

I arrived by cab at Club Malecón, a smoky joint in East Harlem around nine o'clock. When I called him, Raoul agreed to meet me after his performance here tonight. The joint was crowded and noisy. All around me people were clinking glasses and laughing. Occasional raucous singing broke out in Spanish. Men gesticulated wildly, slapped hands and offered each other cigars. Golden light filtering through thick smoke. Absorbing the tropical vibe I sat at the bar and ordered a Cuba libre.

On a small stage a group played guitars and bongos. People dancing in the aisle and around the bar. It was a happy joint, let me tell you, and my spirit soaked it up. I needed something like this.

Around 9:30 PM that group stopped playing. By then I'd had two more Cuba libres and my head had left New York City. I was buzzing through Havana. And if you're ever looking for a place where the bartender didn't crimp on the juice, hit Club Malecón. He was filling my glass with rum, adding coke, it seemed, just for flavoring.

The bongo players went offstage leaving the two guitarists who began to pick furiously at their instruments, a complicated mixture of melody and rhythm. Three men in black rushed onstage followed by three young girls in long red skirts. Castanets snapping a steady rhythm as the dancers launched into furious flamenco dancing. The men clicking their castanets feverishly, the woman raising their long arms and twirling their hands in mesmerizing circles.

This set of dancers was replaced by another group. Just as lithe and even more energetic. By the end of the dance I'd forgotten all my concerns and wanted nothing more than to stay in Havana watching beautiful flamenco dancers.

After four more dances the stage was silent. As the tired musicians left the stage the crowd applauded enthusiastically.

Fifteen minutes later a man sauntered toward me, his face wet, his eyes laughing. As he got closer I recognized him as one of the guitarists. This must be Raoul. I'd told him I would be wearing a black mock-turtle neck with a pin of the Barbados flag on my chest so he could recognize me.

Short and slender, he looked stylish in the tan suit he'd changed into after playing for the flamenco group. He smiled and waved to friends in the club, shaking hands as he passed them.

He joined me at the bar. "You must be Mr. Overstreet."

"Yes." I proffered a handshake. "Call me Blades."

He fingered my Barbados pin. "I used to know a man from Barbados. He was actually born in Havana. His parents moved there after working on the Panama Canal. I guess they must've been originally from Barbados. He always used to say he was from Barbados"

"That's where my grandmother grew up. The Panama Canal."

"Is that right. You speak Spanish?"

"A few words."

"Like my English."

"Your English is perfect. Can I buy you a drink?"

"Not at all. I drink for free." His laughed echoed like a firecracker. He called to the bartender. "Mario. Black Label. On the rocks."

"I enjoyed the show. You play great."

"It's nice to play for my people. I also play jazz in a club downtown, but when I'm up here the energy is beautiful. Beautiful dancers. All Havana girls. If you want to meet them…"

"I'm married."

"That's beautiful. I never remarried after Lourdes. But don't feel sorry for me. I'm having fun."

"How long ago did you leave Cuba?"

"Long time. Fifteen years, maybe. Yeah, It was fifteen years ago I sailed to Mexico. I lived there for two years before coming to America. Buried my first wife there. She didn't want to come to America anyway. She wanted to leave Cuba. Once she get to Mexico she was content. Not me. I always wanted to come to America. I wanted to come to America so bad I had an American dollar bill in my wallet which I kiss every day. Every morning before I ate breakfast I kiss George Washington."

"Are you happy you came?"

He hesitated, then looked at me thoughtfully. "Regret is the death of progress. I don't regret anything. Not even getting divorced from Lourdes. And God knows I will always love that woman."

"Tell me about Lourdes?"

"Ah, Lourdes. She was such a lovely woman. So beautiful. But so troubled."

"Troubled? What do you mean?"

"She was always smiling, but inside she was so sad."

"Why was she sad?"

"I try to make her happy. But I fail." He sighed and gulped a mouthful of whisky. "When I first meet her she remind me of this girl I used to see dancing at this Flamenco school along the Paseo del Prado. That's a street in Havana. That's how I got into playing for the Flamenco. She was so beautiful. I was in love with this girl. But she is already married. And when I see Lourdes, it was as if God bring her to me from Havana. But such sorrow. Her mother was killed by the Sandinistas. Right in front of her eyes. As was her brother. Such sadness."

"Did she get depressed?"

"We all get depressed."

"How did she handle depression?"

"Like anybody else. Drink a little. Sometimes she no talk to me. Sometimes for days it go on like this. Holidays were the worst. Christmas. Easter. Bad times."

"Would she commit suicide?"

"Who knows? For us Catholics that's not a good thing But... my first wife... she take her own life. And I thought she was happy so nothing shocks me anymore."

"Elena said she had half a million dollars in the bank. Where would she get so much money?"

His eyes wavered. He looked down at the table. "I really don't know about that?"

"I think you do."

He sat straight up. "I don't appreciate you calling me a liar, Mr. Overstreet."

"I'm sorry."

He got up. "It was nice meeting you."

"Please, I didn't mean to offend you."

"I have to get ready to play again."

I handed him my card. "If you can remember anything, give me a call."

He took the card, eyed it thoughtfully. "Anything about what?"

"Where Lourdes might've gotten that money."

"This is America. That's what people come here for. To get money."

"Is that why you came?"

He shrugged and walked away.

I was still able to walk out of the bar with enough sense of direction to find the street where I hailed a yellow cab.

When I staggered into my living room there was a woman on the couch sipping tea. I was too drunk to be surprised.

"You sure took your sweet time getting home," she said, reverting to the southern twang she often used when she wanted to be playful.

I unbuttoned my leather jacket as I walked toward her. "I'm so happy to see you."

She met me halfway and caressed my face tenderly.

"Why didn't you tell me you were coming back today?" I said.

"I wanted to surprise you."

I drew her into my arms and we kissed for a long time. I could feel the blood throbbing in her lips. Her breath was sweet and tangy like ginger. She held my face in her hands and her gaze was as brilliant as the blade of a new knife.

I shucked my coat on the floor and she led me to the sofa. She wove her long-boned fingers into mine as we sat next to each other. I lift her onto my lap. She stroked my brow. I stroked her hair. Her hands trembled with tenderness.

"How's your father?"

"He's feeling much better. It was a miracle. We can't explain it. He came out of the coma and asked for ice-cream."

"You actually gave him ice-cream?"

"No. The doctor wouldn't let us."

"Don't worry. He'll be eating ice-cream in no time."

"I see you've been drinking."

"Loneliness."

"Where were you?"

"I went to meet a Cuban musician in Spanish Harlem."

"Someone for your club?"

"No, he's the ex-husband of the judge's housekeeper. Appears she might've hanged herself."

"Oh my goodness."

"Her daughter thinks otherwise."

She lifted my chin up to peer into my eyes. "Could you file all that away for tonight? I need your full attention from now on."

I smiled. "Done. Let's go upstairs and take a shower together. We haven't done that in a long time."

On impulse I bent and picked her up in my arms. She shrieked with laughter and delight. I walked gingerly up the stairs with my precious cargo.

22

It was a windy morning. As I parked the Volvo I saw the homeless man from the park stumbling along the sidewalk. I watched him trip over his feet and fall, reeling against a trash can. He got up and stumbled again, pitching headfirst into a heap of newspapers on the sidewalk.

I got out and walked toward him. He saw me and tried to sit up quickly but was unable to move fast enough. He sat back down on the sidewalk, swaying as if he was in a swing. When I got close enough I heard him swearing to himself.

He looked frightened, his eyebrows arched in bewilderment. Having lost his hat in the series of falls, he rubbed his bald head.

Seeing him in daylight was shocking. It was hard to determine what the original color of his baggy pants might've been. He had a floppy face, his forehead slatted and high. Looking at him you'd think he'd just emerged from being buried in a grave.

I reached down to help him up.

"Get away from me," he screamed.

I stepped back. "I was offering you a hand."

"I'm fine just where I am. What do you want?"

"Nothing. You okay?"

"I remember you."

"Yeah."

His smiled exposed black spotty teeth. "Yeah, you gave me money the other night."

"Did you get something to eat?"

"Bought me a plate of fried wings and rice from the chinks."

My voice tipped my surprise and disgust. "The who?"

He scowled. "Nigga please. Don't pretend you don't know who I mean. Everybody around here know who the chinks are."

"Would you want them to call you nigger?"

"Don't care who call me what. Look at me. What difference does it make?"

I turned away.

He said, "Hey, help me up, will ya?"

I turned back, but hesitated.

"Come on, don't be a nudge," he growled.

I grabbed hold of his elbow and pulled him to his feet.

"Thank you," he said.

"What's your name?"

"Jersey."

"Jersey. You need anything? You had breakfast?"

"I had breakfast." He took a step and stumbled, steadied himself and laughed. "But I ain't know what I'm having for lunch. Or if I be having any lunch."

"When I come back I'll buy you lunch," I said.

He rolled his eyes. "Man, who you think you jiving?"

"No jive."

He laughed. "I'll be right here waiting."

I don't know why but I put my arms around his shoulder. He didn't move.

I left him and went to ring Elena's bell.

She had cut off her hair. Gold bracelets jingled from her wrists and her ears were filled with gold rings. She was wrapped in a tight black dress, her eyes dark as a river at night.

"Would you like some coffee?"

"Sure," I said.

We were sitting at the white ceramic-covered kitchen table. She got up and strode over to the coffee pot, poured two cups of coffee and came back. When she walked everything was controlled, but not contained.

"I spoke to Raoul last night," I said.

"What's he like? I never met him."

"Seems like a nice guy. He loved your mother very much."

"That's nice. My mother didn't talk about him."

"She didn't tell you anything about him?"

"No. Hardly mentioned him."

"He wasn't quite sure your mother wouldn't have committed suicide."

"You think he knows my mother better than I do?"

"There's no evidence that she was murdered."

"You have me. Her daughter. And I tell you she wouldn't do something like that."

"Raoul said she was despondent at times. Possible reasons might've been seeing her family killed. Those are some heavy irons to be lugging around."

Elena put her elbow on the table. "What Nicaraguan family doesn't have a story like that? If it all drove us to suicide there wouldn't be anybody left in the country."

"According to the coroner's report. Your mother died around eleven or twelve."

"That's about the time I got home. You think she might've been alive when...?"

Her voice broke off.

"I know you said you'd had a lot to drink, but try to think. Was there anything different or odd about the way the apartment looked when you got home?"

"Other than the TV was on and there was nobody watching it. No."

"Was the door locked?"

"Yes, it was locked."

"There was no sign of forced entry."

"I remember unlocking it."

"Was she dating anyone?"

"My mother had sworn off men."

"Really? Why?"

"She'd had enough. Men placed too much emphasis on sex and not enough on feeling. On love."

"Is that what she said or is that your interpretation?"

Elena laughed and said assuredly. "My interpretation. She would've told me if she had a boyfriend. She went out... but alone."

"How often did she go out? Every week?"

"No. Not that often. A few times a month. Why're you asking these questions?"

I thought of telling her that her mother had had sex just before she died. "Do you know most of her friends?"

"She didn't have many friends. She went out because she liked to watch dance. And the movies. Not to make friends. She was a very private person. My mother didn't have a secret boyfriend, Mr. Overstreet, if that's what you're getting at."

The way she said it made me believe her. In that soft moment I got the impression that she knew her mother in a way that only a daughter could. If the semen found in Lourdes' body wasn't her boyfriend's, whose was it? Was it consensual sex? Were drugs involved? None were listed on the coroner's report.

"That night, did you see anyone leaving the building as you came in?"

"No."

"What'd you do after you found the body?"

"I called, Javier... my boyfriend."

"Who called the police?"

"Javier. I couldn't think. I remembered going to wait for him in my mother's room. She paused for a while, her head bowed. Then she looked at me and her eyes were animated. "I just remembered something about my mother's room. It was very cold. I went to close the window thinking I didn't want her to be cold. That she hated to be cold. I was in such shock, because she wasn't even in the room. She was already dead."

"Was it opened wide or just a crack?"

"Was wide open."

We got up the same time. She led the way to the bedroom.

It smelled of wild flowers. On the dresser was a beautifully decorated wooden bowl of potpourri. The bed had been pushed against the wall.

I turned to Elena. "You moved the bed?"

"Yes, I was looking for a watch my daddy gave me. I couldn't find it anywhere. And I remembered the last time I saw it my mother was looking at it in here."

"What kind of watch was it?"

"An old fashioned silver pocket watch."

"Did you find it?"

"No."

I opened the window. Cool air spooled in. A group of young children marched in a tight unit down the street, their voices full of excitement. Three women walked not far behind, ever watchful as they passed Jersey still sitting on the sidewalk, swaying as if he was listening to some distant band.

I leaned over the ledge and looked down. A twenty foot drop. And there was no fire escape. Hard for someone to climb from the ground up to the bedroom without a ladder. I saw bits of paper and other garbage on the ground. Something sparkled in the light. I strained to see better but still couldn't make out anything clearly.

I closed the window. "I'm going downstairs to look around."

"Why? What's down there?"

I shrugged. "I don't know. But looking around certainly can't hurt."

She tapped her foot on the floor. "Are you coming back up here?"

Impatience. An affliction of the young.

"I don't know. Depends on what I find."

She folded her arms around her body. Scratch marks like tiny veins etched the dark skin of her neck. She looked at me; an immense and weary silence gashed her face.

I touched her arm. "You're going to be okay."

"I feel so small and anonymous in this city."

"New York can do that to you."

"I feel sometimes like I'm drowning."

"Where're you going to bury your mother?"

"I'm taking her back to Managua."

I could see in her face the groping for a way to understand what had happened to her. She bowed her head. I put my arm around her shoulder to say hang in there and then went out through the door.

I had to scramble over a chain-link fence to get to into the area under Lourdes' window. The first thing I noticed was a silver men's pocket watch partially hidden by a crushed beer can. I picked it up and looked at it. The Stanhausen had a shiny silver house; the handsome face showing off fancy Roman numerals and three dials. I dropped it into my pocket and took inventory of the garbage-strewn area.

Pennies and other coins had been trampled into the soil. Scraps of paper. A tattered wool cap. Pens. A pair of glasses. Beer cans. Plastic soda bottles. Used Q-tips. An empty Tylenol bottle. A broken syringe.

I used the wool cap to pick up the broken syringe which had a tiny bit of sediment in the barrel.

I wrapped it carefully and stuffed it into my jacket pocket. After clambering back over the fence I got Elena to buzz me in.

Upstairs, she met me at the door with a glass of milk in her hand.

I dug the watch out of my pocket. "Is this your watch?"

She took it and flipped the silver cover. "You found it down there?"

"Yes. Half buried under an empty. Like somebody had stepped on it, pushing it into the ground."

She put the watch to her ear and her face broke into a smile. "Still working. My grandfather got it from a German guy in Cuba when he went there to work. He gave it to my father before he died. How do you think it got down there?"

"I was hoping you might have the answer?"

She wiped the watch on her dress. "I have no idea."

I unfolded the cap and showed her the syringe. "Did your mother have any kind of illness that would require her to use one of these?"

"That's a syringe..."

"Broken... But yes."

She looked confused. "What kind of illness? You mean like diabetes or something?"

"Yeah."

"She was very healthy."

"Did she have a drug habit?"

"She would never use drugs."

"You sure?"

"You think I'm lying to you?"

"Just trying to cover all the bases."

"You also found that down there, under my mother's window?"

"Yes."

"You think my mother used it?"

"I don't know. Maybe your mother didn't leave the window open. It's possible that if she was murdered, whoever killed her escaped through the window when they heard you come in. There were no signs of struggle. No marks on your mother's skin. So, if she was murdered, the question is, how did they subdue her? Maybe they used some kind of drug."

"With that syringe?"

"I don't know."

"But why would they leave it behind?"

"Maybe it dropped when they jumped out of the window."

"Was she was killed for my watch, you think? Ain't worth that much."

"I doubt it."

"You think somebody found out about her money and thought she kept it here?"

"If that was the case, the house would probably have been searched."

"And it wasn't."

"Exactly."

"Maybe I came home before they could do that."

"I doubt it. You would've seen or heard something if you'd interrupted them in their search."

Her eyes widened. "Is there something you're not telling me?"

I folded the syringe and put it in my coat pocket and turned to go.

She grabbed my arm. "What is it?"

"I've told you all I know."

Her hands dropped to her side. "I'm sorry."

"It's okay."

"Mr. Overstreet." Her eyes were wet. "Thanks for not doubting me."

I called River as soon as I got outside. She picked up on the first ring.

"Whaddup, Blades?"

"Do you always sound like this in the morning?"

"How? Like I'm being abused?"

"Yeah, that's it. Are you?"

"Yeah. By fools like you who don't understand that I like to sleep late."

"How much later can you sleep? It's almost time for lunch. And since we're on the topic of lunch, do you have time to meet me for lunch?"

"Let me see if I have time to fit you in today."

I laughed. "Your contact who got you the autopsy report."

"Detective Brady Petersaw."

"He doesn't sound like a brother."

"He isn't."

"Who is he?"

"A hard-luck homicide cop who wants to retire to Arizona."

"You still got his number?"

"Sure. Why?"

"Need him to run something I found as Lourdes' through the lab."

"What is it?"

"A syringe."

"Was she doing drugs?"

"I don't know."

"There was nothing about drugs on the report."

"I know. But let's talk to him."

"Alright. I'll hook it up."

I started to sing. "The sun is shining. On a bright yellow morn. Do you like Bob Marley?"

"You had some last night, didn't you? Anais is back."

I laughed. "Talk to you later."

23

Jersey refused to let a noisy lover's spat nearby ruin his lunch. I'd bought him a cheeseburger, fries and coffee from a greasy spoon around the corner. We were sitting on what he called his favorite bench in the park. Not far away on another bench a man and a woman were going at it, rehashing their infidelities with dramatic outbursts and flapping arms.

I sipped from my Styrofoam cup of coffee and watched Jersey demolish his food with amazing speed.

"If you don't slow down you gonna choke, my friend," I said.

He laughed without pausing.

"Where do you sleep?" I asked.

He pointed to a spot about fifteen feet across the park. "Over there. See that spot between those two benches?"

"Why don't you go to the shelter?"

He spat to the ground and rolled his eyes. "Man, only crazy people go there."

"Is that right?"

"Yeah, that's right. Do I look crazy to you?"

"Not at all. Do you have any family?"

"I don't need no family. What is a family good for but trouble? Suck you of your spirit. You're better off by yourself."

"I have a family."

He looked at me. "You want a medal?"

I smiled. "Do you spend all your time in this park?"

"Sometimes I go around to the church on Broadway. The priest has sandwiches and soup on Wednesdays. But my life is here in this park. What ain't here is in my head. Memories."

"Of what?"

"I used to play with Miles, you know."

"You played with Miles? As in Miles Davis?"

"What, you hard of hearing?"

I laughed. "That must've been awesome."

"Also played with Mingus for a stretch. Didn't like him. Great musician. Bigger asshole."

"You didn't like Mingus?"

"You have a problem understanding me or something?"

"What instrument did you play?"

With his fork and his index finger he began to etch a rhythm on the bench.

"Drums?" I said.

"I flipped the baddest sticks on the east coast."

"What happened?"

"What you mean what happened?"

"Well…why'd you stop playing?"

"I gave it up."

"Just gave it up? Why?"

"Love took me down."

"Love?"

"Wiped out my will to play. I found love and lost it. When I lost love I lost everything else too."

"She broke your heart?"

"I broke my own heart. I didn't know what I had. Man, don't ever let that happen to you."

"Do you know anyone in that building across the street?"

"There's a woman lives on the first floor. She lets me take a shower sometimes. Gives me food when she has it. I also know the woman who lives above her. Speaks Spanish. She was nice. Gave me food… and sometimes money. Always said good morning. I heard she died."

"Her name was Lourdes. She died three nights ago."

"She a friend of yours?"

"You can say that."

His eyes squeezed shut. "Man I knew this was too good to be true. You buying me food and shit. You a cop ain't you?"

"No. But I used to be."

"Now you a P.I. or something, like in the movies? You got a gun on you?"

"The night Lourdes died did you see any strangers going into the building?"

"Man, I ain't the doorman."

I crushed my Styrofoam cup and got up. "Thank you for your time."

He wiped his mouth with the back of his hands. "You mad at me or something?"

"You can't help yourself. Why should I expect you to help me."

He stuffed fries into his mouth and chewed for a while. "The only people I seen going in there were the cops."

"Cops? When?"

"I don't know what time it was. You see a watch on me?"

"Approximately. Do you have any idea? Was it dark?"

"I guess maybe ten… eleven o'clock. They passed me as they went into the building."

"You were coming out?"

He chewed and nodded.

"What were you doing in the building, if you don't mind my asking?" I asked.

"I mind."

"Did they speak to you?"

"I asked one of them for a cigarette. He told me he would arrest me for smelling bad. I laughed and told him to go fuck him mama."

"I guess they were in uniform, right? That's how you knew they were cops?"

"You're a bright, nigga," he quipped. "The blues brothers."

"They were two of them?"

"Two white males. One short. One tall. I didn't get a good look at their faces, so you can skip that question."

"And you didn't see anyone else going into the building?"

He drained his coffee. "You should've been a lawyer. They like to ask the same question over and over even after you give 'em an answer. Answer is still no."

I opened my wallet and gave him 20 dollars. "Thanks."

"For what?"

"The conversation."

He looked up and snatched the $20. "Anytime. All you gotta do is bring the food."

I heard him laughing as I walked across the damp concrete to the park gate.

As I drove home I placed a call to an old pal, Lieutenant Wilson, who worked out of the 75th. I asked him to find out if officers had been dispatched to Lourdes' residence on the night she was killed.

He told me he'd check dispatch and get back to me.

My phone rang moments later. It was Raoul. He wanted to see me. We agreed to meet around 9 P.M. at a Latin jazz club called Aquazul in the East Village where he played on occasion.

After I hung up I wondered if this Aquazul would be as much fun as Club Malecón. I was enjoying this education Raoul was giving me about Latin clubs in my city.

His Al Davis haircut, a cross between an afro and a beehive, seemed misplaced on the wide-shouldered but useless-looking body, gone slack from neglect. When he sat down his body sagged rather than settled into the seat. He had a very dark, deeply-lined face, and his brooding eyes gave him a villainous look.

Observing his sour demeanor made me wonder how River got Detective Petersaw to hand over a copy of the coroner's report. But then, that's what made her a good investigator.

We met at a Cuban restaurant on McGregor, where Petersaw informed us he ate lunch every day, where the oven-fried pork chops were the tenderest he'd ever tasted. It was a few blocks away from the 77th where he'd worked homicide for the past ten years. A promised promotion to a lighter precinct in Manhattan never came.

The 77th was still one of the most dangerous and deadly in Brooklyn. This situation offered plenty of overtime which helped when it came to paying the tuition bills of his two sons in college, but he was getting way too old for fifteen-hour shifts, battling shitheads in the drug-infested neighborhoods ruled by the 77th.

The restaurant was as run-down as the street it was on. But it appeared to be clean. The Mexican waiters were efficient and friendly, smiling as convincingly as those Method-actors working the fancy reservation-needed places in Manhattan.

It could easily have been one of those joints found in immigrant communities across the borough, which got passed from entrepreneur to entrepreneur. For most it'd be their first taste of business ownership, a stepping stone to economic freedom and prosperity. The money used to buy the restaurant or bodega wouldn't have come from a bank loan, but from sophisticated system of resource-pooling known in many communities as a "susu": a group of people would get together and agree to commit a certain amount of money into a pool each week, with one person chosen to serve as the "bank". Every week one person in the group would get to withdraw the total from the bank, the process continuing each successive week until every one got a turn. It not only built trust among the immigrants, but also gave them opportunities to buy things they would ordinarily not be able to afford because of lack of credit or capital.

Petersaw sat opposite us, drawing closer to a plate piled with enough pork chops and yellow rice to feed a lion. The size of the portions once more emphasized to me why we're one of the fattest nations on the planet.

"We appreciate you meeting us at such short notice," River said, snapping into a burger.

The detective nodded and started eating, lifting his head only to gulp mouthfuls of Pepsi. He didn't like Coke. Not sweet enough.

After wolfing down half the pork chops in brisk time, Petersaw looked up, smiling. "Man, I haven't eaten since last night. I usually skip breakfast because of this condition with my stomach. Can't eat anything early in the morning without gagging. You'd think I was pregnant or something."

"Have you seen a doctor?" said River.

"Fucking doctors. All they do is take your money. Give you some pills and tell you to come back in a few days. Then they take more money and give you a different set of pills. Who needs that?"

"We'd like to talk to you about that autopsy report," I said.

Petersaw had resumed eating. "What's your name, again?"

"Blades Overstreet," I said.

"Oh, yes. You worked narco, right?"

"Years ago," I said.

He stopped chewing and glanced up, catching my eye, smiling wryly before sticking a fork of rice into his jaw. "I remember your case. How's retirement working out?"

"You should try it," I said.

River kicked me under the table.

"Six more years, my friend. You ever worked homicide?" He said.

"I don't like looking at dead bodies," I said.

He turned to River. "How about you?"

"I got homicide a month before I resigned," River said.

"Why'd you resign?" Petersaw asked.

"Long story," River said quietly.

Petersaw studied her face for a moment. "I did four years in narco. Worst experience of my life. Was hell, man. Nearly gave me a heart attack. My blood pressure went off the charts. On top of that it broke up my first marriage."

I tried to imagine him chasing after a drug suspect who'd just ditched his stash in the sewer and was about to escape with what little residual evidence might be left on his person. Wasn't happening.

"Narco can be rough," River said.

"It's a shit job, I'll tell ya that," Petersaw said.

I said. "About the report…"

What report?"

"The autopsy. Lourdes Calderon. The Nicaraguan woman who was murdered on Livonia."

His face clouded and he glanced at River. "She's a suicide."

"Did you try to find out who she had sex with just before she was killed?" I said.

He straightened his shoulders slowly. "We talked to her daughter. She didn't know of any boyfriend. We tried to find friends who might know if she had a boyfriend. Couldn't find any… friends."

"Didn't that alarm you?" River said.

Licking his fingers. "Why should it? A lot of these immigrants keep their personal lives a secret. Even from family. Anyway, I ran the man's DNA through FBI database as a favor to her." He looked at River. "And got no hits. So either he isn't a criminal or he's never given a sample. Either way, he's not on our scope, whoever he is." Petersaw picked up his fork, then put it down again. "Look, I've seen this type of stuff before."

"What type of stuff?" I said.

"Woman with no friends. Despondent over the death of somebody close to her. She loses it. Only there's no coming back for her."

"She had sex and then hung herself, that's what you believe?" I said.

"You got any evidence otherwise?"

River was about to take another bite of her hamburger. She put the burger down and wiped her hands on a paper napkin. "Does that make sense?"

"Maybe the sex was bad."

"No woman kills herself over bad sex," River snapped.

"It was just a joke... Christ," Petersaw mumbled. "Look, you wanna know how many deaths we get called out on every day? Too many. Too many accidentals. Too many homicides. Too many suicides. Too many people dying unnatural deaths. Suicides are common among immigrants. They come here and discover it's not as easy as they thought. They get homesick. They get lonely. They feel lost. Sometimes they lose it."

I unfolded the cap with the broken syringe on the table.

"What's that?" Petersaw said.

"Something I found. Can you run this through the lab. See if you get a match for Lourdes' DNA. Or the man she had sex with," I said.

Petersaw said, "Where'd you find that?"

"On the premises."

"That makes it evidence. You should've called us," he said.

"It isn't evidence if you don't think a crime was committed," I said.

"It's probably contaminated now."

"Look, don't you wanna find out if somebody else had a hand in Lourdes' death? I would think you'd wanna be sure," River said.

He drew the wool cap toward him. "Gimme a week."

"A week?" River said.

"Lab is short-staffed. Takes time," he said.

River leaned across the table to look into his face. "C'mon Brady. You can do better than that. I still got that friend working in the Knicks front office. I think they're playing the Lakers this weekend. I'm sure I can hit him for two more tickets."

"Call me in three or four days," he said, without smiling.

"I'll call tomorrow. Then I'll call the next day if you have nothing," said River.

I drained my coffee and waited to see if River would finish her hamburger. She had eaten about half and was looking at the rest of it with a measure of disgust. She pushed the plate away, downed the rest of her coke and wiped her mouth.

Petersaw was still fighting with his pork chops; he seemed determined to eat the whole thing.

Good luck to ya, pal. A horse couldn't finish the portions they served here.

I pushed my chair back and stood up.

River waited until I had cleared the table before getting up. "Thanks Brady."

Petersaw stood up and shook River's hand. "Anytime, sugar. Don't forget those tickets."

He looked at me and nodded.

24

Aquazul is a smallish club with seating for no more than 25 people. When I arrived to meet Raoul the joint was as quiet as a bank after 5:00 P.M. Hardly anyone in the place. Lights dim. Everything in shadow.

I parked myself at the circular bar and ordered a shot of Black Label. The bartender sported a silver nose ring bigger than Dennis Rodman's and his head was wrapped in Kinte cloth. Pirate with an African twist, I suppose.

I sat alone sipping my drink. Over in a corner the piano player seemed to have his eyes closed. I recognized the Oscar Petersen tune he was playing: Sweet Georgia Brown. The other patrons sat in deep silence as if in a trance.

I looked at my watch. 9:05. A few minutes later Raoul shuffled in, his face solemn, his hair slick and shiny and dark. Too much dye. Even in the masked light his face appeared ashen.

He sat next to me without speaking and unbuttoned his coat. I noticed he was shivering. He craned his neck to get the bartender's attention and having done so ordered whisky. Then he turned to me and whispered in a soft voice that he was not feeling well.

"Sorry to hear," I said.

"I'm on blood thinners," he said. "Bad clock. I feel cold all the time now. The weather has been terrible. I think it's going to snow again. That's what the forecaster said last night. And he's never wrong."

"Really? Which forecaster was that?"

He sipped his drink. "Univision."

"That's the all-Spanish station, right?"

He nodded, his mouth suspended on the tip of his glass. "It's a very good station. Lots of news you don't see on the English stations. The networks only report from one point of view. America's. They don't see the rest of the world."

"What rest of the world?"

He looked at me puzzled and we both started to laugh at the same time. I said, "You have some information for me?"

He brooded, rubbing the corners his mouth. "I been thinking about my relationship with Lourdes. I was trying to remember the good times we had. She loved to dance the tango. Oh, you should see her. The passion. The energy. We had good times."

He paused as if distracted by a memory. He sipped his drink and glanced around the room. His gaze drifted gently back to my face. "She was very supportive about my work as a musician even though I make very little money. All the time she come to see me play."

"So what happened?"

"I don't know. In her heart she no happy, I think. She missed her family. She used to talk about bringing Elena to America all the time. It no her fault. She try to be loving to me. Waited on me hand and foot, as you say. Then things started to change. She started going out a lot. Alone. All the time going to Spanish social clubs and dances. I think she having an affair. I confront her. She telling me don't bother her or she will leave me. I am very shocked. And so scared to lose her. But the jealousy eating me inside. I hired somebody to follow her, yes. You would do the same, no?"

He paused. I shrugged non-committedly.

He continued. "Yes, she meeting a lot of men, he say. But it no seem like she having an affair."

"What was she doing?"

"She was working for this woman. I see her picture on the news the other day. The one who the paper say was running a fake marriage thing with the judge Lourdes worked for."

"You mean Odessa Rose?"

"You know this woman?"

"I've made her acquaintance."

He stared straight ahead with a great remoteness as if numbed by what he was thinking. "Lourdes was recruiting Latin men for that woman."

"Are you sure about this?"

"This Odessa Rose is big boss of something. She offering Lourdes plenty money. Too much to turn down, she say. She could do many things with this money. Bring her daughter here. Send her to best school. Build a house in Nicaragua for her sister and nieces. I think it is bad idea, but she tell me stay out of her business. I blame that woman for making things bad between us."

"I'm beginning to believe Lourdes was murdered."

"Because of the things she was doing for that woman?"

"Maybe." I finished my drink. "When do you start playing?"

"I no play tonight. Another drink?"

I nodded.

He waved the bartender over and ordered drinks for both of us. "You know, Lourdes told me she always wanted to come to America. Even before the Sandinistas killed her family. She used to work in a hotel in Managua and met many Americans. She even learn some English before she get here. She feel she could make much money here. She did find a way to make mucho money, sí. But no find happiness. That's the funny thing about this country. Plenty money but also plenty sadness. Plenty more than you'd think. Plenty more than there should be. It's strange. When you come from poor country you expect everyone in America to be happy. After all, it's got everything. To come here is to go to Heaven. But then you get here and you see that people still no content. They don't enjoy people the way they should. In Cuba we have nothing else to enjoy but our people. Each other. Americans, they enjoy the things they can buy. Everywhere you go people just living for themselves. Families don't enjoy families. Families don't even see families. It's sad."

When the drinks came I realized I was no longer in the mood. Perhaps I was tired. Might've been the stuff he'd just said. Whatever it was, I felt a wave of sadness surround me. I needed fresh air. After one sip of the whisky, I pushed it away.

He looked at me and gave a knowing nod.

I drove back to Brooklyn with my mind drifting all over the place. I tried to think of my wife waiting up for me, ready to drown me in her infinite sexual flavor. Anais' image refused to stick in my mind. It was quickly replaced by my sister's enflamed eyes. I heard her voice, restless and surprisingly frail. My sister, fortified by her stubborn intelligence has always been cocky. And a bit mysterious. No one knew she was even dating until she announced that she was getting married. And then her husband was nothing like I would've imagined. Wasn't nerdy or didn't have a cloven hoof. He turned out to be a television producer who dressed in jeans and polo shirts. He liked sports and drove a gold 69 Corvette.

The bass on the Volvo was racked to the limit. It didn't have the most advanced sound system, (truth is it was pathetic). The radio was tuned to BLS. Barry White had recently died and the silky-voiced male DJ promised to smoke all of the Love Man's joints that night. The persuasive, I've Got So Much To Give, was wrecking the airwaves at that moment.

My sister's voice kept drifting behind the Love Man's playful growl. I didn't want to entertain her caution to leave the past in its graveyard. Would rather listen to Barry sing passionately about the lifetime it'd take to give all his love, actually. Because that's how I felt about Anais. But I couldn't shake Julie's voice. Couldn't shake the feeling of sorrow.

As I weaved through traffic on Flatbush I remembered that tonight Toni's going-away party. Hadn't really thought seriously about going, but at that moment it occurred to me that I owed him a proper apology. It was hard to condone his involvement in the drug business, but the optimist in me wanted to believe that perhaps I could get Toni to change.

I called Anais to tell her I was making a detour. She was already in bed, half asleep.

My first look inside Toni's house left me stunned. It was spectacular... and then some. The huge double-wing front doors opened into an enormous room with a pearly diamond glow. The ceilings were as high as a cathedral's; the wood floors mirror clear. Mostly black and white paintings on the shocking white walls. I looked around for Toni. Didn't see him, but saw a couple of faces I thought I recognized from television.

It was early by New York party standards, but the drinking and mingling had started: brawny men and skinny women with faces molded with models' vanity were well on the way to drunkenness.

I found Toni in a bedroom upstairs with two other men, clustered around several tidy lines of coke on a GQ magazine. One lanky man, holding the magazine close to his face, was feeding the white powder into a nose as gorgeous as you could imagine. Entering the room, I smiled, knowing that his nose wouldn't stay gorgeous for long if he kept filling up his pockets with that rock.

Toni looked up at me and smiled, but I could've been anyone. Didn't appear that he recognized me. The stiffness of the smile and his clouded pupils told me he was gassed. As he took the magazine from the man next him, I turned to leave. My guess was that a lot more powder would be consumed here tonight. This place might just turn into a madhouse later. I didn't want to be anywhere near it.

"Blades, where the fuck you going?" Toni said.

I stopped.

Toni spoke to the other two men. "Why don't you girls go down stairs and make sure everybody is having a good time?"

The two men got up and sashayed past, snickering as they went by.

"Come and sit down, Blades." Toni said.

I remained in the doorway.

"What's the matter? You afraid to sit on my bed? You think I'm going to attack you?"

"Where's your boyfriend?" I said.

"Around somewhere. Come on, Blades. I'm not going to bite you."

I sat on the edge of the bed. "When're you leaving?"

"Day after tomorrow."

"So you're going through with it?"

"Why not?"

I shrugged. "Listen, about the other day…"

"I'm happy you came," he said, resting a hand on my thigh.

I removed his hand and smiled. "You don't want to hear my apology?"

"I'm still kinda angry."

"That's why I want to apologize."

"Will it be sincere?"

I got up. "I get a little carried away sometimes, you know that."

"A little carried away!" he exclaimed. "Fuck that, Blades. What are you? A child? You don't know me as well as you think, you know. You think you know how I roll, but you don't. Not really. You think it's okay to disrespect me because to you I'm some kinda lowlife faggot."

"That's not how it is."

"Really? Then how is it, mister big mouth?"

"I came here to apologize. You don't want my apology. Then I guess I'll bounce."

"You bounce, muthafucker. And you better keep bouncing."

"What is that? Some kinda threat?"

"If you feel threatened, Blades that's your business, but it's not me that's threatening you," he said, with an air of superiority.

"You're a drug dealer, Toni. I don't care that most of your clients might be rich rim-jobs from the entertainment industry. I know you still got action in the projects and on the corners. Drugs make people do bad things like hurt innocent people."

"I don't need your sermon, Blades. Moralizing muthafuckers like you who think it's their job to tell people how to live their lives do more harm that all the drug addicts out there." He lowered his face to the magazine and snorted a line of coke. When he looked up his eyes gleamed with cocaine madness. "I bet you had a lot of girlfriends when you were in high school, didn't you. Bet you were one of those jock types that the girls couldn't resist."

I remained silent.

"I didn't," he said. "No surprise there, right? I didn't have any boyfriends, either. I was too scared. I didn't know what to think. But I was bursting inside to express my sexuality. I didn't want to keep my interest in boys a secret. But I knew I had to. I couldn't tell my grandmother. Dance kept me from going over the edge. It took all my scattered energy and fused it. One day, when I was about fifteen, this family friend, an older man…about forty or so, I guess. He offered to give me a lift home from church one evening. As we were driving he started asking me about school and stuff. Then he asked me if I had a girlfriend. I don't know what I was thinking. Maybe I was happy that he paid an interest in me. But I told him that I didn't like girls. That I was attracted to boys."

Toni snorted another line of coke and rubbed his nose with the back of his hand. "We were driving through Prospect Park. He pulled the car onto the grass. Muthafucker sucker-punched me in the face and started screaming and choking me. I was a skinny kid at that age. He was so strong. It's hard to tell you how humiliating it was to be raped. All the time he was raping me he was screaming how God was gonna punish me. It took thirteen stitches to sew me back up. I couldn't shit for months. Still my grandmother wouldn't believe me. Told me that I was lying. That the man in question would never do that.

"I didn't care about anything after that. Dance didn't matter anymore. I started taking drugs. Then I started selling. I got to know the suppliers. I just lived my life like it didn't matter.

"About five years later, I saw him late one night on the subway and followed him. It was winter. Very cold. Heavy snow. I followed him for about three blocks in the snow. I caught up with him and when he turned to look at me I shot him in the head."

A flat silence weighted over us. For a while I just looked at Toni, studying his face. All the time wondering why he told me that story.

"You got some balls, Toni," I said.

"Not for long if I have my way."

I forced a laugh. "Suppose I decided to go straight to the police?"

"Hey, if you do, you do. I guess then I'll know how it really is, mister big mouth. You wanna bounce? Don't let me hold you up."

For a long while I sat in my car thinking about the shit Toni had laid on me. I had no doubt that he'd told me the truth. The reason he chose to tell me was what had me scratching my head. Was he trying to scare me? Or was there some other meaning behind his story?

Toni's rivals in the game who made the mistake of underestimating him usually didn't last to talk about it. Those who took the way he dressed as some kind of weakness usually paid a stiff price for their error. It's not that Toni's look was some sort of act, some ruse to throw off his rivals. Far from it. What you saw was what you got. To a point. Beyond the outward appearance, Toni had something else going. Brains. His craftiness. And lots of money. Once he'd figured out how to stay two steps ahead of the law by creating legitimate businesses to wash the dirty money he went about eliminating the paradox between his lifestyle and the toughness required to be a big player in the game. Insulate yourself from the streets by having loyal lieutenants who were bright, but not too ambitious. Treat them well. Be ruthless with your competitors; generous to your underlings. So that not only did he have all the muscle and protection he needed, it was hard to penetrate his organization.

What did Toni want from me? Was his confession an expectation of true friendship? Could I really be friends with a drug dealer? If not what would be the fallout? I really didn't want to have to look over my shoulder any more than I had to. And certainly not for this asshole. One day I was going to have to reckon with Toni and his drug-dealing, and I had a feeling that day was coming soon.

25

I swallowed several shots of Jack Daniels before calling the Foder residence, identifying myself at the sound of Zoe's voice.

Zoe snorted into the phone. "Do you know what time it is?"

I looked at my watch. It was after midnight. "I need to talk to you. Can I come out to see you?"

"You can't be talking about coming out here now."

"Now is fine, if it's a good time for you."

"You must be crazy."

"I take it now is not a good time. How about tomorrow, then?"

"We don't have anything to talk about."

"I believe Lourdes Calderon was murdered."

There was a deep silence. I thought I heard her gasp but it was so soft I could've imagined it.

"When can we meet?" I asked.

Another naked silence.

I said. "I believe her death is connected to your father's murder."

"Leave us alone, Mr. Overstreet."

"I'm prepared to park in your driveway until you decide to talk to me."

Her voice shook with tension. "Tomorrow. In the city."

"Where? What time?"

"Eleven o'clock. The T Salon."

"Where's that?"

"Look it up."

I heard the click before I could reply. She was gone.

The T Salon was a quaint tea house tucked away on a quiet block in the Flatiron district across from a near empty parking lot. The entire block had the appearance of tranquility, almost as if it didn't belong in this heaving commercial part of town. Next to the parking lot was a tiny shoe store. No attendant in sight. The women's shoes in the window were pretty though. I'd have to remember to mention the store to Anais.

With its scarlet décor, worn antique-looking chairs and exposed brick walls the T Salon had the atmosphere of an old-fashioned living room that couldn't make up its mind if it wanted to be a boudoir. At first glance it seemed overly gaudy.

Seated at a tiny round table in a tight corner near the window almost hidden amid a jungle of potted plants, Zoe was dressed in a dark suit, her hair dangling loosely around her shoulders. She fiddled with her hands and looked to be nervous, her face an intense mask.

After taking off my jacket, I draped it on the back of the chair. Then I sat across from her glancing at my watch. "Are you always this punctual?"

"It's just a short walk from my office."

"Oh, where's that?"

She curled up her eyelids. "I'm not here for your company, so let's get on with it. What do you want?"

A gray-haired waiter wobbled over with a menu, handing it to me.

I sidestepped Zoe's bristles and offered her a generous glimpse of my teeth. "You ordered?"

"I come here all the time. I usually get earl gray with lavender."

I handed the menu back.

"I'll have whatever you're having."

"The usual, Marissa," Zoe said to the waiter. "A large pot."

The Hispanic waiter folded the menu in half and walked away with a toothy smile that seemed more sincere than most.

"How's your mother?" I said.

"No less suicidal," she said dryly.

"And you?"

"No closer to suicide."

I laughed. "I guess what they say about you is correct."

"And what's that?"

"That you're the tough one in the family."

"It's easy to be tough when everything's going right. But how tough can anyone be in the face of death? My world is upside down right now, Mr. Overstreet. I don't feel very tough at all."

"A long time ago I used to be a Marine. Recently I find myself thinking about how I would react if I was one of those young Marines sent to fight in Afghanistan."

"You like guns, don't' you, Mr. Overstreet?"

"I feel in control when I have one in my hand."

"Makes you feel like Superman, huh?"

"A lot of bad people out there have guns. Can't fight them with sticks."

"What do you want with me, Mr. Overstreet?"

"I'm investigating Lourdes' death. A favor to her daughter, Elena. You know her?"

Zoe shook her head.

"A really sweet girl," I said.

Zoe just stared at me with impatient eyes.

I said, "You know about your father and Odessa Rose…"

She opened her mouth to interrupt.

"Just let me finish," I said. "What you might not have known is that Lourdes also worked for this woman. One of her recruiters. This operation was big. Taking in millions a year. Your father had intimate knowledge of her organization. Perhaps Lourdes did too. And from everything I've heard Odessa can be ruthless. I believe she broke into your house. And I suspect she might be behind both murders. Do you know if he kept any secret records? Books? Diaries?"

"You talk like my father was some kind of mobster."

The waiter brought us a tray holding a blue teapot and two white cups with matching saucers along with milk and sugar. She placed the tray on an empty table beside us and transferred the teapot and cups to our table. First she poured for Zoe then for me.

"Can I get you anything else?"

Zoe smiled and shook her head. The waiter left and Zoe added one cube of dark sugar to her tea and a bit of cream. She stirred the mixture slowly with her spoon.

I added cream only and tasted. The tea had a sharp tangy taste and was slightly bitter.

"This is not going away, Zoe. Face it. If you're hoping to avoid a scandal that might ruin your father's good name. Guess what? It's already ruined."

She pondered her response for a while, sipping her tea with a distracted but pained look in her eyes. "I ask again. What do you want from me?"

"I want the truth about your father's dealings with Odessa."

"I don't know anything."

"Have you ever met Odessa?"

"Never heard of her until I read the story in the papers."

"Since the FBI moved your father's office to Federal Plaza, have you heard from them?"

"Two agents came around asking the same questions you're asking. Wanting to know if my father kept files anywhere else? I told them he had a safety deposit box. But they already knew about that."

I thought to myself, maybe this was why Odessa seemed so cocky and dismissive of the FBI. Perhaps she knew exactly what she was looking for and where to find it when she broke into the judge's office. But she must not have found it, else why would she want to hire me?

"How about your mother? Would she know something?"

"Leave her out of this."

"Don't you want to find out why your father was killed?"

"I don't really care."

"You don't mean that."

She bowed her head. "I need you to just leave us alone."

"Did somebody threaten you? Is that why you took us off the case?"

"What do I have to do for you to leave us alone?"

"Tell me the truth." I snapped.

"What truth? Whose truth? What if this truth causes other people pain and suffering?"

"It's more painful to live in fear."

She put her hands over her ears as if to shut me out. "I got a call at the house. His voice was as cold as ice. Asked me if I wanted to see my mother dead. Told me that if you didn't stop nosing around that's exactly what would happen. It took all of two seconds. I had tremors for hours afterwards."

"When did this happen?"

"Five days ago. I called your friend to tell him I no longer needed your services."

"Why didn't you call me directly?"

"Because I figured you'd ask a lot of questions."

"Did you call the police?"

"I don't want my mother dead. Can you understand that?"

"You can't let these people intimidate you."

"Maybe you can't. After all, they didn't threaten to kill your mother."

I ignored the bitterness in her voice. "Was there anything distinctive about the voice that you can remember?"

"He had some sort of accent."

"What kind?"

She looked at me sharply. "I would've asked where he was from but he seemed to be in a rush to get off the phone."

I laughed and let her words hang in the air. She sipped tea and I could see her body shiver. It wasn't from cold; the T Salon was quite warm. Whoever it was that put the fear in Zoe had apparently done so with the fluency of a mystic. It might take an equal force to extract that fear. I doubt I had that power.

"You may not care about finding the people who killed your father, but Elena wants to bring her mother's killer to justice and I believe you're hiding something that might help me."

"You're not even sure Lourdes was murdered."

"Oh, I'm sure. Just don't have proof yet. You know more about your father's business with Odessa than you're letting on. I'm beginning to wonder if you didn't work for her too."

She stood up. "I'm not listening to anymore of this nonsense."

"Sit down… Please."

She glanced around the room as if to make sure no one would witness her submission before sitting down.

"Lourdes told me about a young black man who came to your house and threatened your father. She said you were home that day."

"Lourdes must've been mistaken."

"You don't remember it?"

"I just told you."

"Happened about a year ago," I said.

She leaned back in her chair and wiped her lips with the linen napkin. "I'm afraid I have to get back to work."

"Tell me about your work. What exactly is mesotherapy? Is it like Botox?"

Her face came alive with a smile. "It's not Botox.

"But you're getting rich off other women's insecurities."

"Are you always this annoying?"

I laughed. "I blame my insecurity."

The swell of hushed voices around us was building as the salon became more crowded. I offered to pay the bill but she plunked $20 down and refused to budge. She did let me walk her back to her office on Park Avenue South. We shook hands outside and I watched her enter the building before heading to the parking lot at Union Square.

I slogged my way through heavy traffic on the FDR and across the Brooklyn Bridge. It was a bright day if cold; the sky a flat stretch of bluish linen streaked with yellow from the sun's reflection. Across the bridge I headed down Adams Street and found a parking spot two blocks from the club.

Entering the club, I bumped into Komi coming out.

"Blades, how are you, big man?"

"Doing alright. And you?"

"Just buzzing."

I smiled. "If you buzz any louder you'll wake up the whole damn neighborhood. Is Negus here?"

She spread her wide mouth in a reckless smile. "Recovering."

I sort of had an idea what she was getting at. "Laid out, eh?"

Her eyes opened up with glee. "Scorched, would be a better term."

"He knows about you and River, right?"

"He saw us together at the club. And he saw us leave together. And he knows I've been stayin' with her the last few days. The only thing he doesn't know is how often we do it."

I laughed. "So, he cool with your game?"

"Negus is a playa. What playa wouldn't be cool with my game?"

"So it ain't serious, you and Negus?"

She smiled and patted her crotch area. "Why? You want some?"

"Just wanna know my man Negus isn't getting crowned."

"Nigga, please. You don't need to be worrying about Negus."

"What happens if he falls in love with you?"

"Not in the script. Any minute my shit's ready to blow up. My game's too tight for love. If he stays loose, the ride's safe. If not, I'm a hit eject and he's ghost. I ain't looking for no man to take care of me."

"Or woman?"

She laughed and punched a finger playfully into the center of my chest. "That bitch is in love with you. You know that, right? But you too straight."

"I'm married."

She rolled her eyes. "You trippin'."

"See you around, Komi."

"Yes sir." Her voice soared with sarcasm as she sailed out the door.

My meeting with Negus lasted longer than I'd expected. We went over plans to install the new sound system and about bringing a group from Barbados to perform for Valentine's Day.

Afterward we cracked open two bottles of Guinness Stout.

I took a large rip. Nice and bitter. Just what I needed. "Ran into Komi coming in."

Negus smiled. "That's one good looking woman."

"Heard you took her to a sex club."

He laughed. "Komi took me."

I finished my Guinness and opened another bottle. "How was it?"

He chugged a mouthful of stout and settled the bottle down with a satisfied sigh. "Why? You want the address?"

"Anais would put my balls in a meat grinder."

"Maybe she might wanna go too. You never know."

"Oh I doubt that."

"Don't underestimate your woman, Blades."

"Oh, I know my woman."

River called my cell about 3 in the afternoon.

"Blades, I just spoke to Petersaw. He got the report from the lab."

"That was quick."

"You complaining?"

"Not at all. Just impressed with your prowess."

"Whatever. That needle you gave him contained curare. It's a poison which causes muscular and respiratory paralysis. It also had traces of Lourdes DNA. When they went back and checked…"

"Traces of curare was in her system."

"Bingo. Very small. Wasn't enough to kill her. But she probably couldn't struggle when they strung her up. I don't know how it got overlooked in the first place."

"The coroner's office is understaffed, overworked and underpaid."

"Don't make excuses for them, Blades. That could've been your mother they were about to declare a suicide."

"You're right."

"Now that we know it was murder. What next?"

"I can link Odessa to the judge. And I can link her to Lourdes."

"Lourdes and Odessa knew each other?" River asked.

"I'll tell you about it later."

"Wait, when did you find this out?"

"When I spoke to Raoul the other day."

"And you're now telling me this?"

"It slipped my mind," I explained.

"How does something like that slip your mind?"

"Look, it slipped my mind. I'm sorry. What do you want me to say? You need to help me find a way to put Odessa's boys at Lourdes' apartment the night she was killed, not lecture me."

"You're an arrogant bastard, Blades. That's all I got to say."

Before I could respond she hung up.

26

I **woke next morning with** a numbing headache, the smell of apricots in my head and a stickiness on my tongue as if I'd been eating popsicle. Across the street the wet empty sycamore branches looked like fake props on a movie set.

I licked my lips to clear the stickiness away. But my lips were dry. The apricot smell and the stickiness had been part of a dream. Slowly the dream resurfaced.

It happened when I was about twelve or thirteen. Summer. Not long before my father disappeared. The old red and blue ice-cream van which came chugging down our block just before dusk each day was late. Darkness was already feasting on our neighborhood. I'd been waiting on the stoop a good half hour before I heard the familiar jingle.

I liked it better when Jason waited with me. But he and Melanie were away visiting their dad. Still, nothing could dampen my anticipation of tasting the apricot-flavored popsicle I always got.

The temperature had hit 98 that day. The evening was no cooler. Because of the heat just about everyone on my block was still outside. I heard a church bell ringing. The sound was harsh and annoying. Nothing at all like the sonorous chimes of the ice-cream truck.

A bunch of kids were playing touch football under the bright streetlights. Kipland and Leyland, the twins from next door, were riding their bikes up and down the narrow tree-lined street. Sandy-haired Martin Frommer, who later went on to become a pitcher for the Oakland Athletics, was playing catch with his dad. They were waiting, too.

Ten excruciating minutes later, I had my apricot-flavored popsicle. Racing up my steps, I ripped the wrapper off and tossed it into the street. An adult voice reprimanding me for littering. But I didn't look back. Tomorrow I'd probably get a scolding from my mother after the neighbor ratted me out. But that was tomorrow. Right now all I cared about was getting my popsicle into my mouth before it began to melt.

As I entered my apartment I heard angry voices. Mom and Dad were arguing. They did it just about every day now. Determined not to let their adult suffering ruin my treat, I decided to go to my room. There I could blot out their shouting. The popsicle was beginning to melt all over my fingers. Mom got angry when we made a mess on her expensive rugs so, I ran to the kitchen to get a bowl and a napkin to catch the droppings.

That's when I saw them. My mom flattened against the fridge. My dad leaning his heavy body on her so she couldn't move. The big gun in his hand gripped tight. I stopped dead. My heart flew to my mouth. I was about to crap in my pants. My dad's eyes met mine. I saw cold fury.

He lifted up off my mom and came toward me. I looked at the gun in his hand. Then at his eyes. I turned and ran from the house.

All day I tried in vain to get hold of my father. I had to speak to him. This time I was sure it hadn't been a dream. No, this had happened. I'd witnessed my father trying to kill my mother.

I called his house and left several messages. Got no call back so I hollered at Noah who was no help. He had no idea where my father was.

Late in the afternoon I drove to the Crown Heights apartment where he'd moved not long ago. Rang the bell and banged on the door so hard I almost broke it down. Nothing. Where else could I look? He'd been dating a singer who lived in the Village, but I didn't have her address or a phone number.

Driving back from Crown Heights my phone rang. Lieutenant Wilson, my friend from the 75th.

"Blades, how're things?"

"Fucked up. But you know that already."

He laughed. "I checked into that thing for you."

"What'd you find out?"

"Nothing."

"Nothing?"

"No blues dispatched to that location within the last six months."

"Are you sure?"

"Positive. Check your information again."

"Thanks Pardna."

I turned the car around and steamed toward Atlantic Avenue. Seems Jersey had given me bad information. Should've known better. Still, it wouldn't hurt to question him again.

The streets of Brooklyn were oddly calm. The afternoon seemed anchored in silence. The absence of noisy trucks and delivery vans hurtling along this artery, which connected to Queens and by extension Long Island, helped to preserve the illusion of stillness and tranquility.

Tension ripped through my muscles. My grip on the steering wheel was tighter than it needed to be, and I was driving faster than I should've been. I knew this but was unable to do anything about it. My body had become one long blade of rage. I thought of turning around and going home. What I needed more than anything was to speak to my father. Get this shit out in the open. Over and done with.

I was driving at a furious pace. And without discretion. Flying through yellow lights. Passing cars on the left or right. Didn't really matter.

A voice in my head telling me to slow down. But when was the last time I paid heed to small voices? The struggle between confusion and clarity was one that has raged in me for years. All my life, to be honest. Like a malignancy it had been nurtured by my distorted view of life. Power liberated you from accountability. The kind of bullshit philosophy you develop from being a cop, carrying a gun, knowing you could pound on criminals with impunity.

I don't remember ever having a conversation with my father about what I'd witnessed that summer evening over twenty years ago. Nor with my mother. Might there have been a conversation and like the incident itself I'd simply buried it into oblivion?

I swerved to pass a slow moving bus.

Shit!

My way was blocked by another car moving just as slowly.

I jammed on the brakes.

Damn!

Traveling way too fast to stop.

My muscles clenched. I swerved the car to the left. The wheels began to skid. The car sidewinded across the street and over the median. The Volvo slammed against the sidewalk and flipped, skating on its side.

I could hear my blood screaming in my ears. Pain shot up my right side. That's when I flew through the black hole.

27

I woke up to brightness: The jarring intensity of hospital lights and the static glare of my Anais' eyes. I blinked a response to her demanding, frightened gaze. She opened her mouth. I imaged sound leaving her throat but somewhere between her mouth and my ears the sound died.

I stared and I blinked. That's all I could do.

She left the room and came back with a nurse. My head was as heavy as a truck. I could not lift it up. Sun's long tantalizing rays crept through the window and I couldn't even move my head towards the warmth.

The nurse whispered something to Anais and withdrew from the room. Anais sat on the bed and took my hand in hers, her smile wavering between worry and relief.

Anais began to speak and though I was aware that she was speaking to me her words seemed stuck in some tunnel beneath me because I wasn't really hearing her clearly. All I could do was respond with a smile.

She kept talking until the nurse returned with a doctor. The doctor's gown was mint white and for some reason I wondered if this was her first day on the job. She proceeded to prod my eyelids open peering into them with a point of light. Unexpectedly, my mind circled back to a speech made by a former president about a thousand points of light. I laughed out loud and everyone was startled.

Anais began to cry. The doctor patted my wife's shoulder as if to say everything would be all right. That's when I felt the searing headache and closed my eyes.

Day 1 in the hospital:

I'd been unconscious for about 3 hours after the accident. Anais had gotten a call from the police and rushed to the hospital, arriving minutes after they wheeled me in on a stretcher.

Keeping that old Volvo around might've saved my life. I'd escaped the accident with a cut on my brow, a bruised knee and a concussion but no broken bones. Because of the concussion the doctors decided to keep me hospitalized for further observation. I called Noah and River. Left a message for my father. Didn't bother to call my mother as she was coming back in a few days and I didn't want to spoil what was left of her vacation.

Day 2:

Up and walking around. Tests in the morning. Results inconclusive. Want to go home. Doctors order more tests. I say no. Anais said yes. I dare not argue with her.

Noah and River come to visit. No word from my father.

Day 3.

More tests. The first tests come back negative. The headaches should go away in a few days, the doctors tell me. I call my father again. Still no word from him. Where the hell could he be? Afternoon discharge. Anais picks me up around 2:30 in the afternoon.

Anais was tight-lipped throughout the ride home and her face no longer housed the concern I'd seen in the hospital but had become stern and matriarchal. I could feel a lecture coming.

"How's the Volvo?" I asked.

"The Volvo? You should be concerned with how I am," she replied.

I knew what she meant and couldn't fashion a plausible response.

"Why were you driving so fast?" she said.

"Who told you I was driving fast?"

"Police figured you were going about seventy-five."

"That's impossible."

"That's highway speed."

"I wasn't doing more than fifty." I said.

She looked at me, incredulous. "Why were you driving that fast?"

I had no explanation and was smart enough to keep my mouth shut.

The doctors said I should take it easy for a while but after two hours lying around the house my head started hurting again. I wanted to have a beer but Anais' hawk eyes had me covered at all times. The doctor had given me strict orders not to drink for a few days. I called River and told her I needed a ride to Georgia Avenue Gardens.

River picked me up around 6:30. Wearing a long black leather coat and black gloves, she looked like she'd just stepped off the set of Shaft. Swelling around my knee made walking difficult. After getting into her truck I flexed it several times to loosen it up.

River's face was tighter than a drum all the way across Empire Boulevard.

"Why're you so serious?" I tried to joke.

"Don't mess with me, Blades."

"What's up with you?"

"Were you trying to kill yourself the other day?"

"I swear. Suicide was not on my mind that day."

"Well, something was on your mind. Either that or you're a worse driver than I thought."

"I was testing the roll-bar safety feature on the Volvo."

"You know what, Blades. You ain't even funny."

We stopped at a Caribbean restaurant on Empire Boulevard. River stayed in the truck while I went inside to order a plate of ox-tails and rice.

I hobbled back to the truck where River was screaming into the phone. With some difficulty I pulled myself up into the seat. I heard Negus' name mentioned and assumed she was beefing with Komi. I waited impatiently for the fight to end.

She shifted her eyes to mine as she hung up. "What's wrong now?"

"Nothing," I said.

"Why you look so bothered?"

"Can we go?"

She rolled away from the curb. "You don't even know if he's there."

"He's there."

"What makes you so sure?"

"He sleeps there. Now stop grilling me. It's giving me a headache."

She looked at me, confused. "Don't get tight with me? I'm part of this investigation, too, you know. In case you forgot. Shit! You got a problem with me asking you questions?"

"As a matter of fact, I do."

"To hell with you, Blades. I ain't just following you around because you look good. If I see you doing something that don't make sense I'm a call you on it. That's how I am. Get used to it. You afraid of a strong black woman, eh?" She laughed.

"I'm afraid of clichés," I replied

"Really? There's no bigger cliché than your Big Chief Cochise act? You don't automatically get to run things because you got pipe, you know. The problem with this fucking country is that most men seem to believe that. And you've been acting that way. Not sharing information. Calling me when you want me to do shit but getting all hot and bothered when I dare to ask what's going on. What's that about?"

I was silent for the rest of the trip. She was right. I couldn't argue. This was happening to me way too often. First Anais, and now River shutting me down with airtight arguments. Maybe I was nothing but a cliché.

Ten minutes later we curbed across from the park and got out. Light breeze stirring from the south. Street real quiet. Too quiet. And the park seemed unusually bright. Too bright.

Some activity near the entrance. Candles at a makeshift altar. A few people milling around the burning candles.

A darkened squad car was parked a few yards away.

Before we crossed the street I said, "I'm sorry if I've appeared too self-absorbed."

"It's alright, Blades. Just don't start acting like you got some kinda control over me."

We ambled across the wide street with a little more space between us than usual. That's when I saw the yellow police tape blocking the mouth of the park. We were approaching a crime scene.

A woman peering through the iron fence surrounding the park hawked and spat into the creviced sidewalk. She was very short, no more than 5 feet. River walked up to her and said hello. The woman turned around to see who was addressing her. She had a dark flat face, no ridges or curves, even her nose seemed to be on the same plane as the rest of her face. Her neck was decorated with gold jewelry.

"What's going on?" River said. "Why the cops got the park on lock down?"

"Nigga got shot. What you think?"

"I was supposed to meet a friend in the park," River said

"Not this park. Not tonight." The woman laughed, but it was an unhappy laugh.

"Do you know who got shot?" I said.

The woman flashed scorn at me, her face becoming immediately impenetrable as if the thoughts she had been forming had simply vaporized. She hawked and spat at my feet, then walked away.

"What the hell was that?" I said, more to myself than anything else.

"You still got that male supremacy cop shit going on," River said.

"What?"

"You got the look of tyranny, Blades. It's like shit on your face. You can't hide it."

"That's bullshit."

"Then I guess it must be your night to piss off the female gender."

I strolled over to the squad car. The officers must've seen me coming because the window on the passenger side rolled down as I got there.

A pasty-faced young cop, his good-guy smile plastered across his face, stuck his head outside. "Hey Pardna, what's up?"

"Hey, name's Blades."

"Can I help you?"

"I was supposed to meet a friend in the park."

The smile faded. "There's nobody in the park."

"Who got tagged?"

"No ID as far as we know. Just some old homeless dude that nobody cared about. Probably won't get ID'd. Potter's field will be his next home."

I heard him laugh as I turned away.

I walked back to the car thinking of what the cop had said about the old man being Potters Field's next resident. I thought about Jersey. And I thought of the pain of imagined lives which was at the core of this city's mythology.

So many people come chasing dreams; so many end up hiding from nightmares. Too broken to leave. Too tired to drag themselves out of town. Too drugged or afraid to dream anymore.

28

There were no names on the doorbells so I rang both 1A and 1B. After a few minutes of waiting I jammed my finger on them again.

River glanced at me, her face tight. "Relax, Blades. Somebody's coming."

Seconds later an old woman appeared at the door shaking her head.

You could tell she must've been an extraordinarily beautiful woman when she was younger. Her lineless face still held the mystery of youthfulness though her eyes had that New York City restlessness that came from mistrust and sleepless nights.

She cracked the door and stuck her head out. "Yes?"

"My name is Blades Overstreet. This is River Paris."

"Hello Mrs. Eversley," River said.

The old woman smiled. "Hello. I remember you."

"Yes," River said. "We spoke a few days ago. How are you today?"

"I'm doing alright. Just watching Law and Order on TV."

"Do you know an old man who hangs out in the park across the street. Goes by the name of Jersey?" I said.

Her face became passive, her eyes questioning, and she did not answer right away. "Are you a police officer?" she said finally.

"No. I'm a friend of his," I said. "Do you know him?"

"I should. He used to be my husband."

I glanced sideways to River and then back to the woman. ""When was the last time you saw him?"

She tugged at the front of her grubby green sweater. "Come in."

From under her disheveled hat, I could see silver curls creeping out. She moistened her lips and stepped back from the door to let us in.

We followed her a short distance along a dim corridor lit with a flickering florescent bulb. Wouldn't be long before that shit conked out. Mrs. Eversley stopped in front of apartment 1A. She had left the door unlocked.

We walked into a large room with an orchid-themed decoration. The red curtains painted with white orchids seemed homemade. The volume on the television was up high. Law and Order was wrapping up. Mrs. Eversley walked over and turned the set off.

"Sit down," she said, bundling herself into a yellow recliner.

River and I settled on the couch.

"How long were you divorced?" River said.

"Over twenty years. Though you wouldn't think so the way he behaved. And I'd kicked him out five years before that. He wasn't right in the head. Even after the divorce he still wouldn't accept that I didn't want him back. That fool refused to go on with his life. Set up house in the park across the street and decided he wouldn't go anywhere unless I came with him."

"Maybe he was just crazy in love," River said.

"Crazy is right. But just plain crazy. If he was really in love he would've done the things he needed to do to keep me, not drive me away."

"But you let him come here to take a shower," I said.

"After a while he became pitiful. I felt sorry for him. His sister came and put him in the hospital but he ran away. His family washed their hands of him after that. I even offered to get him help. He say all he needed was me. He wasn't a bad person. He never hit me or anything like that. He just didn't know how to get himself right in this world."

"Did you let him sleep here?" River said.

"When it got too cold. I'd let him sleep on the floor. He was so used to sleeping on the ground he couldn't sleep in a bed."

I said. "Is there any other place he'd be other than the park?"

"Not that I'm aware of."

"He said he was a musician," I said. "Played with Miles and Mingus."

Mrs. Eversley laughed. "Played along with their records is more like it. He wasn't that good. He tried out for Mingus and got rejected. I don't know if that sent him over the edge."

"Do you remember the last time you saw him?"

She took off her hat and set it on her lap. "Not since the night he had that argument with the police officer."

"What night was that?" I said.

"Maybe a week or more."

"Was it the night your upstairs neighbor Lourdes was killed?" River said.

Her back straightened. "You said, 'was killed'?"

"Yes. We believe she was murdered," River said.

"Oh my! We were told she committed suicide."

"That's what everybody thought," I said.

She squirmed and her expression became agonized. "Who did it?"

"We don't know. You said Jersey had an argument with a police officer?" I said.

"That's what he said. He was outside the building and asked the officer for a cigarette."

"Did you see them? The cops that night?" I said.

"No," she said.

"Do you eat oxtails?" I asked. "I brought a plate for Jersey. Be a shame for it to waste."

"You can leave it here. I'll give it to him if he comes by. Or tomorrow when I go out."

I handed her the bag. She handled it as if it were a sodden piece of cloth or a bomb.

We followed her back to the entrance, saying thank you at the door before watching it close after us. River pulled out her pack of Marlboro's and lit a cigarette.

"He's dead," She said, matter-of-factly.

I didn't reply. Truth is I was thinking the same thing.

A ballet of red rear lights danced ahead of us along Eastern Parkway. River kept glancing into the rearview mirror with an intense look on her face. At Kingston Avenue she jammed the gas, blasting past a black Mercedes barely negotiating around a van, and just merging into traffic by a horse's hair.

"Hey, take it easy," I said.

Her nostrils flared. "I think we're being followed."

I shifted to peek into the side mirror.

"Black Escalade," she said, excitedly.

"You sure? That's not an inconspicuous vehicle to tail somebody."

"I can't vouch for the intelligence of the driver, but we're being followed."

"When'd you pick it up?"

"Back at Broad Street."

We came to a red. River slowed down and tailed around a compact into the outer lane, but instead of stopping she throttled the accelerator. With a burst of power the truck slashed across traffic making a sharp right turn and onto a narrow side street.

"Shit!" I exclaimed.

She turned to me her eyes wild. "See if the muthafucker can top that."

"You must be crazy!"

"Not even close."

"Think you should let me drive. I wanna get home in one piece."

"You? Drive my truck? After what you did to your car. You gotta be on some weird shit to think I'd let you at my baby. Besides, do you still have a license?"

I couldn't help but laugh.

She checked the rearview mirror again. "I don't see him."

We slid quickly down the dark quiet street. I looked out the window to see where we were. A hushed street yawned before us.

"What street is this?"

"I this it's Ralph," she said.

We seemed to have crossed onto the set of The Twilight Zone. Not a spark of life on the street. Darkened apartment buildings. Empty lots. A few houses here and there. Not even a stray dog roaming. Steam rose around the rim of a manhole cover. Everywhere black.

We drove in silence for about five minutes before River pulled over and killed the engine. We were on a block of darkened warehouses. The hum of fear swelled in my head. I didn't like the idea of stopping if indeed someone out there was trying to find us.

"Why're we parked?"

"It may not have seemed that way, cause I did it so smooth, but that move I made back there was pretty stressful. I need a cigarette."

River rolled her window down before lighting up. After taking a few deep puffs she tossed the burning stick into the street.

"Who do you think would be following us?" River said.

"I don't know. Assuming somebody was following us."

"I know when I've picked up a tail, Blades."

I laughed. "You know how to pick up a tail, I'll give you that much. I've seen the tail on Komi."

"You're really a nut job."

"Take me home to my wife," I said.

She rolled up her window. Before she could kick the ignition I heard the heavy vroom of an engine roaring toward us. A sudden blaze of headlights. Instinct propelled me into action. I ducked my head. Next came the crash of glass and the reverberating *pop-pop-pop* of gunfire as I frantically tried to open the passenger side door.

I scrambled outside, rolling onto the sidewalk with River right behind me. My bowels coiled and uncoiled with dread as I groped for my gun.

But the vehicle didn't stop. It kept on going.

I looked at River as the distant echo of the powerful engine reminded us of how close we'd come to being tagged.

"Let's go," I said.

Next morning Anais and I finished breakfast around 9:30. With a maternal tap on my shoulder she got up and began clearing dishes from the table. I drew her to me.

Beneath her terrycloth robe she was naked. We'd made love before breakfast and she hadn't bothered to dress. Her breasts hung heavy like dark mysterious fruit. Legs trim and muscular from dance classes which she took two or three days a week. She eased herself into my lap, her smile sprinkled with seduction. I felt a stirring in my loins. So this was why she hadn't bothered to get dressed. I hadn't satisfied her this morning.

The phone rang. Anais picked up. Chesney calling from Newark airport. Anais handed the phone to me. The weak cell phone connection made Chesney's voice sound as if she was dipping in and out of a tunnel.

I felt myself swell inside, my stomach going soft as waves of emotion swept through me. Despite the difficulty making out what she was saying, hearing my daughter's voice was pure joy. I had missed her beyond description. Like the night misses the moon, I told her. She giggled at my corniness.

A momentary break and then I heard my mother's voice on the line. I desperately wanted to ask her about that night I saw my father standing over her with a gun in his hand but realized that right then wasn't the time. We spoke briefly and I hung up.

Anais must've picked up something in my tone because her expression changed immediately. Her eyes, a minute ago filled with the spark of sexual possibility, had quickly lost their soft edge. A revolt had occurred. The minute I rang off she pinned me to the mat.

"What's going on between you and your mother?"

"What do you mean?"

"Your face changed when she got on the phone."

"Changed how?"

"I don't know. It got strange. Like you had thoughts tangled up in your head that you didn't want me to hear."

"If you don't make it in acting," I said, "you should try your hand at psychotherapy."

Her index finger poking hard into my chest. "Don't patronize me, Blades."

"There's nothing going on, Anais. I'm just tired and in pain."

"You weren't in pain last night when you were out playing cop with that woman."

"I was in pain then too. Just didn't cry out hard enough for you to hear."

"Well, that's your problem, isn't it?"

"I love you, dear. But sometimes, you do get on my nerves."

She got up from the table. I thought she would kiss me but she just wrapped her robe around her body and disappeared up the stairs.

I took a cue from my wife's questioning and decided to spend the morning trying to untangle my thoughts. The thing was I didn't know where to begin. These flashes of memory had awakened a hunger in me. And anyone who's been hungry knows it's the hardest sensation to ignore. The need to know, the hunger to unravel secrets can encircle you with the raw power of dreams. The only therapy for ignorance was knowledge. And I needed to know the true nature of my parent's relationship. How did it affect me? And how much of it had I forced into a dark corner somewhere in my mind.

I was tired of lying awake at night feeling that dark glaring eye searching my soul. I was tired of feeling as though I was sweating, not outside but inside my body. I wanted to wake up from this nightmare.

I found the number Anais had given me for the therapist in Park Slope and called without hesitating. If I thought about it much more I knew I would've changed my mind. Again. The receptionist took my personal information and told me the earliest appointment would be in two weeks. I said yes and hung up feeling remarkably relieved.

29

He met me at the door wearing a white open-necked cotton shirt and crimpled black pants. I shook his hand and limped passed his dry smile, leaving a terse "Hi Pops" for him to ponder. I turned the corner at the end of the hallway and into the living room where I flopped into an antique mahogany settee.

Following me into the cozy room, my father stood a few steps away from the television, his face puzzled. My attitude should've made it clear that I was not here to view his latest masterpiece in charcoal or oil or whatever medium he was working in these days, nor his collection of antiques.

My eyes drifted across the room. He'd acquired a few new pieces since my last visit, including the chair I was sitting in. The two shiny walnut bookcases on either side of me were also new.

At some point during the twenty-odd years my father was unofficially missing he'd acquired a thing for antiques. And since his return he has added collecting New York City memorabilia to his list of leisurely pursuits. The latter left me shaking my head and wondering about his sanity or at the very least, his good taste.

A massive nighttime shot of the Empire State Building commanded the wall over an unused fireplace. It seemed odd to me, perhaps even corny, for my father—once a renegade for revolution—to have a poster which represented the virtues of the establishment so prominently displayed in his living room.

"So where were you?" I said.

"North Carolina. Went down to check out a couple of warehouses."

"Warehouses?"

"Antique furniture. The south is good for antiques because of the plantations. Much of the furniture is still floating around. Most of it European designs."

We lapsed into silence, amplified by the forlorn look in his eyes.

"Are you okay?" He said.

"My knee hurts."

"Other than that, you're okay?"

I heard the thudding toll of a bell somewhere in the neighborhood. For some reason being here and getting to the point of my visit was proving to be very difficult.

"The doctor said I had a concussion." I said.

"How did it happen? The accident."

"I was driving too fast."

"In a hurry. That's always been a part of your personality."

"How would you know?"

If he was surprised by my response he didn't show it. He simply nodded his head in an I-have-it-all-under-control way. The way I remember him nodding many times when the police came to our house to ask questions about his Black Panther activities.

"I wasn't always absent, you know. I did raise you until you were fifteen. I do know a little something about you. And I know this. You were built for speed. That's why you preferred basketball and football. Power and speed. When you were twelve this kid from the neighborhood challenged you to a race around Long Meadow. He was older than you. Fifteen, I think he was. Remember that?"

"Vaguely."

"You whipped his butt pretty good. Left him by about ten yards."

"Guess you and I are both good at leaving people in the dust."

"No need to go there, Carmen."

"I was just complimenting your athletic ability," I said.

He laughed. "Yeah. Of course. You want a drink?"

I pulled myself up. "No, I wasn't really planning to stay long. I just wanted to see you. To say... I called when I was in the hospital and you never called back."

"You just got here, Blades."

"Don't wanna overstay my welcome," I said.

"Don't be silly. Come on. Sit down. Have a drink."

"I really should go."

"I know there's something on your mind."

I said nothing.

He reached for a nervous smile, but let it slip away after a few seconds. "I could tell the minute you walked in. You looked like you had come to execute a search warrant."

"I'm not in humorous mood, Pop."

"I'm sorry you feel so tormented, son. I wish I could help you."

"Well... Actually, you can."

"What?" He smoothed his hand over his scalp. "Is this about me and your Mom again?"

I said nothing.

"Don't you have anything better to do with your time, Carmen?" He turned away and when he looked at me again his eyes were drawn deep into his head. "Come on, son. Don't pick up that shitty stick again."

"What am I supposed to do, Pop?"

"I don't know. But I don't see the point of dragging up that muck."

"Easy for you to dismiss, isn't it?"

His voice flattened with a sigh. "How far down do we have to go, Carmen, before we can look each other in the face and feel like we belong in the same room together?"

"That's up to you."

"And you have no part in the transition?"

"Do you have any idea what it was like all those years not knowing? Not knowing if you were alive? Not knowing why you abandoned us?"

"And do you have any idea what it's like not knowing if I was going to wake up and find somebody with a knife to my throat?"

"You could've called once to say you were okay," I snapped back.

"I'm sorry. I can't say it any better than that. I'll say it as often as you need to hear it, but at some point you're going to have to believe me."

"There was a time when I came into the kitchen and you were leaning on Mom against the fridge. You had a gun. Remember that?"

His eyes widened. "Come, son."

My voice rose hesitantly. "Do you remember that?"

"I don't remember."

"You're a liar. You tried to kill her."

"This concussion seems to have tilted your brain past crazy."

"Nothing's wrong with my brain. I was there. I remember."

He turned to walk away. Instinctively I grabbed his arm. In an instant he brushed my hand away. Probably reflex. But the effect on me was cataclysmic. I stuck my hand in his chest, pushing him violently. He grabbed my arm and pulled me toward him. This only incensed me further. We stumbled to the fireplace and my head struck the wall. My hands flew up to his neck and closed around his throat, my fingers burrowing into his tightened muscles, squeezing hard.

He groaned. "What're you gonna do, Carmen? Kill me?"

I released him and stepped back, breathing hard. My knee buckled from the tension and I slumped to the floor.

He walked around me the way a bullfighter parades around a beaten bull before finishing him off. I could feel his shadow over me. I must've looked pitiful. I felt pitiful. What the hell did I just do?

Reaching down he grabbed me firmly by the elbow and lifted me up. We eyed each other square on, no more than a few inches apart. I could see the tiny rucks in his face left over from the chicken pox he'd contracted as a teen. His face was closed with a look of exhaustion. As if he'd retracted into a shell.

An ugly pain scatted up the back of my leg. I felt as if I was going to fall. Then my father put his arms around me and hugged me.

Tears crowded behind my eyelids. Sounds lumped in my tight throat. I tried to squeeze everything back. My father's arms wrapped around me. Tears broke loose and tumbled down my cheek. But at least I was crying silently.

It took me about five minutes to pull myself together. I don't know what my father was thinking because he said nothing. The weird thing was that I wanted him to hold me. It felt strange but necessary.

After a while he released me and stepped away. "I can deal with your anger as long as you don't try to choke me again. You're too strong for me. But if you really wanna know what happened between me and your mother that day, ask her. And that's all I'm gonna say about it."

30

Around 7 P.M. I arrived at Diego Ercolo's gallery on 27th Street. Earlier in the day, Mr. Ercolo had called. I'm in the telephone book. Said he had information which might help me find the judge's killer.

The place was crowded and he was nowhere in sight when I got there so I walked around trying to make sense of some of the art on the walls. I was having a very hard time of it until my second glass of wine. Then I stopped caring.

The gallery occupied the top floor of an old building in Chelsea, once a thriving Hispanic neighborhood. Much of the poor Hispanic population were displaced when gays moved in during the '80s, bringing art, chic restaurants and theater, making it cool to live in Chelsea. The buzzards of gentrification followed: lawyers, investment bankers and young executives, whose real interest was the escalating property values.

It was hot and bright in the gallery. No one was looking at the art on the walls. Can't say I blamed them. The large number of mostly white men clung together in asymmetrical groups, chatting and laughing in between sips of wine from plastic glasses. White light smashed white walls. Camera bulbs flashed. Were they here for the Dali Shoe exhibit or for the drinks? Were they amused by the Epdidymus installation—an innocuous video of someone's scrotum sac—or to discuss the latest stock market trends? Did they know that the entire process of sperm formation to maturation is estimated to take about 72 days, information served up on the card under the display? Did anybody care?

As folks buzzed around the strange installations I stood by the window sipping wine. Frankly, I found the bustle down on 9th Avenue far more interesting where trucks and vans came and left the U-Haul depot with regularity. Friday must be a good day for moving.

Lightning flicked its tail across New York and then slunk back in the darkness. Seconds later, thunder rattled the night. I felt a hand on my shoulder and looked around. Diego Ercolo stood smiling like a man who'd been promised 27 virgins.

His tan suit was a cut below designer level but expensive enough. Too much splish-splash with the cologne, however; it had a musky bitter smell. Burned my nose like incense.

He extended his hand. "Mr. Overstreet."

I absorbed his overpowering handshake. Too strong. A sign of insecurity.

"Mr. Ercolo."

"Did you take a look around?"

"Yes, I did."

"What do you think of the exhibit? Truthfully."

I tried to be polite. "I really don't know."

Combing three fingers through his thick hair. "You don't know? That's so boring. You can hate it, but please don't be boring. We're not showing sitcoms here. Art is supposed to stir your passions. Whether it be anger or pain. Or love. Art should get under your skin. It should provoke you. Only humans can appreciate art, Mr. Overstreet. You know why? Emotion. We get a rush, a release of pleasure when we encounter something beautiful: the brightness of a color, the variation in the use of language. It's that human ability to have an emotional response which makes art spectacular. It's what makes art important."

"What kind of emotion does watching a video of a man's balls stir in you?" I asked.

His eyes slid like oil off my face. "You hated it, but that's okay. Next time, say so."

"Maybe it's not art to me."

He smiled. "That's fine. Come, let's go into my office."

His office was at the back of the gallery away from the noise and commotion of the exhibition. This was where he hid the more conventional art, including some Chuck Close prints. He waited for me to enter then closed the door.

The noise from the party outside disappeared as a talon of white lightning clawed at the window with a muffled savageness, lingering in the air for several seconds, as if God was trying to send a message about what He thought of the art inside.

Diego went to the window and peeked out. "Looks like a storm."

"You said you had some information for me," I said.

He turned around. "Yes." Reaching into his pocket he pulled out a pack of Camels. "Mind if I smoke?"

I shook my head.

He sat behind an uncluttered antique-looking desk which had the sheen of a well-groomed pet. "Have a seat, Mr. Overstreet."

I sat in a chair opposite the desk, facing him.

He lit a cigarette, took a deep drag and blew a thick cloud of gray smoke into the air. Leaning back in the chair as if thinking hard on something. "You know, the great thing about this country is the opportunities it gives you to remake yourself. Over and over. Or even to get lost."

"I don't want to curb your desire to wax philosophical, Mr. Ercolo, but as you pointed out, a storm's brewing. I'd like to get going before the storm comes."

"I'm Argentinean. As is Maria… Mrs. Foder. The difference is: I was born there. She wasn't. She was born in Germany. Her father was a member of the Nazi party. My mother worked in their home in Argentina. I used to visit the house with my mother. That's how I got to know Maria… Mrs. Foder. When we met here, she didn't remember me until I reminded her that I was the boy who used to hide behind the maid's skirts whenever she was around. She was already in her twenties. I must've been no more than twelve or so. But even at that age I recognized her incredible beauty. Don't you think she's a beautiful woman, Mr. Overstreet? Even now in her sixties. The most beautiful woman I've ever seen."

"You said her father was a Nazi?"

"Yes. He fled to Argentina at the end of World War Two. Maria was about four, I guess, when they came. They lived in a villa near the sea. She was his only child. His wife had died during the trip across the Atlantic. He never remarried. When Maria left to come to the States it crushed him. He died not long after. Crushed me too. It was a week before my fourteenth birthday. I thought I would never see her again.

"How did you find out about her father? I can't imagine he flaunted his former life."

"He changed his name and created a new life for himself in Argentina, but couldn't let go of his past. He kept pictures of himself in his Nazi regalia hidden in a vault in the basement. Somehow my mother found them and after he died she took them. I don't know why. I suspect she was secretly in love with him. She was impressed by his art collection, most of which was probably stolen. I found the pictures many years later in our attic."

"And you came here looking for Maria."

"Yes and no. I came primarily to go to law school. But I did try to find her. She was already married by then. And even more beautiful than ever. The irony of course was that she was married to a Jew."

"What happened when you got here?"

He blinked. "I tried to get close to her, yes. I became her lawyer. But she kept her distance. All that changed a few years ago when I was hired by Miss Rose to represent her in a transaction involving a great sum of money."

I sat straight up. "Are you talking about Odessa Rose?"

He leaned away with a deep sigh. "Yes. I rue the day I met the woman."

"Go on."

"Unfortunately, I wasn't completely professional. I'd borrowed a lot of money to open the gallery and was in great debt. I took some of Miss Rose's money to tide me over."

"You stole from her? I hope for your sake she didn't find out."

"Oh, but she did. She sent some thugs to teach me a lesson. One particular guy, not very big, but I could see in his eyes that he enjoyed hurting people. That he would've gotten even more pleasure killing me. He was particularly fond of hitting me in the genital area. They stripped me naked and he held my scrotum in his hands and squeezed them until I passed out. When I awoke they threatened to kill me if I went to the police. Ms. Rose sent me flowers the next day. And came to my house with chocolates. I didn't even know she knew where I lived. I offered to repay the money but that's not what she wanted."

"What did she want?"

"She wanted a judge. I told her I didn't know any judges who would take bribes."

"Are you kidding me?"

He chuckled. "I knew a few but after that experience I wouldn't have let her near my worst enemy. This woman is a piranha. I thought of going to the police. But I still hadn't paid her back her money and even if I cooperated with the police I was sure to get disbarred for what I did. That night an idea came to me. I saw a way to give Miss Rose what she wanted. To get her off my back. And a chance to get me what I wanted."

"You gave her judge Foder."

"Yes."

"How did you know he'd flip?"

He ground the stub of his cigarette into a bronze ashtray and lit another one. After the first puff he smiled. His eyes dwindled to nothing. "The judge had a reputation to uphold. He gave money to many Jewish organizations including the Simon Wiesenthal Center where I think he was on the board. I told Miss Rose about Maria's background. I was pretty sure Maria hadn't told him about her father. If word got out that he was married to the daughter of a Nazi, I suspected it would've been very embarrassing."

"And you thought that when he found out his wife had lied, he would leave her."

"Yes. And it happened exactly that way. Miss Rose got her judge. You see, Maria had not only lied to her husband, but on her visa application as well. She'd also lied about being born in Argentina. She'd lied about who her father was. The judge and Maria separated. Though it was brief."

"And did she come running to you?"

His smile was as hollow as a riddle. "She was distraught and upset about the whole thing. I consoled her for as long as she allowed."

"Didn't she suspect that you might've been behind the revelation?"

"Why should she? As far as she knew I had no idea who her father was."

"Then why're you telling me this story?"

"Because, Mr. Overstreet, I'm afraid for my life. I believe my house is being watched and I'm being followed. Ms Rose wouldn't hesitate to do me harm if she felt I was cooperating with the police."

"Are you?"

"No. That's why I called you. She's got spies everywhere, even in the police department."

"Did Odessa kill judge Foder?"

"Why else would she be following me?"

"You have proof?"

He stubbed his half-smoked cigarette. "No."

"How do I know Odessa is the only client you stole from? For all I know you killed judge Foder and figured if you can pin it on Odessa, you'd get two for the price of one. Get the judge out of the way. Odessa off your back. And you can get to live happily ever after with your obsession."

"She's not an obsession, Mr. Overstreet. You know nothing about love."

The conversation had clattered to a foggy silence. He stared at me, his cheeks whitened, the corner of his eyes laced with lines of bitterness and regret. Perhaps he was right. What the hell did I know about love? I'd only loved one woman and had come close to losing her a few years ago. Yes, I was a novice when it came to love.

"There's something else," he said.

"What's that?"

"Maria told me the judge had molested his own daughter when she was thirteen. That's how she got him to take her back. She threatened to go to the police."

"Let me get this straight. She blackmailed her husband by using his abuse of his daughter?"

"They're a strange family with enough secrets to sink a sub."

I got up and he did the same. We shook hands and he escorted me to the elevator. The crowd had overflowed the gallery into the tight hallway near the elevator bank. As I waited, the din of small talk became deafening. I decided to take the stairs.

31

I arrived at the morgue in the basement of Kings County Hospital around ten-thirty. Sipping coffee from a Styrofoam cup, I waited for the attendant to finish his telephone conversation.

A fleshy man scotched on an office chair behind a thick Plexiglas screen, talking on the phone. He spoke angrily in a foreign language, perhaps one of the Eastern European languages and his loud voice was beginning to get on my nerves. I tried to think of something else.

When was the last time I'd been here? Couldn't even remember. A damn good thing, too. Trust me, there are no Kodak moments waiting to happen in the morgue. Luckily, as a narco, I dealt with few dead bodies, other than those way-past-redemption twisters whose brains had been so fried by crack or heroin they drew breath by accident. But what a drab place! Cold and cramped. Just looking at the bare green walls brought on feelings of nausea.

The attendant finally got around to me. He spoke through the ten-inch square cut-out in the Plexiglas. I asked him if anybody had identified the body of an old man brought in two nights ago from Georgia Avenue Garden in East New York. He typed into the computer. Seconds later he told me that a woman had identified the man as Richard Eversley.

"Who was the woman?" I asked.

"Dorothy Eversley. His ex-wife."

"Can I see the body?"

"You the police or a relative?"

"No, Just a friend."

He looked to be in his forties, a man who ate too much and sat on his butt too long. His voice was so deep it made his stomach quiver. Not a pretty sight.

He said, "Sorry, but I can't do that."

"I bet you have a family." I said. "Lots of friends. Richard Eversley wasn't so lucky. He didn't have much family. And I'm as close a friend as he had."

"Sometimes life tough with family," he said. "I run from Chernobyl. Find job here. Think it will be easy. Get wife. Two kids. Now life very hard."

"Two kids, huh. How old?"

"Four and six."

I pulled two twenties from my wallet and put them on the Plexiglas ledge near his reach. "I'm sure your kids could use a new toy. A video game, maybe."

His gaze trailed from the money to my face. His fist close around the 40 bucks and then he buzzed me through the electronic door. He led me a short distance down a wide corridor into a freezing room with rows of compartments in the wall. He glanced at a sheet of paper in his hand as he walked along the line of compartments.

He stopped and pulled one of the slots open. Jersey's body was stretched out on a slab, his mouth slightly open in surprise, his eyes half closed. There was a hole in his forehead. From the size I'd say exit wound. Death had been quick, it appeared. Almost instantaneous.

"Thanks," I said to the attendant.

Silently he pushed the slab back and closed the compartment. He glanced at me while we walked back. "Nobody claimed the body, you know."

"His ex-wife didn't?"

"She just ID for police."

"Maybe she'll come back," I said.

The attendant opened the door to his cubicle. "Maybe that's hopeful thinking."

"Wishful thinking, " I corrected.

He smiled. "That too."

I thanked him and made my way back to the light outside.

The feeling of wanting to retch stayed with me all the way home. Who would want to burn an old man living off the embers of an old romance? It made no sense. Was it possible that he could've identified Lourdes' killer or killers? Who were the two men he tangled with that night? Real cops or imposters? And how was I going to find them?

I never did get around to calling Odessa to tell her I'd decided not to accept her offer. Somehow, I doubt she'd really expected to hear from me. She never called either to get an answer, which was fine by me. The ambush River and I had escaped a few nights ago might've been a message, a sign of her displeasure. If so, my decision to go see her was risky, but that was exactly what I planned to do.

I thought briefly of calling River to cover my back. Remembering that feather-triggered temper of hers changed my mind. The wrong look in her direction, or the wrong word by any of Odessa's musclemen could provoke an incident.

It was about 9 P.M. when I got to the Pink Houses. The bustle in the brightly-painted lobby area was normal for the projects: animated young boys and girls entering and leaving, watched over by Odessa's cubs.

As I waited in the lobby for security to call up on the walkie-talkie, I took in the photographs and soaked up the mini biographies of famous African-American inventors decorating the yellow walls: Elijah McCoy, who invented an oil-dripping cup for trains, from which the term "The Real McCoy" was coined; George Washington Carver, inventor of peanut butter; Garret Morgan created the first traffic signal.

By the time I'd read all of the entries on the wall, walkie-talkie man had finished his consultation with his higher-up and came over to me. Too damn close. His breath crawled with garlic and his eyes seemed to be secreting some kind of oil.

"Follow me," he said.

The elevator wheezed to a halt on the top floor and we got off. My escort headed in the opposite direction of Odessa's apartment and the skin on my neck began to tingle with alarm. Where the hell was he going?

I followed silently, unbuttoning my jacket for quick access to my gun. I didn't know where he was taking me, but if he turned suddenly, I'd be ready.

At the end of the bright hallway he unlocked a door and held it open. I hesitated.

"She's on the roof," he said.

I paused for a moment. We stared at each other, measuring. I wanted to be sure he wasn't angling to get in back of me.

"Is she alone?" I said.

"Only one way to find that out, dawg."

Mounting the stairs, I passed him, encountering another closed door which I pushed open before stepping out onto the roof. The door closed, leaving me all alone.

A chill bustled across the rooftop and I buttoned my jacket. Two figures ahead of me near the edge of the roof. As I got closer I saw Odessa, seated in a high-back chair, and Mallet, her obedient puppy, standing a few feet to her left.

Mallet approached me, moving briskly, almost running. Without speaking he stuck his left hand in my chest to halt me. His black leather jacket was open. Tucked in his waist, I saw the flash of chrome, the butt slanted for easy grip.

"Hand over your gat," he mumbled.

I stepped back. "Not on your life."

He drew his gun and cocked it. "Give up the shit or step off."

"Mallet, relax," Odessa sang out. "The man ain't here to hurt me. You're here to start working for me, isn't that right, Mr. Overstreet?"

Mallet stared straight into my eyes and I felt my skin walk. I tried to keep my focus on the hacked out stone sockets of his eyes, but couldn't. I had to blink. The man was wound tighter than a slinky. It was painful to watch.

I stepped around him and walked to the edge of the roof.

"I'd like to talk to you," I said to Odessa.

"It's a pretty sight, isn't it?" She said.

I leaned against the wall facing her. "New York by night. Nothing like it."

"No, I meant Brooklyn at night."

I nodded though I knew she wasn't looking at me. Her eyes were still focused toward the expanse of blue-violet lights flickering across Brooklyn. Her head was wrapped in multi-colored African material which a Nigerian friend once told me was called a gele. Her clothes were of similar material and she was wearing plenty of it. She sat amid swirls of fabric in the large chair. Off to the side was a table covered with red cloth, a bottle of wine and two glasses rested on top; one glass half full, the other empty.

"Would you like your money up front or after?" she said.

"You know I'm not about that."

"You're either a very brave man or very foolish."

"I wonder myself sometimes."

She picked up the half-full glass. "So what did you learn from Mr. Ercolo last night?"

"He told me a very interesting story about how you bagged the judge."

"And did he also tell you that he tied the bag?"

"He said you tortured him."

She laughed. "Is that what he told you? I don't know why he's such a lousy lawyer; he certainly knows how to twist the truth with the best of them."

"What is the truth?"

"Would you like a glass of wine, Mr. Overstreet?"

I looked at the empty glass. "Were you expecting me?"

She picked up the empty glass and put it back down again. "I was expecting company but not you. Whenever I come out here to have a drink, I always bring a glass for the only man I've ever truly loved. His name was Reginald." She turned to Mallet, standing a few feet away. "Get Mr. Overstreet a glass from inside."

Mallet shuffled off toward the rooftop exit.

"What's with that one?" I gestured at the retreating Mallet. "What's his story? He always looks like he's auditioning for a Wes Crane movie."

"He's a little screwed up on account of seeing his mother strangled to death by his step-father. He doesn't trust many people."

"I understand he's got an obsession with other men's testicles."

"After his mother was killed he was placed in a foster home. One of the boys tried to fuck him. Mallet took a hammer to boy's nuts. That's how he got that name. You should get to know him. You might find the two of you have a few things in common."

"Such as?"

"Don't sound so offended, Mr. Overstreet. He may not have your refinements, but like you Mallet is a man of principle. If he gives you his word, it's as much as if he gave you his heart."

Mallet returned with a wine glass. He placed it on the table and retreated a few feet away standing at attention.

Odessa got up from her chair, poured wine into the glass and handed it to me. "Mr. Ercolo is playing you, Blades. You don't mind if I call you Blades, do you? He's trying to use you to get out from under his debts. He doesn't like paying his bills. That ain't how things work in America."

"How much money does he owe you?"

"What does it matter to you?"

"Just wondering."

"What? That he might've snatched the judge to pay me off? He doesn't have the guts for something like that. He's the kind of immigrant the conservatives don't mind letting in. White. Educated. Corrupt but not threatening. He, himself, is not a conservative but all his friends are Republican, if you get my drift. He's smart enough to figure how to work the system for his gain. With one thing in mind. Getting rich."

I sipped. "What's the difference between Mr. Ercolo and the other immigrants who make you rich?"

Her eyes constricted. "I just told you, muthafucker. White and educated. Five get you a thousand Mr. Ercolo didn't have a problem getting a green card. That's the difference between him and immigrants who come to me for help."

"And this is based on your intimate knowledge of his situation or just the color of his skin?"

She thumped my chest with her middle finger. "Don't try to get cute with me, alright."

I grabbed onto her wrist. Out of the corner of my eyes I saw Mallet move forward.

Odessa, either sensing his movement or knowing the type of dog she had, put up her hand to check his flow. "It's cool, Mallet."

Mallet stopped dead.

Boy, was he well-trained.

Odessa sat back down in her chair.

I breathed easier but my heart was racing. "Thought you liked to see immigrants succeed."

"You already know I choose my beneficiaries carefully. The ones who've already been manipulated by media propaganda are no use to me. Once they've been corrupted by white America's nasty ways, it's hard to re-educate them."

"Have you looked around you, lately? Taken a walk around this neighborhood? Seen all the wasted lives snuffed out by drugs and violence? We're as likely to get manipulated by the media as any immigrant. What're you doing to educate these people? I suspect they might need your help more than some of these immigrants. Are they a lost cause? Or is there no money to be made off them?"

"You're beginning to sound like them."

"Like who?"

"The Neo-conservatives and self-hating blacks. Next thing you're gonna say is that we should try to be more like the West Indians or the Koreans or whatever immigrant group that's doing the dance of docility. We will not swallow their stereotype just to make them comfortable. Why should we care if white people are comfortable? Why should any black person in America care if white people in this country ever get a good night's sleep? After what we suffered? Personally, I think they should thank their lucky stars that we don't slaughter them in their sleep. Does it bother me that black men rob and cheat and commit crime? Yes. But only because most of their victims are black people like themselves."

"Don't you think it's time we stop pounding away at phantoms?"

She jumped up, or at least tried to. She stumbled and lurched toward me, waving a finger in my face. "You wanna hear about phantoms, muthafucker? My man, Reginald, worked every day of his fucking life. Two jobs. Transit by day and when he left that job he came here and did maintenance for these buildings. Took the pursuit of the American Dream to bed at night. He fucked that bitch more than he fucked me. He'd seen this house in Canarsie he was gonna buy for me and the kids. One evening he was on the roof checking out a leak situation a tenant on the top floor had reported. The cops said somebody was robbed in the building and the perp ran onto the roof. They rushed up here, guns drawn. The only person they saw was Reginald. And those cowards bumrushed him. Now, Reginald was a big muthafucker. Cop or no cop you just don't run up on him. Gun or no gun. He musta whacked one of them. That'd be just like Reginald. And those weak, cowardly bitches threw him off the roof. Never got a day in jail. Justice for black people: Now there's your phantom."

Silence unfolded as her raw emotion settled like a mist around us. We were only a foot or so apart. I sipped my wine, trying to appear unmoved. I suspected I wasn't doing a very good job because I was shaking.

"I don't expect you to understand, Blades," she said, turning away, her voice laced with contempt and a bit of sadness. "You are a product of your environment, like the rest of us. We can't change who we are. You may think you are a black man. But when you look at your lily-white mother can you honestly tell me that you think like a black man?" She circled me in silence, then walked off to stand near the edge of the roof.

I was a hair's breadth away from saying something nasty. Where would that get me? What sense would it make pissing her off any further, knowing that her hungry cub was a few feet away waiting for a meal? Besides, I was there to get information not to engage her in a social debate.

I swallowed a mouthful of wine to wash the bile of anger out of my mouth. "How many men did Lourdes recruit for you?"

She didn't say anything for a minute. "Are you going to accuse me of killing her, too?"

"Did you?"

"I'm through talking to you. Get off my roof. And if you show your face around here again Mallet will have your nuts with his cereal."

She turned away from me back toward Brooklyn's lit up sky. I put my glass down and turned to leave.

"Blades…"

I stopped.

She staggered toward me. "You may have a personal dislike for me, but you can't deny that my work is necessary to even the playing field for non-white people in this country. The police can't pin the judge me. But it appears that he kept a record of our business transactions. Some kind of diary. I'd like to get my hands on it before the Feds do. Now, everybody has a price, Blades. Even you. Get me the diary and you can name yours."

"Don't expect any help from me," I said, walking away.

She called after me. "I'm not going to jail, you understand. Whatever the fuck I have to do, I will get that diary."

Mallet fell into step behind me. Halfway across the rooftop, I stopped and turned. "You want to lead the way?"

He opened his jacket and stuck his thumbs in his waistband so I could see his shiny toy. "Walk up, bitch."

"I don't want you behind me."

"You scared, bitch?" He taunted.

"How's your nose?" I countered. "Word's out on your homosexual tendencies."

"Did you just call me a fag?"

"Take your beef and shove it up your ass, Mallet. You can fantasize about sucking somebody else's dick."

He blinked and I knew I'd clotted his brain for the moment. By the time he'd figured out what I'd done to him I'd be long gone. I left him standing there and descended from the roof.

Outside, a large glossy moon crept from her hideaway. With her appearance Brooklyn's night life and secret operations would soon get underway.

32

There are some tastes that are just comfortable to your palate. For me it's rum, or curry. Then there are others, no matter how you treat them, spruce them up, you can never get comfortable with them. For me that would be anything creamy, like Fettuccini Alfredo. This was turning out to be my Fettuccini Alfredo case.

There was just nothing about this case to sink my teeth into. Everything seemed to have occurred in shadow. Even in a mind-your-own-business town like New York that's not as easy to do as you'd think. Who were these elusive police officers Jersey had seen entering Lourdes building? The police had still not found a match for that DNA found on Lourdes' body. Neither had they been able to find anyone who might've seen the judge's kidnappers transport him to that abandoned warehouse in Long Island City. Lourdes seemed to have lived the life of a secret agent. She had no boyfriend, but she had sex just before she was killed. What did it mean? Was she killed by a secret lover? And then there was that common thread to the two murders. The slippery Odessa. Would she make a mistake?

And then, just like that, the cream turned to cheese.

I was standing in the front yard watching Chesney ride her bike up and down the street when I got a call from River around 5 in the evening. The tension of winter had eased considerably and the day was warm enough for light jackets. Birds had appeared at my window that morning, rehearing for spring.

"Blades, you wouldn't believe what I've just seen?" River chirped.

"Knowing you, that's probably correct. Where are you?"

"Standing outside the Court Street bookstore in Boerum Hill."

"And what is it that's got you so excited?"

"Shaka."

"You've decided to seduce him?"

"Shut up and listen. Tris has been tailing Shaka the past few days."

"Who's Tris?"

"I swear, Blades, you're going senile. Tris is the young woman who works for me part-time. Check this. Up until now Shaka's lived a rather dull life. He goes to a trade school downtown. Some kind of electrician school. That's about all the activity for the past few days."

"How come you didn't tell me you had a tail on him?"

"I told you I was going to keep an eye on him."

"But you didn't tell me that…"

"Stop it, Blades. Stop trying to control everything. You wanna hear this or not?"

"I'm listening."

"Tris trailed Shaka to the cinema on Court. Fifteen minutes later a white woman shows up. They kiss and go inside. Tris calls me. From her description I think I know who the woman is. So I drive down there."

I checked to see where Chez was as an SUV came whistling down the block. "And who was it?"

Chez pulled over to the side of the street and I walked toward her.

"Zoe Foder," River said.

"Are you serious?"

"As a multi-orgasm."

I laughed out. "Where are they now?"

"After the movie they strolled down Court holding hands and right now they're in a restaurant across the street from the bookstore."

"It's time to pay Shaka another visit, don't you think?"

"I do love the view from that apartment."

I hung up and called to Chez. Playtime was over.

For about 2 hours we sat some fifteen yards from Shaka's apartment. River's CD player in the boot of the Expedition was racked with Prince's hits. Cuts from The Gold Experience had been playing for the past hour. During that time we saw our share of New York street dramas; enough to remind me that leaving the NYPD was the best thing I'd ever done.

About ten yards away we witnessed a pimp berate one of his whores, the threat of violence always imminent. I kept praying that he would not hit the woman, because I wouldn't have been able to stay put.

Gold Experience came to an end and Purple Rain kicked up with *Baby I'm A Star*. I banged out a few of the lyrics alongside Prince in my bad falsetto which had River bent over in stitches.

"If you don't stop, I'm going to pee myself," she laughed.

"You know you love it," I said.

"Seriously, Blades. You need to stop. You're ruining my moment with Prince here. I was psycho about Prince back in the day. This man got me in so many situations I couldn't control. Those slow jams? Pure sex."

A solid darkness had settled on the street. The only working streetlight was at the other end of the block. Light drizzling from the upstairs rooms of surrounding buildings and lamps on Nostrand provided the only illumination at this end of the street.

"Can't remember the last time I did something like this?" I said.

River lowered the volume on the stereo. "I don't get it. Why would a woman like that be interested in a loser like Shaka?"

"She's a damaged woman."

"What? Any more damaged than you or me?"

I looked at her. "You think I'm damaged?"

"Who isn't in some way?"

"There's damage and then there's damage."

"The way I see it, if you're fucked up, you'll do fucked up things. It doesn't matter what fucked you up." River opined. "My father didn't rape me, but he messed my head up. It's all the same. He taught me to hate. Trained me to kill. Who knows how much of my real self is buried under all that anger and shit that he poured into my soul. Am I really me?"

"I like you, whoever you are," I said.

River laughed. "That's because you're fucked up too."

"So you think that broken souls attract each other?"

"They'd better. Who else is gonna understand them?"

"You think that's what's going on with Shaka and Zoe?"

"Who knows. It's probably simpler than that. She probably caught the jungle fever. That's all it might be. Or she could be using Shaka. Got him to swipe her abusive father. See, I woulda done him myself."

I looked at her. "We can't choose our fathers, but that don't mean we should go around killing them off because we think they failed us."

A man turned onto the block, his head down and fists stuffed into the pockets of his bubble jacket.

River said, "There he is."

His head was covered by a black wool cap and he walked with purpose, neither glancing left nor right. We waited until he was halfway up the steps leading up to his door before getting out of the truck.

At a dead run we closed on him quickly. He turned around and his body stiffened in panic. His eyes got that deer-in-the-headlight look. I'd seen that look plenty. Suspects caught with vials of crack stuffed into their drawers developed it quicker than anyone.

Shaka was trapped between the urge to flee and considering the chances of getting inside his apartment before we reached him. To flee he'd have to get past us. Out of the question.

Without a plan B he fumbled with his keys in his haste to unlock his door. River and I gobbled up the steps three at a time, two bad wolves breathing down his neck. He managed to open the door, but before he could squeeze inside River grabbed him by the neck.

He didn't even bother to struggle. "Y'all ain't got nothing better to do?"

"What can I say, Shaka?" River started. "I have a thing for bangers who go around assuming the names of African princes."

Shaka snorted. "Hell, I bet you don't even like men. You a sushi eater, I can tell. Shit's written all over your face."

River said, "You're right, Shaka. I don't like men like you. But I'm glad to know that you can read. I bet you can even count to ten."

"Let's go upstairs?" I said.

"You two ain't welcome in my house."

River squeezed his neck tighter. "We ain't asking for an invitation, bitch."

I said. "Look, Shaka. We just wanna talk to you."

"That's what you said last time."

"I promise she won't touch you."

I nodded to River who released him.

He stood for a moment watching us, contemplating I don't know what. There was no escape. Shoulders slumped, he turned and led the way up the stairs to his apartment.

Inside he flicked on the light, took off his jacket and cap, dropped them on the floor and went to sit in the Zebra-striped love seat facing the window.

"What do you do for a living?" I said.

He grunted. "When did you start working for the census bureau?"

"Is she keeping you?" River said.

"What're you talking about?" Shaka sneered.

I said. "What's your relationship with Zoe?"

"Zoe who?"

River stepped forward.

I stuck out my arm to stop her from whacking him across the face.

"Look Shaka," I said. "We saw you with Zoe today. In case you didn't know, Zoe is the daughter of the judge who was kidnapped and murdered."

His face turned to stone.

"What's going on with you and Zoe?" I said.

"Man, I ain't got nothing to say to you."

"That's not a good idea," I said.

"What're you gonna do? Have Zena here drop kick me?"

"Would you rather the police interrogate you?" I said.

"What's going on between Zoe and me is nobody's business."

His eyes searched the ground and stayed there for a while. I waited until he'd given up hope of finding reprieve in the cracks in the wooden floor. When he looked at me again his eyes glowed with anger.

"We know the judge molested Zoe when she was younger. She must've hated him. Who would've blamed her if she wanted him dead? She delivered a million dollars to the kidnappers. Plus she's the only one who ever spoke to them. Coincidence? Maybe. But get this: you had accused the judge of robbing your grandmother of one million dollars. Another coincidence? The cops will have no problem coming to the conclusion that she paid you a million dollars to park her old man."

"They can't prove that."

"All it'll take is for them to find out that you also threatened the judge's life. They'll arrest you. Pull your jacket and decide, hey, this guy's a loser. Let's finish him off. A few hours in the interrogation room with a couple of red-eyed Crackers and who knows what you might confess to."

He fidgeted and looked into my eyes as if pleading for something. "You got a cigarette?"

River dug out her Marlboro's and handed him a cigarette. He silently stared at it before taking it. She lit it for him and he tugged hard, his jaw caving in with tension.

"That day I was at the house she heard what I said to her father. And she followed me to the train station. Came up on the platform while I waited for the train and sat next to me. Said she believed me. That her father was a man who took advantage of people. I was like, 'whatever'. You can't help me, so I don't need to hear from you. But she kept talking to me on the platform. The train took a long time to come and she asked me if I wanted a ride somewhere. I told her I lived in Brooklyn. She said that was okay. That she had to go into the city, anyway. I was like, okay. She dropped me off downtown Brooklyn and then asked me if she could call me. I wasn't feeling her game at all. I thought it was some kind of trick. But I gave her my number.

"She started calling me and we talked on the phone for a couple of weeks. Then we met to go to the movies in Manhattan. I wasn't sure what the hell she wanted from me, but I was digging her company and attention. She was very open with me. She told me that her father started doing shit to her when she was thirteen. She was too ashamed to say nothing. And then one day she told her mother who didn't even believe her. That made her feel whack. Like she was worthless. It stopped when she was fifteen after she threatened to stab him if he ever touched her again. She told me that she wished he would just drop dead. I started to think: I wonder if this bitch is looking for somebody to paint her father? But it wasn't like that. She told me she would try to get my money back."

River said, "How was she going to do that?"

"I don't know. That's what she said."

"Did she ask you to kill her father?" River said.

"Never even came up."

River leaned down, fixing her flint-sharp eyes on his. "Did she talk to you about getting somebody to kill him?"

He averted his gaze and blinked a couple of times. "She hated him. But she wouldn't kill her own father. She ain't that kind of woman."

"I don't believe you," River snapped.

"Forget you!" Shaka said, thrusting his hand into the air.

I could see in River's eyes that she was two spaces away from ramming his shaved crown into the wall.

"Are you in love with her?" I said.

"I dig her, man. She a real nice person."

"But she's white," River jeered.

"She's white, but she ain't no Cracker," Shaka shot back. "Never said all white people are evil."

I said, "Did anybody know about your affair?"

"We're friends. Just friends."

"Did Lourdes know about your friendship?" River snickered.

"Who?"

"Lourdes? The housekeeper," I said.

"I don't know. Maybe."

"Do you know what happened to her?" River said.

He shrugged his shoulders and turned his head toward the wall.

River grabbed his head and spun him around to face her. "Look at me when I'm talking to you. Do you know what happened to Lourdes?"

"Zoe said she killed herself."

River said, "She was murdered. Do you know what curare is?"

"Cu... what?"

"Cu-ra-re. Curare. What, you deaf?" River said.

"I don't know what that is," Shaka said.

"It's a drug. It was found in Lourdes' system," River said.

Shaka smirked. "Never heard of that shit."

River said. "But your girlfriend has, I bet. Here's what I think happened. Lourdes somehow found out that you and Zoe killed the old man and you had no choice but to get rid of her. Zoe gave you a syringe with the curare and you went over to Lourdes' house, injected her with the drug and strung her up."

He began to stutter. "You know what? I want you two out of my apartment right now."

River smiled and leaned her face closer to his. "Shaka, why don't you make your break now? You think this rich girl from the suburbs will protect you if she's forced to make a choice? Trust me she'll spit you out like old bubble gum. Look at your situation. You threatened the judge. You have no alibi for the night he was kidnapped. You're having an affair with his daughter who hated him. Probably wanted him dead. And the ransom was one million dollars, exactly the amount you claimed he stole from your grandmother. We've got you cold."

"You ain't got jack. Not even fumes. Get out of my apartment."

"What you gonna do? Call Five-O," River taunted.

He picked up his jacket. "You stay then. I'll leave."

River grabbed his chin, tilting his face upward, speaking directly into his eyes. "Don't think you can outrun me, Shaka. Expect to hear from us again."

We left Shaka's apartment and drove down Nostrand Avenue. River lit a cigarette and dragged hard, filling the truck with smoke. It was as hazy outside as it was in the truck.

"There's only one thing wrong with your theory," I said.

"What?"

"I believe Lourdes was killed by the person she had sex with. If the semen found in Lourdes belonged to Shaka the police would've matched it by now."

"He obviously had an accomplice."

"It's possible he's telling the truth, you know."

She puffed another gray smoke bubble into the air. "Possible. But I doubt it."

Inhaling River's discarded smoke was becoming way too relaxing. Made me wish I hadn't stopped.

"Why'd you stop?" she said, as if she could read my mind.

"Too much proof that it might kill me. Couldn't ignore the body of evidence."

"Why not? You ignore everything else."

"What's that supposed to mean?"

She glanced at me and puffed a circle of smoke into my face. "You're a smart man. Figure it out."

We pulled up in front of my house. I opened the door and got out.

River killed the engine. "Why're you so scared of me, Blades."

I looked at her. "I believe every man who's ever come in contact with you should be scared of you."

"Give Chez a kiss for me."

I slammed the door and heard the big engine roar to life.

33

I pulled into the Foder driveway around 8 o'clock next morning. Early enough to catch Zoe at home, I hoped. Guessing that Shaka had already warned her, I didn't think she would've agreed to see me had I called.

As I got out of my car Honor burst from the house, unfashionably attired in a puffed-out gray pants suit. Her face was badly made up and she had a blank mummified stare going that would've been perfect were she on the set of Dawn of the Dead. In the bright morning light she looked remarkably unhappy.

With her chest lifted high enough for her to smell her own armpits, she rushed toward my car. "What are you doing here?"

"Good morning to you, too," I said.

"Take that car out of this driveway."

"Is Zoe here?"

"You heard what I said."

"Look, I'm here to speak to Zoe. I don't want to tussle with you."

She unzipped her jacked and whipped out a black pistol from a leather waist-holster. "Who the fuck cares what you want?"

My heart quickened into a heavy thumping beat. Was she crazy enough to shoot me?

"I should shoot you right here for what you did to me the other day," she raged.

"I'm really sorry about that," I said.

"Show me. Get down on your knees and lick my fucking boot."

"Look, we've gotten off on the wrong foot here. You don't like me much, that's clear. What if I just turn around and drive out of here quietly?"

A cloud-lump drifted quietly across the sun and everything quickly darkened. But only for an instant. As Zoe appeared at the door slipping her hands through her coat sleeves, the sun flung the grimy clouds aside and rained bright light down again. I was never happier to see someone.

Zoe saw us she came running out. "Honor, what's going on?"

"He doesn't seem to get the message that he's not wanted around here," Honor fussed.

Honor hovered at the tip of my space, the gun a few feet away from my face. I could've tried to distract and disarm her, but if I failed it might get somebody shot. I took a step back, away from the odor of her pungent perfume.

"Put away that gun," Zoe ordered.

Honor blinked but kept her gun pointed at me.

"Put away that gun," Zoe repeated. "Come on inside, Mr. Overstreet."

I followed Zoe toward the house. At the door I looked behind me to see if Honor was following us. She'd holstered the gun and was walking off toward the garage.

Zoe led me into the living room. "What do you want?"

"We need to talk."

"Talk. But make it quick. I'm meeting a friend for breakfast."

"Shaka?"

She pursed her lips. The pomegranate-dark lipstick made her lips look fuller. It appeared that Shaka hadn't warned her and that surprised me.

"You lied to me about Shaka," I said. "Said you didn't know him."

"So I lied," she said matter-of-factly.

"Did you pay Shaka to kill your father?"

"I wouldn't do that to Shaka."

"But you wanted him dead?"

She paused, then picked up her pocket book from the table. "Yes, I wanted him dead. My father raped me when I was thirteen. I haven't been able to have sex with a man since. I hated him. Are you satisfied?"

She turned to leave the room and came face to face with her mother. Neither of us had seen or heard Mrs. Foder come in. The two women looked at each other for a long time. Zoe's back was turned to me and I couldn't see her face. But her mother's was filled with sorrow.

Zoe passed the older woman and disappeared down the hall. Mrs. Foder walked toward me, the expression on her face as stiff as her back was upright. There was no shortage of pride in this family, it was clear.

"She's an emotional child. Always was."

"Why did you come back to him knowing what he did to Zoe?"

"Do you know there was a time when Jews weren't welcome in the neighborhood? That's one of the reasons Rupert bought this house. His father had tried to buy a house here many years before and was turned away." A dazed, secretive look fell onto her face. "Filled him with sadness, which he passed onto Rupert. It's in this house. Can you hear it?

"Tell me about it?" I said. "Tell me about Zoe and her father."

She sighed heavily and sat down. Her face suddenly seemed deformed. "Demons drove him to do the horrible things he did to Zoe? His family fled persecution in Italy. Because of that his grandfather pushed his father relentlessly. Rupert's father pushed him just as hard to succeed. He never let Rupert forget the persecution his family endured in Italy. His motto was that life was made tougher for people who didn't have ambition. Rupert was the same with his children. He was a good father, but he was tough. Intolerant of laziness and prejudice. The irony of it all is that despite what he did to her, he pushed Zoe to greater success than Chance. She's a doctor today because of him. The greatest disappointment in his life was not being able to get Chance to equal Zoe's accomplishments."

"Did he abuse Chancellor too?"

"Not in the same way, but yes. He constantly berated him for being weak and lazy. And all but washed his hands of him after he married that ignorant woman."

"Seems like you nor your husband approved of the marriage."

"Chance married her right out of college. Rupert wanted him to go onto graduate school. But he refused. Chance is only thirty-five years old. Looking at him, you'd think he was fifty. A few years ago Chance was unemployed. Honor was the sole breadwinner. Then she got kicked out of the police department. They tried to borrow money from Rupert to pay their rent. He refused to lend them money. He told them they could move into the guest quarters here but he wasn't lending them money. His wife was furious. Started insulting my husband. Called him a cheap Jew."

"And he still let her live here?"

"My husband wasn't all bad. He knew what he was doing. He told Chance he could live here as long as he liked providing he saved his money to buy a house. Now they have a house which they'll move into very soon. And they got it with their own money. Without having to borrow a dime from Rupert."

"What about Zoe? Why didn't she leave?"

"Zoe doesn't live here. She owns a penthouse in Manhattan. It's being redesigned, that's why she's staying here."

"Have you had anyone working here recently? Electricians? Plumbers? Contractors? People who had access to the electrical circuits?"

"No. This house is in great condition."

Chancellor came into the room dressed in a white velour track suit. His face was shiny with sweat. He sipped contentedly from a glass containing what looked like orange juice.

He approached me. "Mr. Overstreet. I heard you were here."

I took his clammy handshake.

"Will you excuse me, Mr. Overstreet," Mrs. Foder said.

"I didn't mean to interrupt," Chancellor said. "I was about to go have a shower. I ran into Zoe and she said you were here. I thought I'd say hello."

"Since you're here, I'd like to have a word with you," I said.

Mrs. Foder retreated from the room, her head bowed like a woman bearing a heavy load.

"What can I do for you?" Chancellor said.

"Noah was telling me you write a lot about dysfunctional families, especially relationships between fathers and sons. I can see why."

He squeezed his eyes and made a face as if he thought I was being presumptuous. "What're you talking about?"

"Your mother told me about your relationship with your father."

"Did she? We had a great relationship."

"That's not what she said."

"She doesn't understand men."

"Taking abuse? Is that a manly thing?" I asked.

His face became bored, as if he was fighting back a yawn. "Did we have disagreements? Yes. What father and son doesn't? But we did a lot of things together. He gave me an appreciation of history. Of the power of perseverance. He taught me to fight for what I believed in, even if it meant fighting him. He could be domineering, but it taught me how to stand my ground.

The families in my work are metaphors for America. It's a dysfunctional place. How can you be a writer in America without touching on dysfunction in some way?"

"Did you want him dead, too?"

He looked surprised. "What?"

"Just about everybody in this house wanted the judge dead."

"I loved my father."

"He humiliated you. And he humiliated your wife."

"You're describing the average American father. They're always harder on their sons. Despite that most sons will tell you they loved their fathers."

"I figure someone in this house had a hand in your father's kidnapping."

"How do you figure that?"

"Show me where your fuse box is," I said.

"It's behind the stairwell."

"Show me."

He guided me to a little room behind the stairwell. The door was closed but not locked. He opened the door.

"In there," he said.

"How did the kidnappers cut off the lights?"

"Pulled the fuses out of the box."

"Right. I asked your mother if anyone worked at the house recently. She said no. How would strangers get at your fuse box unless they knew exactly where to look? I've come into this house a few times and each time I came I looked to see if the fuse box was in plain sight. Never saw it."

"Perhaps they got hold of the plans. There are copies at the County Clerk's office."

"That's possible, I suppose. But I believe the people who killed your father also killed Lourdes. The question is why. Professionals who'd gone to such lengths to research the position of your fuse box wouldn't have had any reason to kill Lourdes. She was silenced. By somebody in this house."

"That's a weighty accusation, my friend. Where's your proof."

"Don't have it yet."

"Well, I can't help you. And I hate to leave you hanging but I gotta go shower."

"No sweat. Where's your mother? I'd like to say goodbye."

"Try the kitchen."

Chancellor left me standing behind the stairwell and disappeared through a door off to the right.

I found Mrs. Foder in the kitchen feeding oranges into a juicer.

"Ah, Mr. Overstreet, Have some fresh-squeezed before you leave?"

"No thank you. I just wanted to ask if you knew who gave your husband the information about your father's involvement with the Nazis?"

She stopped what she was doing, her eyes suddenly restless. "Yes, I do. He doesn't think I know. I want him to continue to think I'm in the dark."

"Wouldn't it be easier to just confront him?"

"Easier, maybe. But not as satisfying. He still loves me. He still thinks there's hope for us to be together. Especially now that my husband is dead. He's dead wrong. And he'll never know why."

34

"Did you ever wonder where your mother got all that money," I said.

Elena and I were sitting in her living room. Light streamed through the windows where the blinds had been pulled clear away.

Her eyes fell to the floor. "Every day since I found out."

"And you have no idea?"

"No."

"You had no idea she raked in about two grand for every Latino husband she recruited for a woman named Odessa Rose?"

"Who's Odessa Rose? And what do you mean by recruited?"

"Your mother found Latino men who wanted to get green-card and she hooked them up with this group who got them married to American citizens."

She stared at me in silence. I still suspected she was hiding something.

"Is that why she was killed?"

"What exactly did your mother tell you about the night her boss was kidnapped?"

Elena swept a strand of hair from her eyes. "She was very upset. That's all I can remember. I don't remember anything else."

"I believe somebody inside that house was involved. I think that's why your mother was killed. Did she give you any indication that she suspected someone from the Foder house of having a hand in the kidnapping? Did she talk much about the Foders in general?"

"What do you mean?"

"I mean... like gossip. Something she wouldn't tell anybody but you."

"Well... Yes. Sometimes."

"Like what?"

"I don't know. She talked about a lot of things."

"What kinds of things? C'mon, Elena."

"Mrs. Foder had hemorrhoids and liked watching porn."

I laughed. "I don't think Mrs. Foder would've killed your mother to keep that secret."

"The judge's daughter-in-law was having an affair but didn't know that her husband had found out."

"Did she say with whom?"

"I don't remember. I didn't always pay attention. But my mother kept stuff."

"What kinda stuff?"

"I probably shouldn't be telling you this. My mother... I don't want to say she stole, but she brought home stuff. Pictures. Letters. Stuff like that. She kept them. She has a safe."

"Where is it?"

"In the wall in the back of her closet."

"Do you know the combination? I want to look inside."

Elena led the way to her mother's room. The curtains had been pulled back letting in bright sunlight. Lourdes' picture had been installed over the bed. The room smelled fresh, almost summery.

Elena opened the walk-in closet and pushed clothes all the way to one end of the rack. She stepped in and bent down.

It only took her about 2 minutes to open the safe. She backed out of the closet with her hands full of stuff which she tipped onto the bed.

She stooped down again inside the closet and came out with another handful of papers and other documents.

One last trip produced a rectangular lockbox which appeared to be quite heavy. Her face was flushed from the exertion. "That's all of it. Everything."

"What's in the lock box, do you know?"

"Cash. Lots of it." replied Elena.

No lock on the box. I lifted the lid. Inside were three packages of 50 dollar bills neatly wrapped in plastic.

My guess? Several thousand dollars.

"You weren't kidding," I said.

She sniffled as if she was coming down with a cold. "I checked it for the first time after she died. That's when I realized she had so much money in the bank."

Why was Lourdes hoarding so much cash? Was she planning to flee? Among the documents spread out on the bed were records from several banks (seems like Lourdes had her money spread around pretty good), birth certificates of her children, letters to and from lovers, a divorce decree, marriage certificates, and medical papers. There were copies of bill and receipts for purchases of jewelry and furniture. Photographs. Mostly her family. Several of the Foders, too. One of Zoe and Shaka together. How'd she get that one? One with Chancellor and two men in front of a house. Looked like they were planting grass on a new lawn. On the back of it was written: Chance, Kuzlow and Mateo. A picture of Mrs. Foder in a clown suit. A letter written by Mrs. Foder to her lover. Lourdes should've been working for the CIA.

A Travelocity itinerary caught my eye. It was for travel from New York to Hawaii and back for two passengers. Honor Foder and another name which for some reason struck a familiar note. Bartholomew Temple. I'd seen or heard the name before. The itinerary was for travel to Hawaii on February 22 and returning on February 26. That was the day judge Foder was kidnapped. I looked at the time the flight was scheduled to arrive in New York. 4.00 P.M.

I was under the impression that Honor didn't return to New York until 11.00 P.M. It was possible that the flight had been delayed. Who was Bartholomew Temple? A coworker perhaps?

Elena said, "What're looking for?"

"You want the truth? I have no idea."

She said. "I'm going to clean my face. You want anything?"

"You offering to do my face?"

She smiled. It was not much of a smile, but it was true. "I'd probably ruin your skin."

"You gonna walk out of here and leave me with all this money?"

Teeth again. Bright. "I trust you."

Lifting herself off the bed she drifted through the door without much energy in her step.

I chewed over the itinerary, running the name Bartholomew Temple through my memory banks. Today wasn't a good day to test my memory. Most days aren't, but today was worse. Everything was just knotted up. But the name had set off bells; I kept staring at it, thinking I was going to remember where I'd seen or heard it.

I went through the jumble of papers once more. Nothing else caught my eye. The itinerary I kept. Stuffed that into my jacket breast pocket. Everything else I left on the bed and went to find Elena.

The bathroom door was open so I stuck my head inside. Her hair was pulled back into a bun. Whatever she had on her face smelled of eucalyptus. It was green and covered her face and neck. Her eyes strained through the green mask.

"Is that as much fun as it looks," I said.

"I like pampering myself."

"Pamper away. I'll get out of your way."

"I hope you found what you wanted."

"I'll call you later."

I didn't know what news I would have for her later. But maybe it was okay to call her without news. I'd like to think she wouldn't have minded.

River said hello with liquid licorice in her voice. She was obviously expecting someone else.

"Blades, sorry. I thought you were… Never mind. Whaddup?"

"Bartholomew Temple. Mean anything to you?"

"Sure. How can anybody forget a name like Bartholomew Temple?"

"Who's he?"

"The cop who got busted with Honor Foder. I told you about that. Remember. The two of them got caught stealing from drug dealers. Why?"

"Can you get a fix on old Bart for me?"

"What's his load?"

"I think he and Honor are fuck buddies."

"I'm not surprised that she's playing with somebody else's snake. Her husband seems like a nice man. But a little whipped if you ask me. She seems too hot-blooded for a man like him."

"I hope you don't say that about me."

"I don't say anything about you."

"That's the nicest thing you ever said to me."

"That's the last thing I'm going to say to you, too. Bye."

I had a late lunch at home with Anais and Chez who was still bubbly from her trip. Added excitement arrived earlier that morning in the form of a surprise visit from her uncle Gregory just in from Barbados. He was coming back later to take her to the latest Harry Potter flick. Couldn't get the kid to keep quiet after that.

"And, daddy, did you see the present he brought me?" she babbled.

"You're not eating," I said.

All through lunch it was "Daddy this and Daddy that." Finally I told her to ask Anais a question just so she wouldn't feel left out. Truth is my mind was miles away.

After lunch I called American Airlines. Flight 1390 from Hawaii landed in New York on time on February 26. 4.08 P.M. Why did Honor lie about the time she arrived in New York? And what did she do between landing and coming home around midnight? Why was Lourdes in possession of that itinerary? Did she suspect that Honor had something to do with the judge's murder? Honor certainly had the motive and the disposition? The discrepancy between the time she landed at JFK and her arrival home bothered me. I needed to know where Honor spent those eight hours.

Lourdes was killed by someone who had access to powerful prescription drugs. Zoe maybe? Was that why Lourdes had told me about Shaka and his beef with the judge? To draw my attention to Zoe? But if that was the case why then didn't she come right out and say something when we spoke to her? No, whatever Lourdes knew she was unaware of its importance. She wasn't even confident that she'd heard any of the kidnappers use the word cuz.

That's when a dart of inspiration struck me between the eyes. Perhaps Lourdes knew exactly who the kidnappers were. If my hunch was right, then so did I. And I'd seen their faces not long ago.

35

River called me just as I broke from Eastern Parkway onto Atlantic Avenue.

"Where're you?" I asked.

"My office. But get this. Just spoke to detective Grant. They arrested Bartholomew for the judge's murder. Guess you were onto something."

"How'd they nail him?"

"A tip. He lives about five blocks from that warehouse where the judge was found. Apparently a beat cop had ticketed a green Honda parked at a hydrant opposite the warehouse that night. Was Bart's Honda. Detectives went out to question him. Said he was acting odd when they asked him where he was that night. So they asked if he'd mind if they looked around his house. He gave them the okay."

"And they found the gun."

"That's right."

"Bartholomew didn't do it. I'm heading to the Foder's right now. Meet me there."

"Why?"

"There's a killer in that house."

"On my way. Hey, Blades?"

"What?"

"Be careful."

As I got close to Shore Road I could feel the blood throbbing in my neck. Nervous tension was building in my chest. I turned onto Shore Road and eased the SUV up the hill. The houses were shrouded in smoky mist. There was a creepy stillness to the evening as the truck slid quietly through the haze.

I pulled in behind Honor's Ford parked on the shoulder a few feet away from the mailbox. I hefted my Glock for reassurance, racked it and stuffed it back into my holster.

Chancellor answered the door. The strain of the last week seemed to have stripped his face of any color leaving an undignified bearing. His eyes were bereft of vitality, and he looked half-drowsy. His bohemian mop flopped at his neck.

On another day I would've felt sorry for the man.

He smiled when he saw me and stood solid and square in the doorway.

"Can I come in?" I said.

"My mother isn't here," he said. "She went to look at headstones."

"I'd like to talk to you."

His eyes shadowed and I almost thought I saw a flicker of pain. He stepped back.

Inside, I started to unbutton my jacket. Out of the corner of my eye I caught Honor steaming toward us. I twirled to face her.

"You fucking snake!" she screamed.

When I saw the gun in her hand I thought momentarily of reaching for mine. Changed my mind fast. This was a former undercover cop. I wouldn't have stood a chance.

Inches away from us now, she hollered. "I should shoot you in the head!"

But her gun wasn't pointed at me. It was pointed at her husband.

"Calm down," I said.

"Shut up!"

Chancellor's eyes wilted. "Have you gone crazy?"

"You think you're so smart. Thought you could get away with framing Bart for your father's murder?"

"What the hell are you talking about?" Chancellor said.

Her words seemed to blister her lips. "You are the lowest form of slime there is. Killing your father like that. Like he was a pig."

"My father was a pig. But you're not making any sense."

"How long have you known about Bart and me?"

"What about Bart and you?"

"He was fucking the shit outta me while you out playing Shakespeare."

The words hit him like a brick that had crashed through the window. He balled his fists. Anger rose off him in waves. He double-breathed, as if he wasn't getting enough air.

Honor said, "Bart's a real man. He fucks like a man. And if he had to kill somebody he would kill them like a man. Not like a coward."

Chancellor squirmed. The man was trying hard to silence the powerful emotions lashing through his body. Gotta hand it to him. He was good at this.

"It's clear that you're upset," he said. "But I have to say that unless you calm down and explain yourself."

She cocked the pistol. "The only thing I will have to explain is why I didn't kill you sooner."

Chancellor spun a pained glance in my direction. Fat vein throbbing like a worm in the center of his forehead.

I stepped back and to the side so that I was behind her, out of her direct line of sight. "Put the gun down, Honor."

She kept her eyes on Chancellor. "I told you to fuck off!"

I unbuttoned my jacket. "There's no need to kill him. The police will take care of him. And his conscience will do the rest."

"I'm going to kill him. And if you try to stop me I'll shoot you, too. I wanna know how you got Bart's gun?"

Chancellor must've understood what I was trying to do and this restored his courage. "If your boyfriend killed my father I hope he burns."

"Bart couldn't have killed your father because when your father was kidnapped Bart was fucking me on the table in his dining room."

Chancellor sneered. "Then he has nothing to worry about. He's got a tight alibi, right. Or was it loose? It's been so long for me I forgot."

Honor pressed the gun to Chancellor's ear. "You fucking bastard!"

I opened my jacket. "Do you have a key to Bart's house?"

Honor said, "Yes, I do."

I eased my gun out. "He probably copied the key. And when you went away together he sneaked into the house and stole the gun. Took a pair of Bart's boots too. What's he? Size twelve?"

"Yes," Honor said.

"I bet he knew exactly where you were when his father was snatched. He knew you were due back in New York at four and not eleven, because he had a copy of your itinerary. I bet he followed you from the airport, so he knew you wouldn't be coming straight home."

"I should've just left your trifling ass," she said.

"Put the gun down," I said.

"I'm going to kill him," she said.

"You don't wanna do that," I cocked my pistol.

Hearing the click she took her eyes off Chancellor to glance at me. Chancellor snapped his hands upward, clutching her wrist. Crack. The force shattered a bone in her hand. She yowled like a trapped animal. Chancellor twisted the gun toward her. The gun went off.

I saw the flash and instinctively dropped to one knee. Honor slumped to the ground. The sound of the explosion echoed in the tiny space.

My gun was pointed at Chancellor. He now held Honor's gun in both hands pointed down at me. The slack scaly skin beneath his jaw quivered.

My heart was pounding so hard against my chest I could hear it.

There was a stillness in his eye which made me shudder. This man could've easily been an assassin.

"Is this what you call a Mexican standoff?"

"'cept neither of us is Mexican," I said.

Out of the corner of one eye I could see blood trickling toward me. I got to my feet, keeping my eyes locked onto Chancellor's, looking for any change, any sign that he might pull the trigger.

"Why did you kill Lourdes?"

"That nosy bitch. You've figured out this much why don't you try to get a rope around that one." He laughed at his own sick joke.

"She remembered that a man named Kuzlow once worked for you. And somehow she recognized him as one of the kidnappers."

"Yes. She called me. Said she thinks one of the men was Kuzlow. His friends called him Kuz. I'd hired him and his friend to do some landscaping work on my house a few months ago. Kuzlow had taken a liking to her, and she him, I suppose. She said he looked her over the way Kuz did. Women. So fucking vain. Only a woman would remember something like that. I convinced her not to talk to the police until I'd had a chance to speak to the two men."

"I suppose Kuz and Mateo killed Lourdes. Where'd they get the cop uniforms?"

"They're both auxiliary cops in Greenpoint."

"Why would she let them into her house if she suspected them?"

"She didn't. She kept a set of keys here for emergency. When she quit she forgot to take them."

"Where'd they get the drug?"

A grin slowly took shape at the tightened corners of his mouth. "I have ways."

"Humor me."

"I forged Zoe's name on a prescription."

"He raped her before he killed her, did you know that?"

Annoyance flashed in his face for a second. "What does it matter? She's dead."

"What about your mother? Your sister? Can you live with robbing them of their husband and father?"

"You kidding me? I couldn't have done them a better turn. They are far, far better off. And not to sound like a cliché, my father is in a far, far better place. You don't understand, Mr. Overstreet. My father was an evil man. I could never become a writer while he was still alive. He'd made it clear that as long as I intended to pursue playwriting he would leave nothing for me in his will. I wish I didn't have to shoot you, Mr. Overstreet."

"There's one thing I don't understand. Why come to me? Why hire a private investigator?"

"That was Zoe. She was angry when she realized that the kidnappers hadn't kept their word. She wanted to unleash every resource at her disposal. The police. The FBI. Even a private investigator. Anything she could do. That's the way she is. Like a child. Doesn't like it when people disappoint her. I had no control over the police, but I decided it would be in my best interest to hire a private investigator I could get rid of easily. I didn't count on you being so persistent."

The doorbell chimed. I figured it was River.

Chancellor's head turned, his attention drawn momentarily to the sound. I flung myself through the air, my elbow crashing into his jaw and throat, knocking him to the ground. The gun clattered to the floor, skating half way across the room. Chancellor gurgled deep in his throat and was still.

36

The police took statements from River and me, reminding us to be available for further questioning. Honor got the meat wagon. Chancellor left by ambulance with a police guard. River went home. I told her I would wait for Zoe or Mrs. Foder to return.

Half an hour later I got a frantic call from Shaka.

"I think Zoe is in trouble," he blurted.

"What kinda trouble."

"She's gone to get the money back."

"What money?"

He was shouting now. "From the people who killed her father. You gotta help her."

"You ain't making sense. Calm down. Who is she meeting?"

"I just told you, man. The people who killed her father."

"And who would they be?"

"Somebody named Odessa. Said she gonna make some sort of trade."

I immediately understood what was going on. Zoe had arranged to sell her father's diary to Odessa for the million she thought Odessa extorted.

"Said she's doing this for me. To get my grandmother's money back," Shaka said. "I told her not to do it. That I didn't care about the money."

I ran to my car. "Do you know where she's meeting Odessa?"

"No. Maybe you can call her cell phone. You gotta help her, man."

I rang off from Shaka, started up my car and sped down the driveway. I called River. No answer. I called Zoe. She didn't pick up, either.

Something about what Shaka said didn't make sense. If Zoe thought Odessa killed her father why would she even deal with them? Unless she was working with the police or the FBI to set Odessa up. She was too smart to try to deal with people she suspected of murdering her father without some kind of plan to get herself out of trouble.

I got Shaka's number off my caller ID and rang him back.

"How long ago did she leave?" I said.

"Ten minutes or so."

"What exactly did she say to you?"

"That her father kept a diary on Odessa which could put her in jail. And she was going to trade the diary for a million dollars."

"When did she tell you this?"

"Earlier today. We were having coffee at Starbucks. She got a call. She got up and walked away from me. She had this strange look on her face when she came back. Then she said she was taking me home. That's when she explained what she was going to do."

"And she said she had the diary with her?"

"I suppose it was in her car."

"Did you overhear any of her conversation?"

"I heard her say something like Flint Print when she was on the phone."

I hung up and dialed the operator. Asked if she had a listing for a place called Flint Print. I remembered that Semin had said that Odessa owned some kind of printing business.

The operator came back with an address: 10 Jay Street. I knew it was somewhere beneath the Brooklyn Bridge.

Turning on Northern Boulevard, I grabbed the first ramp onto the BQE and laid out the X-5, notching 95 ticks. I calculated that I was about 15 minutes away, if traffic remained friendly. As I bulldozed the tight corners, I tried Zoe's cell phone again. This time she picked up.

"Where are you, Zoe?"

She didn't answer and I sensed that she was about to hang up.

"Don't hang up. I know what you're doing. Shaka called me. He's very worried about you. And frankly it's a bad idea. You don't know who you're dealing with. In any event, Odessa didn't kill your father."

Still no reply. Just the sound of wind rushing. She was still in her car.

"Did you hear me?" I said.

"I can't talk to you now."

"Where are you?"

"I can't tell you that."

"Tell me what's in the diary."

"Everything. Names. Payments. Dates. Everything's here."

"If I were you I would turn that diary over to the police."

"I don't have time for this, Mr. Overstreet."

"Listen to me. Odessa didn't kill your father. I can prove it."

"It doesn't matter who killed my father. What's done is done."

Something about the way she said it made me think. It took me about a minute before I realized that Zoe had known who killed her father for sometime. My mind flashed back to that day I found her getting drunk. She must've known it then.

"When did you find out?" I said.

"When did I find out what?"

"That your brother killed your father?"

There was a long silence.

"I have to go," she said.

"I don't understand how you could've kept that to yourself unless you were in on it. How could you stay in that house with him, knowing what he did? How could you look your mother in the face?"

"What was I supposed to do? Sit her down and show her what a monster her son was? Well, in my opinion, her husband was a worse monster."

"Your brother is a murderer."

"And what about my father? What about what he killed in me?"

"Chancellor's going to jail. You may not be so lucky. You may end up with a tag on your toe."

"I have to go now."

"Zoe, if I can't change your mind, let me come with you."

"Why do you want to help me?"

"I don't know. Call me a fool."

"Goodbye, Mr. Overstreet."

I was approaching the Cadman Plaza exit. I threw the phone onto the seat and slid off the BQE screeching to a halt at the red light under the overpass. I tried calling Zoe again but either she was refusing to answer or was she otherwise engaged.

I sped away before the light turned green, zooming along Jay Street, crossing under another overpass and down a row of darkened warehouses. I smelled the river. The Manhattan Bridge loomed ahead just beyond the dead end. I got out leaving the truck halfway in the middle of the street.

It was around seven o'clock. A hungry wind whistled off the water, serving up trash from the empty street. I looked around for Zoe's car. I spotted the blue BMW parked in front of 10 Jay. I hopped the two flights of steps and found the door locked. It was a commercial building. The row of buzzers came with attached names of companies, mostly printing concerns.

I pressed each buzzer. Seconds later a voice squawked over an intercom. I couldn't make out what it said, but I mumbled something unintelligible. The voice squawked again and I replied in the same manner of incoherence. The buzzer sounded and I pushed the door.

It was dusty inside. The walls were plastered white with dust. I scanned the directory for Flint Print.

7th floor.

I slid my gun from its holster as I boarded the elevator. I pressed 7 and waited for the doors to close. I had no idea what I was getting myself into but the Glock offered plenty reassurance.

37

The elevator came to a jerky halt on 7. I mashed myself against the side to make as small a target as possible as the doors eased back. I peeked outside. Around one corner, then the other. Nobody in sight.

I stepped out into the bright corridor. The odor of ink and chemicals stung my nose. Everything was covered in white dust. Floor. Walls. Rolls of paper stacked almost to the ceiling. Several footprints in the dusty floor.

I moved quickly down the dusty passageway. Twice I stopped to pinch off on a sneeze.

Voices. I stopped, drawing behind a 3-foot thick support column. From somewhere off to my left came the rattle of laughter. Then a sneeze. Maybe ten yards away. I slunk down and crept closer, pausing between two huge mounds of paper on dollies.

That sneeze again. He was almost on top of me now, coming around one of the stacks of paper. He came abreast, wiping his nose in a napkin. One of Odessa's overfed pups.

I edged up behind. Caught him completely flatfooted.

"Don't move," I said.

He arched his back, then stiffened when he felt my Glock at his neck.

"On the ground. Face down," I ordered.

"On this nasty floor... " he began.

I drove the tip of my boot in the back of his knee. He fell forward onto his face. I pounced on him, pinning him to the ground, my knee in the small of his back, the Glock glued to the nape of his neck.

"Not a sound," I commanded. "Hands behind your head."

He obeyed quietly. Then I tossed him. I took a semi from his waist, ejecting the clip and the round in the chamber, before stuffing the empty gun in my waist.

"How many up here with you?" I said.

He stood stiff, as if he didn't hear me.

I whispered into his ear. "What're you marinating on, bumpkin? Don't you understand English?"

"Put that gun down and I'll show you the bumpkin."

"Some other time, dawg. Now answer me. How many?"

He was still reluctant to answer until I grooved his scalped just below his ear with the butt of my gun, reminding him who was in charge. Tough guy flinched, but that's all.

"How many?" I repeat.

"Just Mallet."

"Where?"

"Office. Around the corner."

The judge's daughter?"

He hesitated.

I said, "Do you want to leave with a concussion?"

"In the office."

"Where were you heading to just now?"

"To search her car."

I smiled to myself. No way Zoe had the diary in her car. But then again, I thought she was too smart to do anything this stupid.

"Get up."

He sneezed twice before getting to his knees. When he stood and turned around his face was painted white with dust.

"Move," I ordered.

He marched off, as if in slow motion. We walked around several enormous printing presses and more drums of paper. The smell of chemicals and ink became stronger.

To our left, about fifteen feet away, was a room which looked to be an office. There was one glass door, through which dim light filtered. Outside the door were a punch clock with racks of yellow cards next to it, and a water-cooler. Straight ahead, through the wide glass window, I caught a glimpse of the Manhattan Bridge.

I grabbed my pigeon by the collar, halting him. "Is that the office?"

He nodded.

I stayed back about two paces as we advanced. His huge frame partially blocked my view of the door, but I could see enough to be able to tell if it opened.

We reached the door and I ordered him to open it. As soon as it cracked, I whacked him below the base of his skull with the gun butt and shoved him forward as hard as I could, jumping into the room behind him. He stumbled and fell across a desk in the middle of the room where Mallet was shuffling cards. Like a slinky, my guide slid off the desk and didn't move.

Mallet sprang up clawing at the gun in his waist. I swung the Glock in a wide arc. As I swung he arched backward with the flexibility of a gymnast. My gun barely clipped the edge of his chin, his quickness saving him from the full force of the attack.

Having freed his gun, he squeezed off one wayward round as he twisted away from a kick aimed at his head. My heel dug into his shoulder. He flopped onto the desk knocking a computer to the ground. Recovering quickly, he spun around to find the sights of my gun square on his chest.

"Drop it," I ordered.

He froze. Noticing the tight curve of his body, I suspected that he was thinking of making a desperate attempt to lift the gun into firing position.

Let him.

His lips twisted into a perverse smirk. "Or else what?"

The smell of gun powder from his missed shot stung my nose. I said nothing, concentrating on his hands.

"You gonna shoot me?" he sneered.

"That's an option."

"Go ahead. Put one right here." He touched his chest.

It was an attempt to distract me. I wasn't having it. Aiming at his right shoulder I pulled the trigger. The bullet must've struck a bone. His hand went limp; the gun fell to the floor. His eyes became instantly vacant with surprise. I moved to kick the gun from under him.

I'd taken my eye off Mallet for a barely second. With his quickness it was enough time for him to grab a piece of brass pipe laying on the ground next to the chair where Zoe was tied a few feet away.

Swinging the pipe with his left hand, he lunged at me, his eyes wild.

The blow glanced off my shoulder, but had enough force to knock me off balance. I stumbled back. Mallet swung the pipe at my head. I ducked, still struggling to get my balance. He was quicker than I expected and clearly had some martial arts training. A kick caught my ribs, but I was able to grab hold of his leg, twisting it as hard as I could. He tumbled to the floor. Recovering quickly, he rolled over and sprang to his feet.

I tried to aim the gun but he was moving too quickly. He lowered his head and rushed me. This time, I stepped to the left, swinging the gun like a baseball bat, connecting solidly with the side of his head. He stumbled into a file cabinet and folded into a ball to the floor and did not move.

Recklessness isn't bravery.

Visibly shaking, Zoe cowered in a chair to the left of the desk, her hands tied behind her back. She leaned forward so I could release the ropes. Her skin seemed Gypsy-dark under the dim light.

"Let's get out of here," I said.

"I'm not leaving without that money," she said.

"Are you crazy?" I said, gasping to catch my breath.

"Odessa is on her way here with the money," Zoe said.

I looked at her. "You really expect her to give you a million dollars?"

"Why not? She knows I'm not bluffing," Zoe said.

"What's to prevent her from keeping her million dollars, killing you and just taking the diary?"

"You," she said, her face suddenly relaxed.

I felt a quick pressure in my skull, like a lever tightening a wire. I contemplated what she'd said and realized that I'd been skillfully drawn into a trap. It seemed that at each turn Zoe was always one step ahead of me.

"And what's to prevent me from walking out of here and leaving you to paddle your own canoe?"

"You," she said, coolly.

I thought she would smile, but she didn't. Perhaps she was planning to do her gloating later.

"What made you so sure I'd follow you down here?" I said.

"Because you have a lot in common with the women who come into my office seeking redemption."

"What's that?"

"Vanity. They're too vain to accept the way they look. They need approval. You think you're too good to lose. Too smart to have come to the wrong conclusion. Too generous not to help someone in need."

"Did I come to the wrong conclusion about you?" I said.

"What conclusion did you come to about me?"

"That you weren't involved in your father's death."

"You're right about that," She said.

"Honor is dead and your brother is going to jail. You got lucky."

Her eyes clouded and she bit her lip. I thought she would cry. But she aced me again. The silence lasted a long time.

Her voice squeaked. "Was my mother there?"

"No," I said. "You still gonna go through with this, aren't you?"

"The money is not for me."

"What do you see in Shaka?"

"Something you probably would never see."

"And what's that?"

"Vulnerability. He's been taken advantage of and there was nobody to fight for him. I know what that's like. You probably don't."

A cell phone rang. We both looked in the direction of the sound. It was coming from Mallet.

I stretched him out and took the phone out of his pocket. Odessa's intense voice on the other end registered surprise when I said hello.

"Where's Mallet?"

"Taking a nap," I said. "You got the money?"

Odessa's spoke quietly. "So I see you're a player after all, Blades."

"Do you have the money?"

"Yes, I have the money. Do you have the diary?"

"Where's the money?"

"Right here in my lap."

"Great. Now here's how we do this. We'll meet you in front of the 77th. I think you know where that is."

"You gotta be joking," Odessa said.

"It's a one-shot deal, Odessa. Send your group of overfed slackers to the toilet. You meet us in front of the 77th. If I see more than one car, or if there's anyone but you and a driver in your car, Zoe will walk into the 77th and hand the diary over."

"How do I know you wouldn't have the FBI there waiting?"

"Sometimes you just have to trust a brother, Odessa."

"OK, Blades. We'll play it your way."

"Oh, and you better send an ambulance for Mallet. He's gonna be taking some time off for bad behavior."

I rang off and threw Mallet's phone on the ground next to him.

I turned to Zoe. "Where's the diary?"

"We can pick it up on the way," She said.

38

We picked up Shaka and the diary on the way and arrived in front of the 77th about twenty minutes later. Odessa was already there, parked in front of the public school half a block away from the precinct.

Plenty of activity in front of the precinct. Exactly what I wanted. Cops were entering and leaving the station with regularity. Armed with machine guns, two cops stood guard outside.

I drove around the block twice to make sure Odessa's scrubs weren't hiding out waiting to pile on once the play was over.

Parking across the street from the precinct I got out, leaving Zoe and Shaka in the SUV. Odessa's truck was about twenty yards ahead, past the traffic lights. I walked up to the vehicle, pulled on the back door and it opened. I hopped into the seat next to Odessa. The driver looked around.

"Eyes front," I said.

He looked at Odessa who bobbed her head. Then he turned his face with an obstinate grunt.

"Where's the money?" I said.

Odessa picked up a black travel bag from the floor and hoisted it into onto my lap. I opened the bag to make sure there was only legal tender inside. Mostly hundreds and fifties. I closed the bag.

"Aren't you going to count it?"

I reached for the door. "I trust you."

Odessa grabbed my hand. "Where's the diary?"

"Soon's I step out of this truck your diary will appear, like magic."

She said, "You ain't stepping outta here with that money unless the diary is in my hand."

"I step out empty-handed, the diary walks into the precinct. Your play."

Odessa released me.

As I got out I signaled to Shaka. He got out of my car and hailed a passing livery cab which stopped at the traffic light. By the time I reached the cab he and Zoe had gotten inside, leaving the door open. I took the diary, sealed in a manila envelope; he took the bag.

The cab drove off.

I waited until the livery had safely turned down the next block before walking back to Odessa. I rapped on the window and the tinted glass slowly descended exposing Odessa's bloated face.

"Got your diary right here," I said, opening the envelope.

"Hand it over," she said.

"In a few minutes," I said.

"What're you waiting for?"

"Insurance."

She smiled. "Thought you trust me."

"What are you going to do now that you don't have a judge?" I said.

"Greedy judges are a dime a dozen," she said. "Now finding people you can trust, that's a bit trickier. I could use you, Blades."

"My wife wouldn't appreciate that," I said.

She laughed. "I could use her too. Is she an American citizen? One day I will have a hand in electing the president. You'll see."

My cell phone rang.

It was Zoe. "We're safe. Thank you."

"I have one question for you, Zoe," I said.

"What is it?"

"At the T-Salon that day. The story you told me about someone calling your house, threatening your mother, that was a lie, wasn't it?"

The line was dead for a full minute. I could hear her soft breathing.

"It was what you wanted to hear," she said, finitely.

"Have a happy life," I said, and rang off.

I dropped the leather diary into Odessa's lap.

She was smiling. "See you got played, too."

"You've got what you wanted," I said.

"I always get what I want."

"Then maybe you can help me get something off my mind."

"How can I do that?"

"Tell me the truth about Malveaux's death. Did you give him a choice?"

"You don't let go, do you?"

"I hate to leave things hanging."

She cracked a huge smile. "I like you, Blades. Such a sense of humor. If it helps your conscience in anyway, I had no hand in Malveaux's death."

I still didn't believe her, but there was no way I was going to break her down. I leaned away from the vehicle and watched the truck drive away before trudging wearily back to my car.

39

"Did you talk to your father about this?"

My mother and Chesney had just returned from the Georgia O'Keeffe photography retrospective at the Brooklyn Museum. Sitting in her car outside my house, she'd listened patiently while I related what I could remember of that afternoon I saw my father threatening her with a gun. With each word her blue eyes became more coarsened with pain.

"Yes, I did."

"What did he say?"

"He told me to ask you."

"He didn't tell you what happened?"

I shook my head.

She opened the door and stepped into the street. I thought she might walk away, back into the house; instead she leaned on the door, her head bowed as if praying.

I got out and walked around to where she stood. The sunset grazing Brooklyn was the color of ripe papaya.

"I'm really sorry you had to see that, Carmen."

"Was that the first time he tried to do that?"

"Tried to do what?"

"To kill you."

"He wasn't trying to kill me."

"But I saw it! He had the gun in his hand."

"I was very insecure back then. A white woman married to a handsome black man. The women in the Black Panther party hated me. They made fun of me, when he wasn't around. And I knew that they all tried to take him away from me. Every time a woman called the house, no matter how innocent it might've been, I would fly into a jealous rage."

"I knew he cheated on you."

"That didn't help, of course. That day I'd found a chain in his pocket. It belonged to somebody I knew. Somebody I thought was a friend. And on top of that he told me that he wanted to leave me. I assumed that he wanted to leave me for her. And I wasn't about to let that happen."

"What are you saying?"

"I knew where he kept his gun. And I went to get it."

"What did you plan to do with it?"

"I don't know."

"You just wanted to scare him, is that it?"

She paused. "I suppose. I don't know what I was thinking. I just wanted him to say he was going to stay. He said no and I pointed the gun at him. But he wasn't afraid. He took it away. You must've come into the room right after that."

"So he wasn't trying to kill you?"

"No. He wasn't."

"Are you telling me the truth, Mom? You're not trying to protect him, are you?"

"I wish I didn't have to think about any of this, Carmen. I thought it was safely tucked away in the past."

"I thought he was trying to kill you. What's worst, I realized that I did nothing to help you. I ran."

"You were a child. And I'm glad you didn't try to do anything."

"And then I blocked it out of my mind."

"I'm sorry, Carmen."

Expecting her to cry, I put my arms around her. My mother was emotional that way. But her body didn't go limp with the tremors of tears. It remained solid, steady. When I looked into her eyes she was smiling.

"You should apologize to your father," she said.

I said nothing.

She pinched my cheek and got into her car. I watched her drive off before I turned and walked slowly back inside.

There is a tendency for human beings to try to put a positive spin on things. No matter how bad the outlook, when faced with the specter of a failed marriage, or disappointments at work, with our children, or in love, we strive to find a way to hedge the assault of guilt that comes with doom. But that doesn't always work. Sometimes our rationale for survival cannot save us from the unbearable pain we must at times endure. Especially as we get older. There is one question which haunts most of us. Are we as happy as we could be?

Once you ask yourself this question the truly honest person would admit that his life was miserable, and the more pertinent question then becomes: why is your life such a fuck up? What could you've done differently?

I wondered if Jersey ever asked himself that question.

Only a few people attended the service in the chapel at the funeral home on Atlantic Avenue. I paid for the burial and the funeral director assured me he would be given a nice casket. Jersey's ex-wife wife came, as did a few family members who said they hadn't seen him in years.

After the service his ex-wife came up to me. "At least he wouldn't be buried in Potter's Field."

Jersey was buried in a brown suit which I bought; his ex-wife had told me that was his favorite color. Earlier that week the police had arrested a crack-addict for his murder. Apparently he'd seen Jersey with some cash and decided he had better uses for the money than Jersey.

That night, I stopped by River's apartment to give her the $30,000 Elena had paid us for finding her mother's killer. We shared a glass of port and then I got up to leave. River said she was going out to meet Komi and we left the apartment together.

Outside, a bright moon was erect in the sky.

"The police picked up Kuzlow and Mateo in Baltimore. They're being extradited," she said.

"Shouldn't be too hard to get them to flip on Chancellor," I said. "He's gonna pull a long stretch."

"You feel sorry for him?"

"He's better off than his father."

"How are things with you and your father?" River said.

"We're trying to get along."

"That's good."

"I have an appointment to see a therapist next week."

After a pause, she said. "Is that right?"

"Anais is convinced that I need help dealing with all this stuff."

"And you're not?"

"I don't know."

"Well, I hope it helps. When my father was alive, I used to wish I had somebody else as my father."

"No kidding?"

"Yeah. It's depressing, I know. But I'm depressed a lot. But so's everybody else. For shit far less fucked up that mine. Depressed is depressed. No matter what's causing it. Nobody cares about your pain. You gotta deal with your shit or else get out of the game."

"And what game is that?"

"The only game there is. We either love or we die."

She was right, of course.